I'll Be The One

HAZEL JAMES

D1607888

ISBN-13: 978-1532777493
ISBN-10: 1532777493

Editing by JaVa Editing
Cover design by Luminos Graphic House
Formatting by Elaine York, Allusion Graphics, LLC/
Publishing & Book Formatting
www.allusiongraphics.com

Mom, I hope you like my macaroni necklace.

Grandma, I did it. Just like you said I would.

Sweet Peas, here's to ten years and counting.

James

I zip up my jacket, cross the parking lot and pass under the entryway of Edison High, officially declaring me a "Fighting Cardinal."

How do cardinals even fight, anyway? Cougars, bears, wolves... those I get. But a cardinal? What's it gonna do? *You better watch out or I'll shit on your car!*

Despite the lame excuse for a mascot, I open the door knowing today's gonna be a good day. I can feel it.

Overflowing teacher mailboxes and a sign-up sheet for a college visit make the front office look the same as the five other high schools I've attended. The secretary holds up a pair of soggy shoes and complains to the janitor about the overflowing toilet in the staff bathroom. From the looks of it, she's gonna be a while, so I take a seat on the bench, lean back against the wall, and close my eyes.

Just as I start to doze, she clears her throat, gaining my

attention. I crack my eyelids open. "Can I help you?" she huffs before taking a swig of black coffee.

"Uh, yeah," I say. My last school started a full hour later than this one. It should be a crime to make teenagers get up this early in the morning. "I'm the new student. Today's my first day."

She squeals and flies out of her chair. "We haven't gotten a transfer student here in two years. What a delight!"

That isn't hard to believe in a town with a population of 7,117. Make that 7,119 if you add me and Mom. The secretary fumbles around her desk and grabs a stack of papers before rushing toward me. I guess she forgot she was in a bad mood.

"We have your welcome packet all ready to go. I had to go digging through our files to find one. Here's your schedule, the school map, and the file you'll take to the guidance counselor. Just wait here and I'll call for a student to escort you to your first class." She manages to say all of that in less than ten seconds. She's gotta be bordering on a coffee overdose.

My schedule seems easy enough. Trig, Economics, Anatomy and Physiology, English, World History, P.E. and Robotics.

"You just let me know if you have any problems with your classes, River. We looked over the records your mother sent us and tried to fill in the gaps as best as we could so you can graduate on time. You're quite the traveler."

"The classes look fine, but please call me James. No one calls me by my first name. In fact, you can just delete it from my record."

"I'm afraid we have to keep your legal name in our files, but I'll make a note about using your middle name. It's a shame. River is so... exotic!" She claps her hands twice for emphasis.

I fight against rolling my eyes. With a mother who changed her name to Sunshine at eighteen, River seems like an obvious choice for her son's name. Except that I prefer not getting shoved into lockers, toilets or trashcans. I've found being the new kid is hard enough. Add in the first name of River and it's an adolescent death sentence.

"Lucky for me, I'm more of a domestic person." I drop my packet and schedule inside my backpack, close my eyes once again and lean my head against the wall. My escort. Hmmm.

Black... no, brown hair.

Short.

Red shirt.

Black shoes.

Bracelet on left wrist.

For as long as I can remember, this has been one of my favorite ways to pass the time. I think of it as people watching in reverse, and I've gotten pretty good over the years. I was spot-on with guessing my escort at my last school. Right down to guessing how many minutes it would take before she rubbed her boob against my arm. (It was one minute, by the way—or basically long enough to walk out of the front office and around the corner.)

"James, your escort is here. This is Sarah, and she'll show you to your Trigonometry class," Caffeinated Secretary says a few minutes later.

A brunette walks through the door wearing a Cardinals shirt, blue jeans and black Nikes. She can't be more than 5'4". I glance at her arm as we enter the hallway and see a #teamjenna bracelet on her right wrist. I figure that earns me a 4.5 out of 5. Not bad.

"Hey, it's nice to meet you," she says with a smile.

"Likewise." I follow her out the door and down the hallway. "So what's the teacher like?"

"Mr. Barnes? He's pretty cool. He thinks he's hilarious, though. I hope you're ready for pity laughs."

"Who's Jenna?" I ask, as we round a corner and walk through a small courtyard.

"Huh?"

"Your bracelet." I point to her wrist.

"Oh, she's a kid I used to babysit. Last summer she was diagnosed with cancer. She's still in chemo, but the doctors seem pretty hopeful."

"Well that's good."

We enter a hallway and head for the second classroom on the left. The poster beside the door makes me groan.

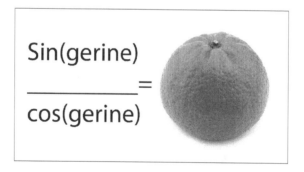

"Like I said—a comedian or something," she whispers as she opens the door.

"I see that."

Right on cue, everyone stares at me.

"Ah, a new soul desperate to soak up the inner workings of mathematics. Hello, Mr. Tennyson. Please take a seat and join us in a rousing discussion of trigonometry in the real world." Mr. Barnes points at an empty spot in the back of the class before turning to face another student. Sarah sits down near the door, and I step past her on the way to my desk. "Mr. Paulson, I know you've convinced yourself you will never use trigonometry after high school. I will bet you ten extra credit points that I can prove you wrong."

Suspicion falls on the student's face. "What do I have to do if I lose? I mean, not that I will because there's no way I'm dealing with this sh—stuff if I don't have to."

"I love teenage confidence. If you lose, you will spend one hour after school this week—on a day of your choosing— helping me pack up last semester's learning materials. I'm retiring at the end of the school year, and I'd like to get a head start."

"You're on." The two shake hands.

"Okay, Mr. Paulson. Tell me what you want to be when you grow up that doesn't require trigonometry."

"That's easy—a rock star." He fields a few high fives as another student shouts, "That's what I'm talking about, Bryan!" The class chuckles, and Mr. Barnes strokes his chin.

"A rock star, quite the noble profession, indeed. Who can resist the dream of being on stage with millions of young ladies in the audience?" He turns to face the class. "You know, I was in a rock band in my college years. I played bass for Broken Elevator. We lived on the fourth floor of our dorm; you'll never guess how we got our name." He chuckles to himself. "We had two paying gigs, and it was the best twenty bucks I ever made."

Bryan laughs. "Wow, Mr. Barnes. I never knew you had such a wild side to you. Now, when will you put that extra credit on my grade?"

"Not so fast, Mr. Paulson. As a rock star, there are a few basics you'll need to understand, yes?"

"Uh, I guess." He taps his pencil on his desk in thought. "Always make sure your guitar is plugged in, never say the wrong city's name, and keep extra protection in your wallet. You know, gotta be safe and all," he says with a grin on his face.

"I see health class did wonders for you," Mr. Barnes mumbles. "You are correct; however, I'd like to get a little more basic than that. You mentioned plugging in your guitar. What does an amplifier do?"

"It makes your guitar louder."

"Yes, it takes your guitar's small amplitude and outputs a similar signal with a much larger amplitude."

"Yeah, sure." Bryan shrugs his shoulders.

"How do you measure amplitude?"

"By the number of girls lined up backstage?" He fist bumps the guy sitting next to him.

Mr. Barnes presses an imaginary buzzer. "Wrong, but nice try. As your parting gift in today's game show, I offer you a one-hour date in my classroom with some cardboard boxes and packing tape."

"No way, I didn't lose. I don't see any math nerds in rock bands. Present company excluded, of course."

"Maybe not, but I do see trigonometry. We can measure amplitude on a graph to see how far away from the X axis the sine wave gets. The farther away, the louder the sound."

Bryan throws his pencil down. "That's messed up Mr. Barnes. That's a trick question or something."

"No one likes a sore loser, Mr. Paulson. I'll see you after

class. Now, who's next?" he says, rubbing his hands together. "I have a lot of stuff that needs packing."

I have no idea what I want to be when I grow up. Never have. I wouldn't say I'm psychic, but I've always known little things before they happen. Everything I predict is pretty mundane; there's no explanation as to why I don't know lottery numbers or answers to tests. I was, however, a hell of a left guard at my last school (it helps to know right where to be to protect the quarterback). There was also that time I knew Brittney Dixon was going to let me get to third base before we moved here. We definitely weren't boyfriend-girlfriend (I don't do girlfriends) but we had our share of fun.

I love third base.

Of course, it would have been helpful to know ahead of time that her little brother was going to walk in. Like I said, there's no rhyme or reason to what I predict. I just sort of go with it.

Sometimes I wish I could see my future, but it hasn't happened yet. When we came here, Mom promised it'd be the last time we moved. *"I think it's time we put down some roots. After all these years, I owe you that much,"* she'd told me. She looked a little sad when she said it. I don't know if it was because she felt bad for maintaining the life of a hippie nomad for so long, or if it was because she was giving it up.

We left Topeka right before Christmas and headed to my grandparents' house—her mom and dad—in a small town outside of Durham, North Carolina. I miss football, even though I only played for three months of one season. Aside from that, there wasn't much in Topeka.

The idea of being "home" is weird considering I've never called any place home. It was always more "where Mom decided to hang out for a few months." I love Grandpa's farm, though. Over the years, we've been there several times between moves or when Mom needed some farm time, which meant she was between jobs or boyfriends. Some of my favorite memories were on that farm. Gran always had a few types of pie to choose from, and I had a whole room to myself. On the first few days of each visit, I'd alternate between eating everything in sight and lying spread-eagle on my bed since I never knew how long I would get to enjoy either of those luxuries. I never want to sleep on another couch or floor again.

Despite the way it sounds, my childhood wasn't bad. Mom made up for her lack of a steady income and parenting skills with love and lots of fun. When we lived in Oklahoma, I was friends with a guy who was being raised by his older sister. A lot of our stories were similar.

The bell rings, snapping me out of my daydream. I consult the map Caffeinated Secretary put in my welcome packet to see where my second period class is.

"What do you have next?" Sarah asks.

"Economics."

"That's just a few doors down in this hallway."

I thank her then head in the direction she pointed. I'm the first one there, so I grab an empty desk by the window and watch everyone else make their way into the room. The teacher sashays toward me, her red curls bouncing with each shake of her hips. I catch two sets of eyes staring at her backside as she walks—one belonging to a guy with muscular arms, smiling like he's the poster child for a dentist's office, and the other to the girl next to him who bites her bottom lip as her cheeks flush.

Interesting.

Feeling guilty, the guy pushes his desk closer to the girl and leans over to kiss her cheek. She glances toward him with what looks like the world's fakest smile and laces her fingers with his.

Oh man, I mentally tell the guy, *your girlfriend is batting for the other team and you don't even know it.* I'm sort of sad for the girl, though. I know what it's like to desperately want to blend in—hard to do when you've been to fourteen schools in thirteen years. With a school this small, I doubt there's a big lesbian population. But I don't feel bad for the guy. Isn't that every teenage boy's fantasy?

"Hello, you must be the new student. I'm Mrs. Mason," the teacher says, passing me a textbook. "I'm glad you're here today. We've got a big project that I'll discuss in a bit. You bring our class count to an even number. That helps. Otherwise I might have had to assign a few students to Utah."

Whatever that means.

She checks off the attendance sheet when the bell rings and then addresses the classroom. "Good morning, everyone, I hope you all had a great Christmas break. Please pass up your holiday homework." She turns my direction as she scans the attendance list. "Don't worry about this assignment…"

"James," I interrupt her before she can call me by my given name. I make a mental note to introduce myself to the rest of my teachers before they commit the ultimate sin.

"Right. James. Like I said, this assignment won't count toward your grade since you weren't here." She points at the other faces in the class. "The rest of you better cough them up. We need to get right into the Dreaded Second Semester Senior Project." I hear a few groans, all of them from guys.

I start thinking about this dreaded project, but it becomes less of an issue when I realize it's getting harder to breathe. A loud ringing overtakes my ears while my brain and heart disagree over how fast it should beat. I have no idea what this means. Maybe it's a natural disaster? I've never predicted anything that big before. Do they even have earthquakes in North Carolina? Tsunamis? Stampedes? I look outside and see blue skies. Is there about to be an airplane crash? Train crash? A code blue? I should've paid better attention in geography or that CPR class.

My heart's beating faster and faster, and I wipe my palms against my jeans. I don't know if I should hide under my desk or try to find a bathroom. I look around; everyone else is passing in their homework as if the new kid isn't getting ready to keel over and die.

Oh, my God. It's the apocalypse. That's gotta be it. The world is going to end, and I'm the only one who knows it. And here I thought it was going to be a good day. Now I wish I would have gone all the way with Brittney. To die a virgin when the opportunity had once presented itself seems like such a waste. I start counting my heartbeats and try to calm the fuck down so I can figure out how to tell everyone else that Jesus or zombies are on the way.

Then the classroom door opens, and I stop breathing.

A girl with long, blonde hair walks in and hands a late slip to Mrs. Mason. "Welcome back, Rachel. How was Cozumel?"

"It was great! We got back late last night. My favorite part was the Chichen Itza tour. Who knew a bunch of old stuff could be so cool? Just don't let Mr. Allen know I said that. He'll probably make me write a report on it."

"I'm glad you enjoyed it, and your secret's safe with me. Turn in your holiday homework and take your seat. It's time to get married."

I watch Rachel dig in her backpack and will my incapacitated diaphragm to remember its sole purpose in life. When she walks toward me, I take a moment to admire her long legs. She smiles, and then her lips are moving. Oh God. I've never hated my lungs so much in my life. I cough and manage to inhale. I swear I smell vanilla mixed with... sunshine? I don't know how to explain it. It's an odd combination, but on her it works. She sits in a desk next to me and stares like she's waiting for me to do something. Her eyes remind me of chocolate. She's the most beautiful girl I've ever seen.

"I'm sorry, what?" *Thank you, vocal cords. Thank you for working and not making me look like an even bigger jackass.*

"Hi, what's your name?" she repeats, drawing out each word.

Shit. I wipe my hands on my jeans again. What's that word people use to get my attention? That thing inside my head needs more oxygen to work properly. I take a deep breath.

Vanilla. Sunshine.

"James." I manage to smile, but it probably looks like the same face I made that time Gran mixed up the salt with the sugar in her apple pie. Rachel looks confused. The teacher starts speaking again and I'm grateful for the distraction.

"All right, class. Let's get into our project. As I mentioned before the break, the senior Economics project is based on real life. You will each be assigned a partner and the two of you will become a couple. You'll spend the next five months dealing with budgets, jobs, bills, pretend families, and so on.

I will place you in different socio-economic classes and you'll see how that affects the jobs you can find, the houses you can afford and the opportunities you have in life. I'll throw in some twists here and there too. Now, let's partner up and get hitched."

She counts off pairs around the classroom and ends up on my row of desks. "Alicia and Scott. Cori and Mike. Rachel and James."

Holy shit. I love this class. I love this desk. I love this assignment.

"Stand up and slide your desks back to make space in the middle of the room." Mrs. Mason grabs a basket off her desk and passes a Ring Pop to each guy in the room. "Gentlemen, please unwrap your rings, stand before your brides and repeat after me:

"I, state your name, take thee, state your bride's name, in pretend matrimony. I promise to be true to our grade for better or worse, in sickness and in health, as long as we both shall graduate."

I slide the Ring Pop on Rachel's finger and make an effort to not jerk my hand back. Sparks didn't actually fly, but I wasn't expecting her skin to feel so soft. So *good*. I've never been pretend married before, but I already know I can never give another girl a ring again. I'm a senior in high school and I'm ruined for life. I want to get married for real and have her babies. I mean, make her have my babies. Shit, who am I kidding? I'd have her babies if she asked me to.

"Okay, let's get the desks back in order and I'll hand out your packets with all of your information. We'll review them together and you can start looking for houses."

I slide my desk back up, bringing it slightly closer to Rachel's. She puts her hair in a ponytail but a few shorter tendrils fall around her face. Fuck, did I just say tendrils? This is not good. I've made it seventeen years without having a girlfriend, and now I have a pretend wife and I'm using sissy words. What's next? I clear my throat and take a deep breath.

"Let's try this again. Hi, I'm James. It's nice to meet you." I smile at her.

She smiles back, and it lights up her entire face. "Hi. Rachel. Where are you from?"

"Nowhere, really, but I moved here from Topeka. Why were you in Cozumel?"

"My dad wanted to celebrate me winning my cross country championship, so Christmas in Cozumel it was. He kept introducing me to the hotel staff as 'Rachel the Roadrunner.' It was really embarrassing," she said, rolling her eyes.

"That beats Christmas on a farm, but you didn't get any of my gran's pie so I win the dessert round."

"Are you kidding? Mexican desserts are the best. Churros, flan, dulce de leche cake...I managed to put on about five pounds on vacation."

"You look perfect to me," I murmur.

Rachel just stares at me. Christ on a cracker. "I said that out loud, didn't I?"

"Yup," she giggles.

I wince and facepalm. "So much for first impressions," I groan.

"That one was weird too."

"Third time's the charm?" I ask with my most dazzling smile in place, praying it doesn't look creepy. About the time

I start silently pleading with the floor to open up and swallow me whole, Mrs. Mason starts talking again.

"Look at the first two pages of your packets. This is where you'll find your profession, your education level, and all the other info you'll need to make it in life. Use this information to figure out where you want to live, what kind of car you want, the type of daycare you'll need and the bills you'll need to pay each month. You need to figure out if you want to rent or own your home; there will be no living with imaginary friends or family. I'll walk around to answer any questions you may have. By the end of the week, you will submit your monthly budgets and give me an informal report on where you live."

Rachel looks at me and points to our packet.

"So, Weird New Guy, what've we got?" she smiles innocently.

"Come on, that's a little harsh, don't you think?"

"Probably, but I couldn't help myself. We almost never get any new students to tease."

"Teasing is the number one sign that you have a crush on someone. Just saying." *That's it, James. Keep your cool.* I can have a conversation with a beautiful girl without making an ass out of myself, right? I mean, I had no problems talking to Brittney... not that she's in the same league as Rachel. Or even on the same planet. God, I wish I knew what any of this meant.

"Let's not get ahead of ourselves; we've only been fake married for five minutes."

"Oh, you didn't know? It was love at first sight. We couldn't keep our hands off each other and decided to elope. It says so right here." I point to the packet and smile.

"Nice try, Romeo." Rachel laughs, and it's the most beautiful thing I've ever heard. She opens our packet and looks over the details. "We're both college graduates and have one child. We live in Raleigh. You're a firefighter and I'm a... news anchor? Seriously?"

"I take it you don't want a career in television?"

"I have zero desire to be in front of a camera."

"So what *do* you want to be when you grow up?"

"That's complicated."

"Let me guess. You want to be a professional bungee jumper, but you're deathly afraid of heights and things made of elastic?"

Her lips twitch upward. "I've already gone bungee jumping."

"Really? I've always wanted to do that. Okay, let's see." I rub my chin. "You want to be a world-famous fashion designer, but you don't know how to sew."

She gestures toward her clothes. She's wearing some type of workout pants—that make her legs look amazing, I might add—and some running shoes. "Now you're describing my best friend. In case you haven't noticed, I don't really care what I wear."

"Wrong, I totally noticed. It's all right, though. I sort of like homely looking girls," I say, laughing.

"Hey!" She playfully smacks me on the shoulder.

"Kidding, kidding! Okay, final guess. You want to be a P.E. teacher, but your dad would never approve of such a lowly profession."

Rachel's mouth falls open. "How the hell do you know that?"

"Just a lucky guess."

She eyes me warily. "Are you psychic or something?"

I used to get nervous when people asked me stuff like this, but I've gotten pretty good at deflecting over the years. "Sorry, my crystal ball's in the repair shop. Perhaps I should have said 'educated guess.' Your dad sprung for a trip to Cozumel over the holidays, which tells me he's got money. You won a championship and your legs look pretty amazing, which tells me you've been running for quite some time. The rest of the guess was just lucky."

She shifts in her desk and a slight pout falls on her lips. "Unfortunately, you're right. My dad wants me to focus on running. He's got this dream of me becoming an Olympic gold medalist. I'd rather do something more worthwhile like work with kids. That's the biggest difference between me and him. I can't think of a better career to have. Running is everything to me. To get a chance to develop that same love in another athlete? That's awesome. And why are you staring at me like that?"

I can't help myself. Passion pours out of her, and I want to go find her dad and punch him in the nuts. "Sorry, I've just never met anyone who was so sure of what she wanted to be in life. I wish I had my shit together like that."

"You don't know what you want to be when you grow up?"

"I do now. A firefighter married to the hottest news anchor in Raleigh who loves to coach our child's track team."

"Well if you get to be married to a hot news anchor, then I get to be married to a hot firefighter. That's only fair."

"Are you saying I'm hot?"

She bites her bottom lip as she studies my face. Sweet Jesus, that shouldn't be allowed. My heart instantly picks up its pace and I draw in a quick breath, suddenly realizing this could end very badly on my part. I know nothing about this girl. Hell, maybe she's crushing on the teacher too. Why is she taking so damn long to respond? And when did I turn into such a little bitch? I watch her expression and sigh with relief when she smiles.

"I don't normally go for guys with dark hair, but green eyes are okay. You've got nice lips too. But my final decision can't be made right now. Hot firefighter status can only be granted after a thorough examination of the abs." She makes a circling motion with her fingertip in the general direction of my midsection. I suddenly wonder what the school dress code says about guys wearing no shirts.

"Well, it's good to know that you're not shy and I'm not entirely repulsive."

She laughs as she tosses our packet in her backpack. I glance at her hands and wonder just what kind of examination she's talking about. I want nothing more than to feel those fingers on my abs. I'm fairly certain she won't be disappointed. I'm not exactly Magic Mike material, but I've never had any complaints.

"No, I'm not, and no you're not. So far."

"Well, we are married now. I'm pretty sure that means I'm allowed to show you my abs. And while we're at it," I say, raising my eyebrows, "you can show *me*—"

The bell rings.

"—where my next class is."

Rachel

I walk into third period with a ridiculous grin on my face. Avery's already sitting in her seat directly behind mine, and her expectant look and incessant pen tapping tells me she's about ten seconds away from Full-On Avery Mode. It's still about two hours early for that.

"Well?" she gestures with her palms upward. "I've been waiting for three and a half minutes! Did you get Sean? Tell me you got Sean. Or Phil. Or Ben. Why am I just now realizing all the cute guys in school have one-syllable names? Come on, Ray. Spill it!"

I glance down at my Ring Pop. "Actually, none of the above."

"Oh, God. Did you get Smelly Warren?" She gently pats my shoulder in a show of sympathy. Avery can be loud, but damn she's sweet.

"Nope, not Smelly Warren. We got a new student, and Mrs. Mason assigned us together."

"You mean I'm not New Girl Avery anymore? Praise the sweet, tiny baby Jesus!" she says, raising her arms in the air. Technically, she hasn't been the new girl since sophomore year, but since we never get new students here, the name just sort of stuck. She moved here from New York City after her mom caught her dad banging his intern on his mahogany boardroom conference table. According to Avery, her mom took a cell phone video of it and filed for divorce. Her dad didn't have any problems agreeing to child support, alimony and a yearly paid vacation for her mom. I guess he wasn't too keen on the idea of the video getting out. Especially since his intern's name was Steven. Now Avery's mom drives an Audi with a license plate that says MAHOGANY.

"Nope, you've been dethroned. And Ave? He's cute. Like, really, really cute."

She squeals, which only makes my grin bigger. "Fresh meat! What's he like?"

"Well, it was sort of awkward at first. It was like he forgot how to talk, and he kept staring at me like I was his source of daylight or something. He did say I was hot though, but he was probably joking."

The last time anyone said I was hot was at a pool party in ninth grade. He was right—I had a fever and spent five days in bed after that. Leave it to me to get the flu in the middle of summer.

"Ray, you *are* hot! This is awesome! Maybe there's hope for prom after all!"

"And, here we go." Avery is the yin to my yang—literally. I'm tall and blonde and she's short and bi-racial—her mom's white and her dad's black. She's been planning for senior prom since the first day of the school year, but I couldn't care less about the whole ordeal. There are far more exciting things to do than spend hundreds of dollars on a dress for one night with a guy who will spend forty-nine percent of his time stepping on my feet and the other fifty-one percent staring at my nonexistent cleavage. No. Thank. You.

"Knock it off Rachel Lynn. I will drag your toned ass to the prom if it kills you!"

"Sure, if you can catch me," I tease. Avery considers running shoes to be a crime against fashion. Case in point: Her dark curls are swept back with some sort of grandma-esque brooch, and she's wearing an off-the-shoulder top, skinny jeans and black Louboutins. The only reason I know the name of her shoes is because she drilled it into my head in an effort to give me an appreciation for designers. (It didn't work.) Regardless, if I tried to wear that shit, I'd fall over. The bell rings to start class, so she starts a note to finish our conversation. Thank God, the teacher is ancient and can't even see the back of the class.

Avery: So what's his name?
Me: James
Avery: Of course it is.
Me: ??
Avery: One syllable.
Me: Yeah, but his syllable is so much better than the others.
Avery: So what does One-Syllable James look like?
Me: Wavy, dark hair. Sort of shaggy. I don't

know if he's due for a haircut or just doesn't care. It works for him though. Green eyes and lips that practically demand some attention. Oh, we had to stand up for the ceremony and get this – he's taller than me.

Avery: Shut up.

Me: I know, right? It's nice not feeling like the Jolly Green Giant.

Avery: Yeah, you're sort of a freak. I meant to tell you that the other day.

Me: I'm not a freak, you're just a midget.

Avery: You better mean that with love. I'm not above shanking you.

Me: I love it when you get all tough NYC girl on me.

Avery: Damn straight. You should have seen the guy at the diner last week who tried to cop a feel. I literally put my boot up his ass.

Me: Good thing your aunt's the owner and your mom's the manager.

Avery: Yes, but enough about my badassery. Do you think you'll actually give James a chance?

Me: Probably not. It's not worth the argument with my dad about how a boyfriend won't distract me from track.

Avery: He doesn't have to know about him...

Me: True.
Avery: So when do I get to meet him?
Me: I'll look for him at lunch. I forgot to check his schedule to see if we have any other classes together.
Avery: OMG. Do you think the teacher knows she's repeated herself four times?
Me: Her hearing aid's probably off.

We both bust out laughing.

We pick up our cafeteria food and scan the crowd. Avery grabs my arm when she sees James. "Holy shit, Ray. He *is* cute."

His backpack is slung over one shoulder, and he's looking for a place to sit. Surprisingly, he looks more confident than nervous, but I still feel the need to rescue him before he makes a huge mistake and sits somewhere bad, like Smelly Warren's table. I walk toward him and can't help but smile. This is the first chance I've had to look him over without him seeing. His jeans hug him in all the right places. God bless you, Levi Strauss.

"Hey New Guy. Why don't you join us?"

"Why hello there, School Wife. Thanks for sparing me a game of eeny-meeny-miney-moe."

"I'm glad to be of service," I say, heading to our regular table. James sits across from me and Avery instantly pounces on him.

"Hi, I'm Avery, your best friend-in-law. I've heard a lot about you already." I kick her under the table.

"Hi Avery, I'm James." He raises an eyebrow toward me and shakes her hand. I wonder if she felt the same jolt I did during the Ring Pop ceremony. If she did, her expression doesn't give it away.

"Nothing exciting ever happens here, so you get to be the feature of our lunchtime conversation," she says before drenching her French fries in ketchup. "Are you up for a game of twenty questions?"

"Sure, this should be fun."

"Question one. Are you a serial killer?"

James busts out laughing. "Well, I see you get right to the important stuff. No, definitely not a serial killer."

"You're pretend-married to my Beef. Her safety is important to me. For all I know, you're on the run from some mass murder you committed out there in... wherever it is you came from," she says, waving her hand in the air.

He pauses, mid-mustard squirt. "Your Beef? Dare I ask?"

"Beef. BFF. Best Friend Forever."

He looks at me with a reassuring glance and continues to drench his corn dog in mustard. "Rachel, I promise you're safe with me. I won't let anything bad happen to you."

For some reason, I actually believe him. My dad's pretty much guaranteed I don't have a wealth of experience in the guy department, but I don't feel the least bit worried about finding myself locked in a trunk on the way to the woods.

"Question two," Avery asks. "What is your stance on chick flicks?"

"I could get on board with chick flicks. Steel Magnolias gets me in the feels every time."

"Shut. Up. That's my all-time favorite movie," I say,

27

pointing my chicken strip in his direction. "Do you have sisters or something?"

"Is that question three?"

"Sure."

"Nope, no siblings. Just me and my mom."

"That explains it." I manage to open a container of barbecue sauce without getting it on my shirt. "Question four. Do you play any instruments?"

"Guitar. Her name is Lucy, and I've been in love with her for about five years." A shy smile spreads across his face and his cute factor definitely goes up a few notches. "She was a gift from my grandpa and has gotten me through some pretty lonely nights."

"Question five," Avery continues. "Why are you lonely?"

He passes a hand through his hair, but I catch a glimpse of the slight calluses on his fingertips before they sink into his waves. "I've moved about a dozen times, so I'm always the new kid."

"I only moved once, but I remember what it felt like trying to make new friends. High school is a hellish place, especially when *some* people," Avery says, glancing at me, "don't appreciate a good fashion sense. You won the lottery with me and Rachey-poo here, though. We'll take care of you." She passes him her can of Diet Coke. "Will you open this? I just got a mani yesterday."

He obliges and asks me for question six. "Diet Coke or Diet Pepsi?" I ask, suspiciously.

"That's easy. Dr. Pepper."

"I think I can live with that. If you said Diet Pepsi, I might have divorced you. There will be no Diet Pepsi in my house."

"My school wife is fanatical about Diet Coke, good to know," he says, making a mental note.

"You don't mess with the Nectar of the Gods and all of its bubbly deliciousness." I clink my can against Avery's. "At least I won't have to worry about you stealing mine. Okay, Ave, your turn."

"Question seven. Do you have a girlfriend?"

"Never had one."

Avery gasps. "Really? You're too cute to have never had a girlfriend. Wait, does this mean you're...."

"Question eight. No, I'm not gay either."

"Well that's good to know. Not that I'd have a problem with you being gay. I could kill for a shopping partner." She pauses and nudges my shoulder. "You know, Ray has never had a boyfriend. Just sayin.'"

The Queen of Subtlety sends a dazzling smile toward James. I know she means well, but *God* she has such a big mouth. Why did I have to tell her I thought he was cute? I let my hair fall over my face. I'm not usually shy, so I'm not sure where this idiotic schoolgirl behavior is coming from. Avery must be rubbing off on me.

"Never had a boyfriend, huh?" He laughs softly and takes a drink of chocolate milk.

"Moving right along," I say emphatically. Those lips look like they have more skill than mine, and I'd rather not be written off as a senior with no experience. Even though I am. "Question nine. If you could get a tattoo, what would it be?

"Well, I already have a few. I'm not sure what I want next though. They're sort of addicting."

"Wait, how old are you?"

"Question ten. I'm seventeen."

"So how do you have tattoos?"

"My mom's a hippie. She went with me and signed the papers," he says in complete nonchalance. "She has a few, so she didn't think it was that big of a deal."

"Alright, question eleven," Avery interjects. "Where are they? Back? Biceps? Buns?" She drums her fingers together and grins wickedly on the last word. As if I'd ever let her see my school husband's buns. James lifts his right sleeve and I see the most gorgeous black and gray tree snaking its way up to his well-defined shoulder. His triceps makes the roots appear 3-D and before I know it, I'm reaching across the table and my finger traces the edge of one root up to the trunk and out to a branch before his shirt prevents me from further exploration. His muscles are as beautiful as his tattoo, and I force my hand away from his arm. Jesus, now I really want to know what his abs look like. And feel like. And taste like.

Taste like? Ugh, I'm turning into a teenage man-eater right before my own eyes. I can just picture it now. *Hi Rachel, what'd you do at school today? Oh, not much. Took a quiz and turned into a cafeteria floozy at lunch.*

"Down girl," Avery warns. "I've seen you have that same look when you drag me to the running store for a new pair of shoes. Oh my God, are you blushing?"

"No!" I retort. Any remote hope I had of impressing James has just died a terrible, gruesome death. Maybe I'll grow up to be the Crazy Cat Lady of running shoes. So much for being the news anchor with a hot firefighter husband. Or the normal, confident girl I was earlier today.

"Don't worry, Ray, I didn't mind," James says as he lowers his sleeve. "But you'll have to wait to see the others. Perhaps when you make your final determination on my occupation?" Those gorgeous lips of his turn upward, and I've never heard my nickname sound better. What the hell is happening to me?

"Occupation?" Avery asks. "You've known each other for a whopping hour and you already have an inside joke? Not cool, Beef."

"It's not an inside joke, Avery. Mrs. Mason's project said he was a firefighter and I was a news anchor. James, uhh, said that I..." I already told Avery that James said I was hot, but that was before he was sitting right in front of me, rendering me as useful as a screen door on a submarine. And now I'm speaking in metaphors. *God.*

"I said I had a hot news anchor wife, but Ray doesn't know if I'm a hot firefighter yet." James grips his heart in feigned injury.

"Duh, she hasn't seen your abs yet," Avery says, matter-of-factly. "If you're not calendar material, you're just a guy who puts out fires."

"I see y'all take this stuff seriously," he says. "It's a good thing I don't mind being objectified in the name of public service."

"Let's find out what we can expect to see in our calendar," Avery asks. "Question twelve. Boxers or briefs?"

"Boxer briefs. Best of both worlds."

Great, now I'm picturing him in just his underwear and a firefighter helmet. How am I supposed to work on this project with him when he's mostly naked in my head? I clear my throat, hoping to clear my mind. "Alright, let's get our minds out of the gutter. Question thirteen. If you had a free vacation to anywhere in the world, where would you go?"

He brushes his lips with his thumb and studies me for several moments before answering. "Fiji."

And now he's mostly naked wearing a firefighter helmet in Fiji. I groan internally. "That's my dream vacation. I'd give anything to go there."

"The man of your dreams is gonna take you there one day," he says with a smile before dropping his eyes. He has lashes for days. How did I not notice that earlier? Oh, that's right. His lips. I silently plead with Avery for some help but I think she's enjoying my spectacular shit show. Things were much better when James was the flustered one. Somehow, I manage to find my voice.

"Question fourteen. Have you applied to any colleges?"

"Nope, at least not yet. I never saw a point with us moving around so much. Have you?"

"I applied for two: NC State and UNC. Though you can never mention State to my dad. He might disown me if he finds out." I shudder thinking about it.

"Why'd you apply there if your dad might disown you? That seems a bit counterproductive to me."

"That was her fault," I say, pointing to my Beef. "She was in Full-On Avery Mode about how I should take a chance and do something bold and daring, and I got excited. My dad went to UNC and has dreams of me attending his alma mater and run in their track program. But I sort of want my own dream. So I applied to both."

"Have you heard back yet?"

"Not until the end of the month. I'm stalking the mailbox though."

"Avery, what about you? Where do you want to go to college?" James asks.

"I've applied to FIT and Parsons. My stuff's gonna be on a runway one day."

"Yup, all the baggage handlers at the Raleigh-Durham airport are gonna wear your stuff," I tease. James doubles over in laughter, and I feel like a million bucks knowing I'm the cause of that beautiful sound.

"Har har har." She finishes her Diet Coke and stands to clear her tray. James jumps up and removes it from her hands.

"You done, Ray?" I nod, and he stacks our trays on top of his and heads toward the conveyor belt. Avery and I look at each other in amazement.

"Wow, Ray. Cute and chivalrous? You should try to keep this one around." I sigh in agreement. Several sets of female eyes follow him back to our table and a surge of jealousy courses through me. Those girls better back off my school husband. I wonder if Avery will let me borrow her shank.

"Only ten more minutes for lunch, ladies. Y'all think we'll have enough time to finish this interrogation?" James asks.

"You say that like you haven't enjoyed the company of two beautiful girls in a one-star dining establishment," Avery says, batting her eyes.

"Oh, I've enjoyed the company. This is definitely the best first day I've ever had."

"Of course it is, silly. I told you, you lucked out with Ray and me. Now, where'd we leave off? Question fifteen?"

"I think so."

"Okay, what's the top item on your bucket list?"

"To save someone's life."

"Wow, you didn't even need to think about that," I say. "How many things do you have on your bucket list?"

"I have several, but that's always been the top one. I can't think of anything greater than that."

"So do you want to be a doctor?" Avery asks.

"Question sixteen. Nope. Definitely not a doctor. I'm going to be a hot firefighter, remember?" he says, laughing. I consider this a sign and make a split-second decision to sacrifice all remaining dignity.

"Question seventeen," I say, before losing courage. "What does your ideal girl look like?"

James lets out a breath. "That's tough. There are so many beautiful girls in the world." He runs his hands through his hair and I cross my fingers under the table because apparently I'm five now. "I could spout off a bunch of crap about a perfect body and gorgeous eyes, but that doesn't mean much. My ideal girl makes me laugh. She makes me want to be a better person and she challenges me. That being said," James rubs the back of his neck, "I've always thought blondes were pretty."

Oh, God. I have blond hair. And I make him laugh. I don't know about the rest, but it's a step in the right direction. My inner schoolgirl is high-fiving herself.

"Aw, you're a romantic. It's a shame we don't know anyone with blond hair," Avery teases. "Question eighteen. What kind of car do you drive?"

"Don't laugh, but I just got my license last week. My grandpa gave me his old Ford. That thing is so ancient, I swear it was built by Henry himself. It definitely won't help me pick up any ladies, but it serves its purpose. And more importantly, it was free."

"That's cool. My cheating gay dad promised me a car for my birthday. That fucker better follow through." James tilts his head to the side, trying to connect the dots of Avery's statement. "Don't worry, it sounds worse than it is," she says, with a pass of her hand. "The bottom line is he said he'd get me a car for my eighteenth birthday and that's next month. All I know is that it better have leather and a big ass pink bow."

"Speaking of birthdays, question nineteen," I ask. "When's your eighteenth birthday?"

"April third."

"No it's not," I say, as Avery lets out a shriek.

"Yes, it is. I may have moved around a lot, but as far as I know my birthday never changed." He furrows his eyebrows as he looks between Avery and me.

"It can't be April third," I say.

"Why not? Is that day reserved or something?"

"Yeah, for my birthday."

"Shut up!" Avery shouts, slapping her hand on the table with each word. "Are you guys serious? I can't stand the cuteness. This is totally a sign or something."

James and I stare at each other briefly, and for a moment, I wonder if Avery is right. Then again, last week she was positive that Tyler McKinney was going to profess his undying love to her, which made for a really awkward standoff when he came to the Sweet Pea on Friday. Damn Avery and her romantic tangents getting my hopes up. I snap out of my thoughts when the bell rings.

"I didn't get to ask the last question," I say.

"Why don't you give me your number, and I can call you after school. You can ask then, and we can talk about our project."

I reach for a pen in my backpack while attempting to hide my grin. I can't wait for it to be tonight. Who cares if he said it was for the project. "Give me your hand." James rests the back of his hand in mine while I write my number on his palm. Why are phone numbers only ten digits? I print slowly to maximize my time. His fingertips brush the inside of my wrist, sending a stream of electricity up my arm, and I concentrate on keeping my whimper to myself.

"There you go." He stares at his hand and then looks back at me and smiles.

"Thanks. See you on the six o'clock news, Mrs. Tennyson."

"Excuse me?

"Tennyson. My last name, and now yours, according to high school Economics."

James heads to his next class, and I find myself appreciating the view as he leaves. I should bake Mrs. Mason some cookies.

"Earth to Rachel," Avery says, waving her hands in front of my face. She links arms with me and spins me around to walk in the opposite direction. "This has been quite the lunch. I must say, I've thoroughly enjoyed watching Rachel I-Don't-Care-About-Guys Wheaton fall apart over one."

"I have no idea what you're talking about."

"Sure you don't," she says, patting my arm. "And denial is just a river in Egypt."

James

The truck door requires more than a tug to open it, and the hinges protest against the cold. I toss my backpack on the passenger seat and crank the engine. I don't know how much life is left in this beast, but looking for a job might not be a bad idea. As the truck warms up, I search the parking lot for Rachel. We don't have any other classes together, which I suppose is a good thing. It's hard to concentrate with her nearby. Hell, I'm still buzzing from sitting across from her during lunch. As far as first days go, I stand by my earlier statement to Avery—this has been the best one I've ever had.

In typical high school fashion, the cliques aren't hard to spot. The jocks park along the football field and the country guys hang out by the agriculture building. The rich kids are in a luxury car oasis at the far end of the lot. But there's still no Rachel, which means I'll have to wait until tomorrow to see her. And that's a damn shame.

I throw the transmission into drive and head out of the parking lot, passing the couple from Economics. Tomorrow I should introduce myself to her. I have a feeling she needs a friend and I definitely know what it's like to be different. When I was eight, I made the mistake of telling someone that I knew things before they happened. After that, I was always the last pick during P.E., and Halloween that year was brutal. Four different kids dressed up as me, complete with muumuus, gypsy scarves, and fake crystal balls. When Mom told me we were moving, I kissed her on the lips and I didn't even wipe it off afterward.

I steer the truck to the line of vehicles leaving the parking lot, but turn toward the stadium at the last minute. The truck groans over a few speed bumps, and I slow near the concession stand. The field is empty, but I park and grab a seat anyway. I've been intuitive long enough to know I'm here for a reason. The cold aluminum doesn't leave much room for comfort, but at least it's warmer than Topeka.

To pass the time, I bring up my Lake Street Dive playlist on my phone and stare at the album cover as the first song comes on. *I'm sorry, Rachael Price. You've officially been demoted to the second most gorgeous woman on the planet.*

Three songs into my playlist, a group of girls walks onto the track—including a leggy blonde with a long ponytail. I do a mental happy dance and lean forward to watch the group warm up. (Okay, I lied. I'm only watching her warm up.) She stretches with ease and chats with the other girls. I can't make out what they're saying but everything is punctuated by laughter. For several minutes, they torture me with displays of teenage flexibility and then stand to take their positions in each lane. I hear Rachel count down and all eight spring forward. She's definitely got a hot body—I saw that when she walked into class—but seeing her in action gives me a whole new appreciation for it. She starts out in the middle, but takes third by the end of the first lap. She passes another runner on lap three. When she reaches the final turn on lap four, she's in first. Her dad was wrong—she's not a roadrunner, she's a gazelle. The only thing more amazing than her body is the smile that takes up half of her face.

Rachel hits the finish line a full six seconds before the rest of the group joins her. She laces her fingers on top of her head and sends quick bursts of breath into the cold air. I have no idea what she ran her mile in, but I know I wasn't watching for very long. The girls settle on the track for a few minutes of stretching, and I figure this is the perfect time to leave before I'm spotted.

I picture her legs at full speed on the way back to the truck and have to adjust myself slightly before climbing into the cab. I remember being so bored during our move to Topeka that I actually read one of my mom's romance novels. Now I have an idea of what "aching loins" means.

I take two pieces of apple pie back to my bedroom and stare at my phone. Is 6:53 too early to call? Or too late? I feel a little like Goldilocks. My finger hovers over her name. I saved her number as soon as I walked away in case it rubbed off. I touch the screen, and she answers on the third ring.

"Hello?"

"Rachel? This is James. I hope it's a good time to call."

"Yup, perfect timing. I just got out of the shower."

Oh God. Rachel. Shower. Naked. Wet. Soap. My brain short circuits and my mouth opens and closes like a fish drowning on land.

"Oh, that's good." It comes out an octave higher than normal, so I clear my throat. "I mean, not that you needed a shower. Or maybe you did. So it's good that you showered. So you're clean and stuff. And I'm going to shut up now." She laughs as I work to remove the foot from my mouth. These mental images aren't going anywhere for a while.

"Yeah, I like being clean and stuff."

I groan. "One of these days, I won't make an ass out of myself. Though, from the looks of it, that may not be anytime soon."

"Cut yourself some slack, New Guy. We'll chalk it up to first-day jitters."

"I've moved too many times to have first-day jitters."

"Hmm... jet lag?"

"Nope, we drove here from Topeka a few weeks ago."

"Well that leaves one thing."

"What?"

"You were abducted by evil aliens who use you for their amusement and force you to say embarrassing things."

I bust out laughing and fall onto my bed. This girl is absolutely perfect. "Yes, that's exactly it. How did you know?"

"Oh, just a lucky guess. But watch out for those probes. I hear they can be a real pain in the ass." I can hear the smile in her voice. "So how was the rest of your day?"

"Not bad. Classes seem easy enough and I didn't get lost. How about you?"

"I had a pretty good day. I did a one-mile assessment after school with some of the girls from track. We're gearing up for an invitational and coach wants to make sure the holidays didn't take too much out of us."

"How'd that go?" The girl with the golden legs has been running through my mind all day. Pun intended.

"I came in at 5:45."

Holy shit. That's only about 20 seconds off my time. "Why don't you sound very proud of that?"

"Eh, it was far from a personal record."

"It's still pretty amazing. You should give yourself credit." Someone says something in the background and she pulls away from the phone.

"No, not under 5:30. Yes, I'll make sure to get it down. Jamie, a new classmate."

Jamie?

"Sorry, that was my dad. He just got home." I can practically hear her eyes rolling.

"Don't sound so excited."

"He's such an ass. Of course the only thing he cares about is my time from today and that it's not fast enough for his liking."

"Wow, your dad sounds like a twatwaffle. Who's Jamie?"

"You are. I didn't feel like telling him I was on the phone with a boy, especially since he's pissy."

"He doesn't let you talk to boys? It's a good thing I'm an outstanding specimen of a man," I say, emphasizing the last word. She laughs, which is what I was hoping for. Her douchebag dad isn't going to ruin our conversation.

"He thinks boys will distract me from running, so generally speaking, I'm not allowed to date."

41

Now Avery's comment at lunch makes sense. "So *that's* why you've never had a boyfriend."

"Yup, good ol' dad."

"Well, I don't think he'll be a problem for me. I don't want to date you."

"You don't?" She sounds wounded and for some odd reason, that makes me smile. We've definitely been flirting, but I still don't know if I'm competing against anyone else. Just because she's not allowed to date doesn't mean she doesn't like someone else. The fact that I don't have any hints into that area in her life is both maddening and perplexing. Normally, I get a sense of whether or not a girl likes me (hence me, Brittney and third base). But Rachel? Nothing.

"I married you today, so the way I see it, we're way past the dating phase. In fact, aren't we supposed to be talking about where we want to live?"

"Wow, you take your homework seriously, don't you?"

"Very. After all, I did make a vow." Now seems like a great time to shove apple pie in my mouth to prevent "Maybe one day it'll be for real" from coming out. Restraining orders aren't very sexy. While I may not know exactly how she feels about me, I know there's no one else I want to third base with. Is it even possible to use third base as a verb?

"I thought most high school guys were afraid of commitment."

"Is this the part where I say 'I'm not like most guys?'"

"But at lunch you said you've never had a girlfriend, so what do you really know about commitment? For all I know, you're a manwhore with a track record of breaking hearts."

Though I'm tempted to go for the obvious ego boost, it doesn't take psychic abilities to know that's not the best idea.

"I know I'll never lie to a girl, and I won't commit unless I mean it."

"Very smooth, James."

"There's nothing smooth about it. I spent all my life watching my mom follow guys around the country. She found out she was adopted in high school and left right after graduation. She fell into the hippie crowd and their idea of free love, which basically meant they were free to come and go as they pleased. I got tired of moving from city to city watching Mom give pieces of her heart away to guys whose promises lasted as long as their marijuana supply. I will never treat a girl the way those guys treated my mom."

I didn't mean to go all truth diarrhea on her, but at least she can't say I'm not sincere. Several seconds pass. I wish she'd say something. Just as long as it doesn't begin with "It was nice knowing you."

"Wow. Um. Sounds like your future girlfriend will be a lucky girl."

Tell her. Quit being a pussy and just tell her.

"What about you? Would you have a boyfriend if your dad wasn't the Joseph Stalin of dating?"

Pussy.

"I don't know. Not that I'd have much of a shot with anyone in school anyway."

"Why not? Did you accidentally kill the school mascot or something?" I take another bite of pie and wonder if I can sneak more out of the kitchen. Growing boy and all.

"No," she laughs. "I'm just not the type of girl a guy goes for. Which is okay. I deal with enough drama in Avery's love life." She tries to laugh that part off too, but I'm not buying it.

"So guys in North Carolina don't like hot blondes?"

"It's not that."

"They don't like girls with crazy dads?"

"It's okay, James. We can change the subject now. I'm starting to sound like I'm fishing for compliments, and that's most definitely not the case."

"I didn't think you were. I'm just trying to figure out what's wrong with the guys here. Oh God, you don't secretly have a penis do you?"

For the next ten seconds, I listen to the glorious sound of her full-on belly laughter, and I can't help but join in.

"James, no!" she yells when she finally takes a breath. "I most definitely do not have a penis."

"Well that's a huge relief. Because that could get really awkward." I *cannot* third base with a penis.

"Ugh, I can't believe I'm discussing penises with a boy on the phone."

"Quit facepalming, Rachel. These are important details we should know about each other."

"How'd you know I was facepalming?"

"I can hear it in your voice. You're blushing so hard, there's heat leaking out of my phone."

"Oh God, will you quit talking about heat and leaking?" She erupts in another fit of giggles and officially becomes the girl of my dreams. I'm grinning so hard my face hurts, but it's a small price to pay for the absolute torture I'm putting her through. She's gonna spill the beans on this "not their type" shit, or else.

"Let's regroup. You're a hot blonde with no penis. What's wrong with the male population at school?"

"You're really not going to let this go, are you?"

"Not a chance, sweetheart."

She sighs. I'm not sure she understands my level of persistence when it comes to getting what I want. I once sold all of my mom's clothes in a yard sale because she said I could get a remote controlled car if I got the money. It's not my fault that she didn't specify *how* I got the money.

"Fine, you win. I don't exactly have the body guys are after. I'm built to be a runner. And that's great, since I love running. It's no big deal, and I definitely don't lose any sleep over it, so you shouldn't either."

"Last I checked, I'm a guy. I'd like to think that means I know a thing or two about what makes a girl attractive. Everything about you is built the right way, trust me." Christ, this girl is killing me. Does she seriously not know how hot she is? That's like people not loving my gran's pie. It's just not possible. Right on cue, my brain revisits the image of Rachel in the shower. Long, wet hair cascading over her soft shoulders, covering her small, perky breasts. Water spilling down her back and over the curves of her ass. Holy mother of God. Her voice snaps me out of my daydream.

"Whatever you say, James."

"Don't get weird on me."

"I'm not. I just feel embarrassed now."

"Well you shouldn't. After all, we're still in the getting-to-know-each-other phase, right? Now we both know you're hot. Man, I sure am glad that's settled." I feign a sigh of relief. Before I can speak again, her dad comes back to her room.

"Tomorrow is fine. It's Avery. A biology report on the study of equine fecal intolerance."

What?

"Do I even want to know what that was about?"

"I make up all sorts of projects so he'll leave me alone. Right now, I don't feel like dealing with any more of his horse shit."

Rachel Wheaton, you are my soulmate.

"What was the last project you faked?"

"Menstruation rituals in South American tribes."

"And why that one?" I ask over my last bite of pie.

"Because he was being a douche."

Choking in front of the girl you have a crush on is incredibly embarrassing. My only saving grace is the fact that she can't see me flailing around my room. I pound on my chest like a dying gorilla and finally manage to dislodge the chunk of apple wedged between my tonsils and my pride. Thirty seconds of coughing later, I'm pretty sure my windpipe is still giving me the middle finger.

"James, are you okay?"

"I'm good," I wheeze. "Just having a disagreement with apple pie and gravity. You gotta warn me next time, Ray. I think I nearly died."

"I can see your headstone now: James: 0, Pie: 1"

"My headstone better say something more heroic than that. What did your dad want this time?"

"He wants me to start running tempo intervals tomorrow to get my time down."

"I haven't even met him and already I can't stand him. Is he running with you?"

"God no, that would be taking him away from all of his important meetings." I'm pretty sure she air quoted that last part. "He hired a personal coach for me and she'll time me tomorrow. He comes to my races, but that's about it. The only thing he cares about is me winning so he can brag some more. Sometimes I wish I could just quit."

"So why don't you?"

"One, because I love running. And two, because what else am I supposed to do with my time?"

"I dunno. Go out with me?" *Shit!* I didn't mean for that to come out. Well, I did, but not right now. I grab my guitar and start strumming to distract her.

"Is that Lucy I hear?"

"Yeah. Do you have any requests?" I plug my earbuds into my phone to free up both hands.

"What's your favorite song to play?"

"It depends on what mood I'm in." Right now, that would be embarrassed. Which is one I'm becoming more and more familiar with today. My fingers move to G major and I play the intro to *Wish You Were Here*. Because I wish she was.

"Is that Pink Floyd?"

"Very good, young grasshopper. What about this one?" I wonder if she'll pick up on the meaning behind the title.

"It sounds familiar. Keep playing."

I start singing the lyrics and she joins in when I reach *My Brown-Eyed Girl*. Maybe one day she will be. That is, if I can remember to breathe, keep my thoughts to myself and not choke on pie.

"This is fun! Play another one."

"Hmm." My fingers absently strum the strings as I think of what to play next. I could use this chance to tell her how I feel, or I could play it safe and come up with some pop radio bullshit. A quick round of eeny-meeny-miney-moe lands on taking a chance. "You may not know this one," I say, beginning a Foreigner song. If she doesn't get the hint after this one, I don't know what else to try. I've never heard a song called "Rachel Wheaton, I like you." With false confidence, I sing the first verse, pre-chorus and chorus of *Waiting For a Girl Like You*. There's no way I can sing the second verse. Not yet, anyway.

"I don't think I've ever heard that song before. I liked it though. You sang it really well. Have you ever performed for anyone before?"

"Nah, I mostly just mess around in my bedroom. With my guitar, I mean. Not anyone else." *Shut up, mouth.* "I mean, not like I haven't kissed a girl before. Because I have. Just not in a while." And clearly, that's not going to change anytime soon. *Jesus.*

Rachel laughs. "You sound really cute when you get tongue tied."

"Making an ass of myself is a gift, what can I say?" So much for impressing her.

"You have nothing to worry about. I'm sure plenty girls will be beating down your door soon. You turned several heads today at lunch."

"I don't care much about other heads. I quite enjoyed the scenery at my table."

"Yeah, Avery is pretty hot."

"That's not what I meant." How can this girl be so clueless about how hot she is? Rather than push my luck, I change the subject instead. "Speaking of lunch, you never asked me question twenty."

"I think I'm going to save it, if that's okay. Since it's my last one, I want to make sure it's good."

"Fine by me. That just means I get to hang out with you more."

"I'd hope so. My Economics grade is riding on you."

"I'll ignore that extremely easy opportunity for a dirty joke. Maybe we should get together this week and go over our project."

"Sounds like a good idea. I've gotta take Avery to the diner on Wednesday. She works there after school a few days a week. Want to meet there?"

"Sure. Maybe I can see if they're looking to hire while I'm there. I want to get an electric guitar. I should probably have some cash set aside for truck repairs, too."

"Is it already breaking down on you?"

"Not yet, but I'm sure it will soon. Grandpa said it's been held together with duct tape and prayers for the last couple of years." We both laugh together.

"I can text Avery to see if they're hiring since her aunt owns it. I'll let you know what she says. I should probably go for now though. I need my beauty sleep."

I do my best to keep her from hearing my disappointment. "You could pull an all-nighter and still not need beauty sleep."

"That's sweet."

"Just stating a fact. Good night, Ray."

"'Night." A moment passes, then another. "Hey James?" she asks quietly.

"Yeah?"

"I'm glad you moved here." Her voice is just above a whisper, but my heart soaks it up as if she shouted it.

"Me too."

Rachel

I can't believe this is actually happening. So what if we only met each other a few days ago? Everything about the way his arms feel around me feels so, so right. He strings a line of kisses from my shoulder to my neck. There has never been a more glorious feeling in the world. His callused fingertips trail across my collarbone, and his hands stop just above my breasts, waiting for permission. I arch into him and kiss his gorgeous lips in approval. His tongue enters my mouth as he cups my breasts and I whimper with need. My hands, starved for his body, reach under his shirt and feel muscle after muscle. Hot firefighter? Check, check, check.

"You are so fucking beautiful, Rachel." He accents every word with a kiss. I run my fingers through his hair and move my lips toward his ear. He groans, grabs my hips, and lifts me up. Instinctively, my legs wrap around his waist and stay there, even after he lays me down on the bed. His weight presses against me in the most delicious way, igniting nerve endings

I didn't know existed. I should really pay better attention in Anatomy and Physiology. Though James doesn't seem to mind giving me a private lesson on the subject. He's a very dedicated tutor.

I return my lips to his and savor every kiss. Fast. Slow. Deep. Teasing. I can't believe I've been missing out on this my whole life. Not that anyone else could ever compare to James. No, he and his tongue are in a league all their own. We roll over and I straddle his hips, grinding into him. I don't know how far we'll actually get, but I'm glad I'm already on the pill. He moans my name, and the sound fills me with power and courage. I rock back and pull my shirt over my head, knocking my hair out of the loose bun I had at the base of my neck. He sits up and sweeps my long locks over my shoulder then covers the black lace of my bra with his mouth, sending a current from my heart to the space beneath my matching panties.

"James," I say, breathlessly. I can't tell if it's a request or a plea. He responds by unhooking my bra. His fingers trace my shoulders and guide the straps down my arms.

"Mmmm," he says, before devouring one nipple, then the other. I suck in a breath and fist my hands in his hair. I knew his mouth was beautiful, but I had no idea it was so talented. So very, very talented.

Garth Brooks comes into my room and starts singing *Shameless*, and while I'm thrilled by his performance, I'd much rather be focusing on James' performance. *Go away, Garth*.

I turn back to James and he's gone. And still, Garth keeps singing. And singing. What the actual fuck?

"Shut *up*, Garth!" I grab my phone off my nightstand and hurl it toward him. My eyes snap open when my phone hits the closet door. Garth is still singing, but now it's muffled by the carpet. I rub my eyes and retrieve my phone to silence my alarm. 6:53 a.m.

It was a dream.

Damn it, damn it, damn it.

If there's a name for the female equivalent of blue balls, I have it. I head toward the bathroom for a cold shower. Only eight more hours until my date with James. And by date, I mean two people meeting at the same public location for the purpose of a school project.

One in which we're married.

I can't wait.

"You sure are smiley today. What gives?" Avery sits down in the front seat and blasts the heat. I'm not sure if she realizes North Carolina is about thirty degrees warmer than New York. Her Yankee blood must be sooo last season.

"Just looking forward to this afternoon." Trying to hide my crush from her is pointless. Avery has a knack for sniffing out important stuff. Clearance racks and secrets are her specialty. Still, I'm keeping my dream to myself. She doesn't need to know I was *this close* to losing my dream virginity. Or that Garth barged in on us. Some things are just far too embarrassing to share.

"Since when did taking me to work get so exciting?"

"Since I'm meeting James there."

"I knew it! Are you two in Economics love?"

"I don't know about that, but I'm definitely crushing on

him. And on top of being hot, he can sing. Like, actually sing."
I think back to the last song he sang me and bite back a smile.

"Huh. So this is what it looks like."

"What what looks like?"

"You, gushing over a boy. I thought I'd have to wait until college to see it. I must say, you're an adorable gusher. I've taught you well." She flashes one of her champion smiles at me.

"Yeah, yeah. I think he was flirting on the phone with me the other night. And he does this thing where he says embarrassing stuff and can't stop talking, and it's so cute," I say, giggling.

"Maybe we can all go to the movies this weekend. I'm hoping Harris will ask me."

"What happened to Tyler?"

"Tyler?"

"You know... last week... undying love?"

"Oh," she says, waving her hand dismissively. "I've moved on. Keep up, Ray."

"Sorry, it's hard sometimes. I should start writing this stuff down. Hey, speaking of your love life, it's January sixth, and you haven't gotten a delivery from Derrick. Think he finally got the hint?"

"God, I fucking hope so. Maybe 'Shove your flowers where the sun don't shine' finally got through that thick, shitty head of his." Avery, despite her small stature, can make a sailor blush when she gets fired up. She and Derrick dated back in New York. When she moved here, they decided to stay together. Everything was fine until last July when he sexted her a picture of his junk. That didn't piss her off, but the caption he sent with it sure did. Avery's name isn't Melissa. She told him to fuck off and lose her number, but ever since August, he's sent her a bouquet of roses on the fifth of every month – their anniversary. He even came to her dad's condo when she visited over Christmas in a pathetic attempt at getting her back. She spit in his face.

Literally.

Like I said, she's fiery.

"Here's to a new year and new beginnings. With Harris, or whoever else," I say, laughing. I pull into the parking lot of the Sweet Pea, and my stomach does a flip when I see James' truck. The door jingles when we walk in and Avery heads toward the back to drop off her backpack. James is sitting in the corner booth and when his eyes lock on mine, I flash back to straddling him in my dream. Sweet mother of God.

"Hello, School Wife." I could seriously get used to being called that. Which is strange, considering I didn't even know him three days ago. I do my best to walk toward him without tripping.

"Hello, School Husband. Were you waiting long?"

"Nah. I wanted to get here a few minutes early to fill out my application. Thanks again for putting in a good word for me. Avery's aunt said I could start on Saturday."

"Glad to help," I say, grinning. "This means you owe me, you know." Me talking to Aunt Devin was for purely selfish reasons, but he doesn't need to know that. "What are you doing?"

"Taking your picture. That smile was too beautiful to pass up. I need it for your profile in my phone."

"First let me make sure it's a good picture." I snatch his

phone from his hand and scroll to the Rs. My name isn't there. "Busted," I say, holding his contacts list up to him.

"Your phone number isn't stored under R. It's under W."

"For Wheaton?

"For Wife."

Well, hell.

I really, really need to thank Mrs. Mason. "Sorry, your name isn't stored under H. Or J, for that matter." He grabs my phone and scrolls through my contacts.

"New Guy? Really?"

I laugh and take my phone back. "It's a fitting name, I think." He's the new guy at school, and in my life. "Now smile, it's my turn." He sticks his tongue out instead, but I save the photo anyway. James and his tongue...

"Good afternoon, Mr. and Mrs. Tennyson. My name is Avery and I'll be taking care of you today. Can I start you off with something to drink?" Avery winks at me and it's obvious that she's really enjoying this. I'm so glad embarrassing me is on her list of things to do at work today.

"I'll have a Dr. Pepper float and an order of chili fries, please. You want anything, Ray?"

"I'll just have a Diet Coke float."

"Coming right up!" Avery bounces away, which is amazing considering she's wearing three-inch heels. She might be a fashionista, but she's great at what she does.

"So. Project," I say, connecting my tablet to the Sweet Pea Wi-Fi. "I looked up our salaries a little while ago, and we're working with $75,000 a year. Today we've gotta figure out where we want to live and stuff."

"Do you mind if I come sit on your side? That way we can both see the screen?"

Um, does a fat kid like cake? I smile and pat the space next to me. James swings around and brings with him a delicious cloud of cologne. For the first time, I notice his shirt. I guess I was too distracted by images of my dream during Economics to pay attention to his clothing.

"Garth Brooks world tour, huh? I didn't know you liked country music."

"I like all kinds of music. Garth is pretty much the man though. How can anyone not like him?"

"When did you see him play?"

"Before we left Topeka. It was such a great show!"

"I dragged Avery to his concert last year in Raleigh. She hates country music. I wouldn't say she's a fan now, but at least she doesn't skip over his songs on my iPod anymore. What's your favorite song?"

"*Shameless.*"

His hands run up my arms and capture my face as he crushes his lips to mine. I grab onto his biceps to draw him closer while breathing in the wonderful scent of woodsy teenage masculinity.

"Rachel?"

My right hand, that traitorous bitch, is indeed grabbing onto his arm. But his lips are nowhere near mine. They are, however, fixed into a smirk.

"Sorry, I um... just wanted to see if your shirt was as soft as it looked." I pull my hand away and sit on it.

"Here you are, lovebirds." Avery sets our order on the table. She mouths "what are you waiting for?" and wiggles her eyebrows at me before walking away. If I could cut my hand off and slap her with it, I would.

56

"So was it? As soft as it looked?" He laughs, and I swear his green eyes sparkle. I grab my float and turn my attention back to my tablet.

"Like I was saying, we have $75,000 a year to work with," I say, ignoring him. "Do you want to live in a house or an apartment?"

"I could live in a shoebox with you and still be happy." I look over at him. The sparkle in his eyes has been replaced by an intensity that makes me forget how to breathe for a moment. I'm not sure how this boyfriend thing is supposed to work, but if it has anything to do with those piercing green eyes and him licking his bottom lip like that, I'd like to sign up.

"That may get a little hard during the holidays, though. I vote for looking at houses for rent." He nods, and I open a new browser window.

"Oh look, this one is nice!"

"It's also next to the interstate," he says, pointing at the map. "Too much traffic. What about this one?"

I scan the photos. "No backyard for our child. Oh, let's look at this one!" I open a listing for a three-bedroom, two-bathroom house on a cul-de-sac. "Wow, that's a huge kitchen. And there's a deck that we could barbecue on."

"The master bedroom looks really nice too." He enlarges the photo and bites the side of his lip. Somehow, I manage to keep my groan to myself. I imagine massaging his shoulders after a long day at the fire station and falling asleep in his arms with our feet tangled in the sheets. Wow, I'm really taking this fake marriage thing seriously.

"Yeah, it's a nice bedroom." My gaze alternates between his lips and his eyes and I don't think I've ever wanted to kiss anyone this badly in my life. I have no idea what kind of Topeka voodoo this guy is practicing. Instead, I take out my angst on my Diet Coke float. "So it looks like we've solved the problem of where we're going to live."

"What's up next?"

"Car shopping."

I keep my hormones in check (I'm still sitting on my hand), and we make our way through the rest of the list. I look around to signal Avery for our check when I hear the door jingle.

"Fuck."

James looks toward the door and his mouth hardens into a line. "This guy is up to no good."

"You know Avery's ex-boyfriend?"

"No, he just looks like a creepy asshole."

"Pretty much."

Derrick scans the restaurant and walks toward Avery's mom carrying a bouquet of roses. His black hair is longer than it was last summer, but his good looks haven't changed much. When Avery moved past the anger stage of their breakup and entered the sad stage, she cried over the beautiful children they'd never have. I tried to remind her that at least she wouldn't be fighting three other women for his child support. Puerto Rican god or not, Derrick is bad news.

"Hi, Mrs. Murphy. Is Avery working today? I wanted to give these to her." Did he never get the message that her mom hates being called Mrs. Murphy? Not that he has permission to call her by her first name, either. That's reserved for people she actually likes.

"Hello, Derrick. She is, but she's on the clock and doesn't have time for socializing."

"It's okay, I'll wait until her shift is over." She gives him a look that says "You'd better not" (I may also be confusing it with the "Go fuck yourself" look) and checks on one of her customers.

I grab my phone and send Avery a warning.

Me: New York City sent its trash to the Sweet Pea.
Avery: Very funny, Ray. I'm telling the chef to spit in your next Diet Coke float.
Me: I wish I was joking. And ew. You're walking to work next time.
Avery: Fuck.

Avery's mom heads toward our table. "Sorry I'm just now coming to say hi, kiddo." She lowers her voice. "Did you know this douchebag was coming today?" Her head nods in Derrick's direction.

"No, I had no idea."

"He better not stay long and he for damn sure better not make Avery upset. That worthless piece of shit has caused enough trouble for her." Clearly, I have no idea where Avery gets her mouth from. She glances toward James and looks back at me.

"Oh, sorry. James, this is Mandy, Avery's mom. Mandy, this is James, resident New Guy and my partner for the senior Economics project."

"Oh, you're the one Devin just hired."

"That's me. It's nice to meet you ma'am."

"I'm not old enough to be a ma'am. Mandy's fine." She winks at James. "I've gotta get to the back. Y'all have a good afternoon." She passes Avery on her way and plants a kiss on the top of her head.

Avery walks around the counter, stops six feet away from Derrick and crosses her arms. "What do you want?"

"To bring you these and tell you Happy New Year." He holds the roses toward Avery. I have to admit, he's ballsy. But mostly, he's just stupid. I hope he's wearing a cup. I never knew there was such a thing as designer combat boots, but Avery's feet are living proof. Derrick's balls should run and hide.

"It was a Happy New Year until you walked in. Did you not understand my message at Christmas?"

"I know you're angry, and you have every right to be. I made a terrible mistake. But there is no other person in the world for me, Avery. We're meant to be together. I love you. I'll do whatever it takes to get you back."

"Go to hell, Derrick. And take your flowers with you. You wasted a trip to North Carolina. Now get out of the diner before I call the cops." She jerks her hand toward the door.

"I'm not leaving until you take your flowers. And please read the card."

"Fine. Whatever." She grabs the flowers, shoves Derrick out of the diner, and walks behind the counter with a wicked smile. "The garbage disposal was fixed earlier today and I'm so glad I have something to test it with." Avery shreds the bouquet, card and all, then brushes her hands off and walks to our table.

"Let this serve as a lesson for you, James. Either keep your pecker in your pants or type the right girl's name when you sext her." She lays the check on our table as if it's a law enforcement citation.

"Duly noted," he says, swallowing, as Avery walks away. "Rachel, I promise that I'll never send you a picture of my penis. And now that we know you don't have one either, I'll sleep well at night knowing you won't send *me* one."

Facepalm.

"I'll take Embarrassing Topics for 400, Alex," I say, smiling. "How much is my float?"

"Don't worry about it. This is our first date, so it's on me." He smiles again, but this one is different. This one has hope behind it. I know, because I'm wearing the same one.

"First date, huh? I feel a little cheated. I'm missing out on the part where you drive me home and kiss me on the front porch." Or at least, that's what Avery tells me happens.

"I could always follow you home, but I'd feel like a stalker. And then there's your dad…"

Oh yeah.

That.

"He's not even home half the time."

"What about your mom?"

"Mom's too busy with all of her councils and committees. She's like June Cleaver on crack."

She's not a bad mom by any means; she's just not a very active participant in my life. I'm much closer to Mandy and Aunt Devin, and that's fine by me. The women in Avery's house are loud and fierce, and I love them dearly. They are the family I choose to have. I once told Mandy how glad I was that her husband had a gay affair so she and Avery could move here. She laughed and said she was too, because her new Audi out-performed him on every level.

"Well, since I can't drive you home today, we need a first date do-over."

Yes, yes, yes, yes!

"I think I could tolerate that, since you're new and don't really have any friends yet. I wouldn't want you to be sitting at home bored out of your mind," I tease.

"Maybe we could finally settle this hot firefighter debate." He does the lip-biting thing again and nudges my shoulder with his. My hand flies out from underneath my leg. Before it can get me in trouble again, I use it to tuck a strand of hair behind my ear and rest it on the table.

And.

Then.

He.

Grabs.

It.

I squeeze my eyes shut, certain that I'm hallucinating again. But when I peek, it's still there. *What do I do?* Maybe this is what Christopher Columbus felt like in the uncharted waters of the Atlantic. I look at James, but I still can't think of anything to say. Well, nothing comprehensible anyway. He grabs a pen out of his backpack and turns my hand over. I watch his face for a hint of what he's doing, but he offers no clues.

"What are you writing?"

"Something for you to read later," he says with a small smile, closing my hand. I try to sneak a glance while he puts his pen away but his eyes snap back to me. "No cheating!" He clamps his hand over mine. "And since you can't be trusted, you leave me no choice." He opens my fist with his fingertips. We sit there for a moment, palm to palm, before he laces his fingers with mine. *I'm sorry I called you a traitorous bitch, hand. You're the best hand I've ever had.*

"And when do I get my hand back, Mr. Tennyson?"

"When I walk you to your car and you leave."

I would have settled for "never," but I suppose this will work too. I put my tablet in my backpack one-handed, but I can't close the zipper. "Ahem. A little help since you're holding my hand hostage?"

"I'd be happy to. After all, marriage is about teamwork, right?"

Yes, marriage is all about a lot of things. Like talking about penises and holding hands. I sling my backpack on my free shoulder and we head to the cashier. Before we can even make it past our row of booths, James tugs my hand back. A few moments later, a waiter drops a tray full of food.

"Wow, good save. Thanks!" I'm having a pretty good non-first date, and I'm glad it didn't end it with sweet tea, country fried steak and gravy down the front of my shirt. James leads me around the mess to the front of the restaurant. If I would have known he was going to hold my hand all the way to my car, I would have parked somewhere farther away. Like the end of the parking lot. Or the next town over. When we reach my car, he doesn't let go. Instead, he leans me against the driver's door and takes my other hand.

"Thanks for meeting me today."

"Anything for Economics." We share a quick laugh. Then he squeezes my hands and I forget about laughing or breathing or standing. Thank God he's propping me up against my car.

"I know this isn't officially our first date, but I still really want to kiss you." His eyes dip down to my lips and he brings his face closer to mine.

"I think I could tolerate that. But I've never had a boyfriend before." Closer.

63

"We already talked about that." Closer.

"That means I've never kissed a boy. I could be a terrible kisser and ruin our non-first date." Closer.

"You worry too much." Closer.

I close my eyes. Seconds later, our lips touch. James lets go of my hands and cups my face. His mouth opens, so I open mine. His tongue reaches out, so I do the same. He leads me in this dance, our mouths exploring and tasting each other. He's smiling when he pulls away, and presses his forehead to mine.

"See, like I said. You worry too much."

I think I'm supposed to say something profound, this being my first kiss and all. So far, all I have is...

"Wow."

I feel his chest moving as he chuckles. "Yeah, I know what you mean."

"So I'll see you tomorrow in class?"

"Yup. I'll be the one with the big smile on his face. You can text me later if you want." He kisses me one last time before I unlock my door.

I could worry on the drive home about my dad and track and rules about boyfriends. I could stress about figuring out how to spend time with James without being caught. But I don't. Instead, I replay my first kiss over and over and over.

I pull into my driveway and reach for my backpack when I remember the writing on my hand.

I just wanted to see if your hand was as soft as it looked.

I laugh and reach for my phone.

Me: So was it?

James: Nope. It was sort of dry. You should get some hand cream.

James

Rachel is the best kisser on the planet.

Rachel

Rachel Tennyson
Rachel Lynn Tennyson
Mrs. Rachel Tennyson
Mr. and Mrs. James Tennyson

James

"Good morning, son." Gran shuffles into the kitchen in her signature pink terrycloth robe and matching slippers. I'm pretty sure she's bought the same set from QVC since 1986. I bend down to give her a hug and realize she fits entirely under my chin now. Her hair is much thinner than it used to be, but she still dyes the gray away. Her robe all but swallows her. If I didn't know better, I'd swear she was shrinking.

"Hey, Gran." I wipe the sleep from my eyes and yawn. The coffee pot beeps, and I say a silent thank you to the person who first combined coffee beans and hot water.

"Did you forget it's Saturday? This is the first weekend I've seen you this side of noon."

"No, today's my first day at the Sweet Pea. I wanted to get some coffee before I took off. You want some?" I hold the coffee pot in her direction.

"No, but I'll thank you for some tea."

I reach for a tea bag in the cabinet and set the kettle on the stove. For as long as I can remember, Gran's had this kettle. It's one of the things that make her kitchen *hers*. Along with her pies, Gran's kettle has been a constant in my childhood memories. "Remember when you used to make me hot chocolate because I didn't like tea? Except that I wanted to drink out of one of your fancy cups?"

She gazes upward, lost in memory, and laughs. "You were so particular too. It had to be the blue china cup or you'd pitch a fit the size of North Carolina. You'd say it's because—"

"The blue cup makes it taste better," we say in unison.

"And I'm still right," I say, holding the same cup, this time filled with black coffee.

"I don't know how you and your grandpa drink that stuff without any sugar or milk. It's a wonder it doesn't set your innards on fire."

"Maybe you should try it out of the blue cup," I tease. The kettle starts to sing and I pour Gran's tea.

"So who's the girl?"

"Who's what girl, Gran?" She quietly stares at me and I can't help but smile. "Her name is Rachel."

We've talked every night this week and usually text for a few hours after her phone curfew. She's the most amazing person I've ever met and I'm still mad that I went almost eighteen years without knowing her. I feel like I've been cheated. "How'd you know I like a girl?"

"Son, you've had your phone glued to your hand or your head all week, and you've been walking around here grinning like the Cheshire Cat. Now you're up at 6 a.m. on a Saturday and you're not even cursing. She must be something special."

"She really is, Gran. I can't explain it. I've only known her for five days. That's not even long enough for milk to spoil. But I can't get this girl out of my head."

"James, don't let timelines keep you from your feelings. The heart knows what it wants. It's the head that usually gets in the way."

"Well, in our case, it's her dad. Rachel runs track and he doesn't want her dating because he thinks it's a distraction." I hate not being able to take her out or be with her after school. Don't get me wrong, I'm grateful for FaceTime, but we're gonna have to figure something else out soon.

"You just focus on Rachel. All of that other mess will work itself out."

"How did you and Grandpa meet?"

"Oh, it was such the scandal," she says, her shoulders shaking with laughter. "I was engaged to George Calloway. He was the sheriff's son, you know. Two weeks before the wedding, I was working my shift at Ruby's Drive-In and this handsome fellow comes up and orders himself a chocolate malt. I'd seen him around town, but we ran in different circles. I teased him because he was alone on a Friday night. You know what he said?" She pauses and takes a sip of tea. "He said, 'I'm just waiting on the right girl,' then he winked and walked away. I didn't see him again until the day of my wedding. George and I were at the altar and the preacher got to the part where he asked if anyone had any reason for us to not get married. Here comes your grandpa bursting through the door, straight out of a movie. He ran down the aisle and said, 'Pearl, you can't marry this man because I'm in love with you!' I tell you, the whole church gasped, and my mama passed out cold. George's daddy threatened to have your grandpa arrested for disturbing the peace."

"What did you do?" I can't help but laugh thinking about my quiet grandpa running into the church like a love-struck fool.

"Well, I asked him what his name was, for starters. Then I looked at George and said, 'I'm sorry, but I'm gonna have a chocolate malt with my friend Jimmy. I grabbed a hold of your grandpa's hand and I never let go. That was fifty-five years ago." She sighs with contentment.

"Just like that, you walked away from your fiancé for someone you didn't even know?"

"Like I said, it was a scandal. But I already knew the most important thing about your grandpa—his heart was pure. I didn't know until I met him that I was never in love with George. I felt like my life began in that church the moment he barged in. Your grandpa saved me from a life of mediocrity and replaced it with love and passion and adventure." She squeezes my hand. "You're an old soul, just like him."

"You said that was fifty-five years ago?"

"That's right."

I count backward in my head. "That made you 18 years old. How on earth did you know you were ready to get married at eighteen?"

"The heart knows what it wants. You just gotta be smart enough to listen to it, James."

"Thanks for the advice, Gran." I down the last of my coffee and put my cup in the dishwasher. "Hey, what kind of pie are you baking today?"

"Blueberry and cherry."

"Mmmm, my favorites." I lean over and kiss her on the cheek.

"That's what you say about every pie I make," she says, swatting me on the shoulder.

"Why don't you consider selling them?"

"Please, I'm no Betty Crocker."

"You're right, you're Pearl Glenn. Betty Crocker doesn't have squat on you." I grab my keys and head out the door.

"Order up!" Fletcher Strickland hits the bell, signaling me. He's pretending to be a blond-haired, blue-eyed Wanya Morris as the radio belts out *I'll Make Love to You.* As I get closer to the window, I see him singing into his spatula and realize he's changing the words.

I'll cook eggs for you
And some hash browns too
It's gonna taste so right
When you take a big bite
I'll cook eggs for you
And some hash browns too
Here's a slice of rye toast
And some orange juice

"That was quite impressive," I shout. Fletcher nods and smiles, then assembles the ingredients for the next ticket. I knew we'd get along about fifteen minutes into our shift when we both started singing along to the chorus of *Livin' on a Prayer* by Bon Jovi.

"Here you go," I say, setting the plate down on table four. "Eggs Benedict, two slices of rye toast, and hash browns. Does everything look okay?"

The man in the chair just stares at me. I tap my finger on my ear in response, and he flicks on his hearing aid.

"Does everything look good?"

"Yes, it does, young man," he says, surveying his plate. I refill his OJ and leave him to his breakfast.

"How ya doin' Fletcher?" I ask across the window.

"Just another day in paradise, dude." He flips a pancake like a pro and starts an omelet for table twelve. It's like watching a teenage Emeril Lagasse.

"How in the world do you do that?"

"What, this?" he asks, flipping another pancake.

"Now you're just showing off," I laugh.

"I've been doing this shit since I was eight. My mom had surgery, and my dad can't cook to save his life. So I got in the kitchen and sort of fell in love. I'm going to culinary school next year, but Devin's letting me cook here in the meantime. I think she likes it because she can pay me minimum wage and I don't bitch about taking the early weekend shifts." He plates the omelet and pancakes, and I make my way to table twelve. Judging by the early morning crowd, Devin and the customers are well aware of Fletcher's skills.

"Here y'all are." I set the pancakes down in front of the girl from Economics and the omelet in front of her guest. "It's Gretchen, right?" She was out of school on Thursday and Friday. Judging by the look on her boyfriend's face during class, there is trouble in paradise.

"Yeah." She exchanges a panicked look with the girl sitting across from her.

"I'm James, the new guy in second period."

"Hey, James." She looks over my head, past my shoulder, anywhere but my face. It doesn't take a psychic to put two and two together.

"It looks like you're getting an early start to your day. Whatcha have planned?" I ask, trying to lighten the mood. We haven't officially talked until now, and I don't want our first conversation to end badly.

"Oh, just going to the Outer Banks with my best friend, Lainey," she says, gesturing to her guest.

"The Banks in January? That's hardcore."

"We're not swimming," Lainey says. "My parents have a timeshare out there, and no one ever uses it this time of year. We're loading up on chick flicks and ice cream."

"Uh oh. Isn't that what girls do after a breakup?" I ask, looking at Gretchen.

"Yeah, I broke up with Billy a few days ago."

"I'm sorry to hear that."

She shrugs her shoulders. "He just wasn't the right... person for me."

"It's about time," Lainey says as she covers her omelet in pepper. "There's no use in being with someone who doesn't make you happy. Especially when there are people out there who *will* make you happy." She gives Gretchen a knowing glance.

"Well, it looks like you'll have some good company this weekend. Me, I'm cleaning out my closet after I get off work. I figure it's important to really get in there and see what's what, you know? Gotta make sure I get rid of all the stuff that's just not 'me' anymore."

Gretchen and Lainey stare at me quizzically. Hopefully, they understand the meaning behind my message. Gretchen deserves to be happy.

"I don't think I've seen you at school, Lainey. Do you go to Edison?"

"No, I'm homeschooled."

"How'd you and Gretchen meet?"

She smiles, the first one I've seen all morning. "We actually met in a chat group. I know, it's dumb," she adds quickly.

I don't tell her that I know it was a "Lesbian teens in Durham" group.

"No way, it's always nice to connect with someone who shares the same interests as you. I can tell you two have a very special friendship, and I hope y'all have a great time this weekend. Let me know if I can get anything else for you before you head out." Fletcher rings the bell for the next order, and I return to the window.

The diner gets busier as the morning progresses. A few more waiters and cooks show up, and Devin stopped in to see how my first day is going. Fletcher and I have been hanging out in between orders. I think I have the pancake flip mastered, but I could use some more practice with omelets. We ad-libbed a few duets and earned some applause from the people sitting at the bar. I found out he plays guitar too, so we're planning to hang out one day soon and jam. As far as jobs go, this one has been pretty cool so far. At noon, Avery walks in for her shift, and Fletcher's face lights up like Christmas.

"You're totally busted, bro."

"What'd I do?"

"Nothing, but you might wanna turn down that smile a couple of notches."

"What smile? I'm not smiling. I'm making a BLT. This is some serious shit right here. Requires intense focus and dedication." He methodically flips three slices of bacon to prove his point.

"My mistake. I could have sworn you were focusing on the pint-sized waitress who just came on shift." I throw a crouton at his face and head to the front of the dining room where Avery's rolling silverware in napkins.

"What's shakin' Avery?"

"Hey, Beef-in-law. Your first morning going good?"

"No complaints from me. I've been chilling with Fletcher getting some culinary lessons in between taking orders. He's pretty damn good." The door jingles, and Rachel walks through. My morning just got infinitely better.

"Fletcher? Yeah. He's a great cook," Avery says. She looks at him and smiles, so I consider this an open opportunity.

"I've only known the guy for a few hours, but he seems pretty legit. I was thinking of catching a movie tonight. Maybe you, Ray and Fletcher can come to?"

"Fletcher is way out of my league. I'm sure he has better things to do than go to the movies with me."

"Who said he was gonna be your date?" I wink at Rachel. "We have a budding bromance, you know. You should hear us sing sometime."

"So you mean your school wife has competition?" Rachel asks, playfully.

"I'm pretty sure I was planning on putting the moves on Fletcher," I say. "I *guess* I could consider putting the moves on you instead."

"Ugh." Rachel makes a face. "That sounds like an evening of pure torture." She leans toward Avery and covers the side of her mouth with her right hand. "I heard James is the worst kisser *ever*," she whispers loudly.

"I don't know about that," I say, looking directly at Rachel. "The last girl I kissed didn't have any complaints." I don't know what she's told Avery, but I don't want to spill the beans if she hasn't.

"Like I said, Fletcher probably has other things to do," Avery says, interrupting our stare down. "He's never really talked to me, so I'm pretty sure that means he's not that interested."

"Don't worry, I'll charm him with my boyish good looks," I say, flashing a smile. We stop at the kitchen window on the way to Rachel's table. "Hey, Fletch! Avery, Rachel, and I are going to a movie tonight. You in?"

"That depends. Chick flick or action movie?"

"Not sure, but you can hold my hand if you get scared."

"In that case, I'm in!" He laughs and flips a burger with the same finesse he's had all morning. I turn to Avery and smirk.

"Oh, there's just one thing. I'm gonna drive Rachel in The Beast, but there's only room for us two. Can you take Avery?" Fletcher jerks his head toward me in a panic and drops the second burger.

"Uh, sure. That's no problem." The look on his face says he might murder me a little bit.

"Great! Avery can text you her address before her shift is over."

"I don't have Fletcher's number, James." Avery near-whispers. This is the quietest I've seen her since we met.

"Easy fix," I say, holding my hand out for her phone. "Fletcher, what's your number?" I punch in the digits and send him a text from Avery's phone. "There, problem solved. Now, right this way, Mrs. Tennyson, your table is ready." I leave Avery and Rachel staring at each other and laugh to myself on the way to the same booth we sat at on Wednesday.

"James, what the hell?" Avery whispers loudly when they catch up to me at the booth.

"What?" I ask with my best innocent face.

"I don't need a pity date!"

"Please, do you really not know that Fletcher likes you?"

"He's said about fourteen words to me since he started working here! And he graduated last year. What would he want with a high school girl?"

"Avery, trust me. If tonight backfires, I'll take your next two Saturday shifts."

"No way are you getting my tips." She folds her arms across her chest.

"Fine, if tonight backfires, I'll take your next two Saturday shifts *and* I'll give you the tips I earn." I extend my right hand. She hesitates, then shakes it and walks away.

"You seem mighty certain of yourself, Mr. Tennyson. Are you sure this is a bet you want to make?" Rachel asks.

"The look on his face when she walked in—and the fact that he dropped the burger he was flipping—are all the assurance I need. I got this in the bag."

"It looks like you're making the most out of my parents being out of town tonight," she says with a sly smile. Her weekend plans were the topic of our conversation last night. Her dad has some benefit in Charlotte so they're getting a hotel for the night. I don't particularly like sneaking around, but he leaves us little choice.

I grip the edge of the table and lean in. She still smells like sunshine and vanilla. God, I could get intoxicated off her scent. "I figured since you're staying the night at Avery's, it was a great night for a date. And this time I can drive you back and kiss you on the porch," I add in a low voice.

"You already know how our date is gonna end, huh?" she whispers. She keeps looking down at my lips and for a few blissful seconds, I remember our kiss in the parking lot. Why can't it be tonight already?

"Yup, I consulted my crystal ball. You don't stand a chance, sweetheart." Her chocolate brown eyes swallow me up, and I'm struck with the best idea I've had in a long time. "Hey, what are you doing when you leave here?"

"Not much, just hanging at Avery's. I'll pick her up when her shift is over, and we'll go back to her house to get ready for the movies."

"Can she drive your car back to her house?"

"Why would she need to do that?"

"Because I get off in thirty minutes. Why don't you come home with me and hang out before the movies? I want to spend as much time with you as possible while I can." I bite my lip and pray silently. She stares at me for three full seconds, then smiles and pulls out her phone.

"That sounds like an excellent plan." She sends a text to Avery then picks up her menu. "I should order some lunch before you get off shift."

"Just make sure you save some room for dessert. Gran will have fresh pie when we get back to my house."

"An afternoon with my school husband and his gran's infamous pie. How did I get to be such a lucky girl?" She closes her menu and flashes a beautiful smile at me before I take her order and head back to the kitchen.

"One last ticket before you go, Fletcher. Make it good. This one's for my girl."

"Rachel's your girl?" he asks, grinning.

"Not officially, but yeah. She's it, man." I glance toward her booth. She's dressed in her typical track pants and running shoes, and her hair's in some froofy half ponytail thing that girls do. She is seriously beautiful.

"You're sure Avery's alright with going with me tonight?" Fletcher asks. You wouldn't think a good-looking guy like him would be nervous, but I can see him chewing the inside of his cheek.

"I promise, she's stoked. She seems to think that you're not interested in her, though. You gotta step up your game, bro."

Fletcher assembles the ingredients for Rachel's lunch. "Dude, she's the main reason I applied to work here. She just seems so... I don't know. Untouchable. Guys are always chasing after her, and I have no idea what she'd want with a nineteen-year-old short-order cook who still lives at home with his parents after graduating. She probably thinks I'm a loser."

Fletcher needs to get his mind out of the defeated zone or tonight is going to royally suck. "There's nothing wrong with living at home to take care of your mom."

"How'd you know that?" he asks, mid-wrap.

Shit!

"Um, you mentioned it earlier this morning. Must have been before your caffeine kicked in. She's not gonna think you're a loser, I promise."

He exhales. "If you say so." He plates Rachel's turkey wrap and fries. "Thanks for helping me out, dude. I've wanted to ask Avery out forever, I just never know what to say around her so I usually don't say anything at all."

"No sweat, Fletch. See ya later tonight."

I set Rachel's plate and Diet Coke on her table. "Your lunch is served, Mrs. Tennyson."

"Are you ever going to stop calling me that?" she asks, giggling.

"Not unless you want me to." My fingers brush hers when I hand her the bottle of ketchup.

"It doesn't bother me any." She turns an adorable shade of red, and I can't help but laugh.

"Well that settles it. I'm gonna grab my stuff while you finish lunch. I'll be back in a few."

"Make yourself at home." We walk into the house and I toss my keys on the kitchen counter. "I'm gonna grab a quick shower and wash off the nine layers of grease before we have pie. You can hang out here, or in my bedroom." We walk down the hallway past the living room and powder room. The house is eighty-nine years old, but Gran and Grandpa have remodeled it over the years. I'm glad they kept the wood floors and the original fireplace. I swear to this day that I saw Santa Claus there the Christmas that I was five. Now I like to play my guitar in front of it.

"My room's around the corner here." I push open the door and watch her enter.

Rachel Wheaton is in my room. *Holy shit.*

"Wow, I admit I didn't expect to see a clean room."

"Cleanliness is next to godliness."

"Are you saying you're a god?" she teases.

"Hey, if the shoe fits..."

"Go shower, grease boy. I want pie." She playfully shoves me in the chest.

Part of being a teenage boy is strategy. In this case, I grabbed a new pair of jeans and boxer briefs before my shower, but my shirts are still hanging in my closet. After my shower, I casually walk across my room for a shirt and feel Rachel's eyes follow me.

"Sorry, forgot to grab a shirt." I look at her over my shoulder and her mouth is hanging open a bit. I reach for a navy blue crew neck shirt and slip it over my head. Mission accomplished in three... two... one...

"Wait!"

I turn around before putting my arms in the sleeves. "What?"

She hops off the bed and makes a beeline for my right side. Her fingers trace the lyrics running the length of my ribcage. It feels amazing.

"What is this?"

"One of my favorite songs."

"Which one?"

"I'll show you after we eat our pie." I lead Rachel back into the kitchen and take two plates from the cabinet. "Do you want cherry or blueberry?"

"What are you having?"

"Both," I say, flashing her a smile before removing the glass pie covers.

She laughs. "Clearly, you have issues making a decision."

"Wrong. I had no problem at all making my decision." I slice a thin piece of each pie and push the plate toward Rachel. "You'll thank me and my decision-making skills in a second."

She takes a bite of blueberry pie and moans. "Oh mah goh, zhish ish amazhig." I totally know how she feels. Gran's pies are the shit.

"Just wait until you try the cherry."

We eat the rest of our pie in silence. Rachel finishes her last bite of cherry and sighs. "James, I've never had pie that good in my life. Why isn't your grandma selling this stuff?"

"I know, right? Maybe we can talk to Devin about Gran selling her pies at the Sweet Pea." I load our plates and silverware in the dishwasher and take Rachel's hand. "Come on, I'll show you that song."

We lay on my bed and I move through my phone to find *Just Ask*.

"You've probably never heard it, but it's amazing. Gives me goose bumps every time. My tattoo is the third verse."

I push play and bring Rachel into the world of Lake Street Dive. On cue, the goose bumps start at three minutes and eleven seconds in. She lifts my shirt, and as the third verse plays, she traces the lines of my tattoo.

"That's a really beautiful song," she says when it's over. "What made you want the lyrics as a tattoo?"

"You promise not to laugh? I'm about to get musically nerdy on you." She crosses her heart with her fingers. "This song is one of the sexiest songs I've ever heard. The way she holds that note out? And then starts in with the third verse? I sort of feel like she's making love with the song." I did *not* just say that. I clear my throat and continue. "Anyway, like I said, it's a nerdy thing."

"I don't think it's nerdy at all." Her fingertips graze my stomach as she lowers my shirt. Did she do that on purpose?

"I got the third verse tattooed because at the time, I wanted to capture that feeling and use it as a reminder."

"Of what?"

"That the girl I fall in love with should make me feel like that part of the song." I bring my lips to Rachel's. She's so warm and soft. Our tongues caress each other lazily and I run my fingers through her silky golden hair. This girl, this moment, is perfect. "Thanks for not laughing at the reason behind my tattoo."

"No way. It's beautiful." She lifts her head and stares at me for a beat, then drops her eyes. "I hope one day you find that girl."

I think I already have. And she's right here. And you're her.

"Yeah." I kiss her again and she settles her head on my chest. I wonder if she can hear how fast my heart is beating. I run my fingers up and down her spine and focus on regulating my breathing.

"This is nice," she murmurs, before yawning. I close my eyes and breathe in the smell of sunshine and vanilla and drift off to sleep with Rachel in my arms.

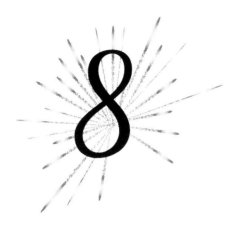

Rachel

I've always loved that moment where you're floating between sleeping and being awake. Where you have enough time to savor your dreams before you open your eyes to start the day. Like right now, where I swear I can feel James' arms around me. He's got this woodsy smell to him that's insanely sexy and comforting. I keep my eyes closed and take one last deep breath. I haven't slept this good in a long time. I picture his delicious lips as I stretch my body. Muscles satisfied and relaxed, I let my arms fall out to the sides.

"Ow!"

My eyes snap open and I bolt upright. I'm not at home. Or at Avery's. I'm in James' house. In his room.

In his bed.

My hands jerk to my face in search of drool, and I offer up a mental high five to God when my fingers come back dry.

"Sorry, I forgot you were there."

"And now my ego is crushed. Pardon me while I go stick my head in the oven."

"No! Sorry, I guess I was sleeping deeply and forgot where I was. Please don't kill yourself on account of me," I giggle and settle back down into his arms. This must be what heaven feels like. Or nirvana. Zen. *Something.*

"You know," he says, turning my face to his. "This was a momentous afternoon for us."

"How so?"

"Because we just slept together."

"Oh my God, you're terrible." My head bounces slightly on his chest as he laughs.

"I'm a guy, what can I say?"

"Hey, what time is it?"

James glances at his phone. "Four-thirty. What time does Avery get off work?"

"At six, then she'll go back to her house and get cleaned up. I figure we can stop by there first so she doesn't have a heart attack before Fletcher picks her up."

"Sounds like a plan. Do you wanna eat here with us?"

"Sure, I'd love to."

"Come on, let's go see what Gran's got cooking." Whatever it is smells amazing. James sits up and grabs my hand. Our fingers entwine, and I don't know how I went seventeen and a half years walking around by myself.

"Hello, son."

"Hey, Gran." James kisses her on the cheek. "Whatcha cooking?" Their kitchen looks so much homier than mine. Mom and dad love stainless steel, but Gran's appliances are all antique white. It fits in perfectly with the butcher-block countertops and copper Jell-O molds along the far wall.

"Sweet potato chili and homemade cornbread."

"Is it okay if Rachel stays for dinner?"

"Only if you properly introduce me."

"Sorry. Gran, this is Rachel, my... Rachel." Oh my gosh, he's adorable. Technically, he's not my boyfriend. Even if he was, that word sounds so cheap. It's like saying Michelangelo is just a guy who paints and sculpts things. I wonder if there's word for "I'm not in love with you yet, but I'm pretty sure I will be soon."

"Hello, James' Rachel." Gran chuckles and shakes my hand.

"It's nice to meet you, Mrs..."

"Call me Gran. You're welcome to stay for dinner. Why don't you two get the cornbread started? The recipe is in the box on the counter." She turns back to the pot on the stove, humming as she adds more spices and tastes the chili.

James and I do as we're told. There's something so domestic about being in the kitchen with the guy you like. Maybe it's because of our Economics project, but I admit I'm enjoying the opportunity to play house this afternoon. I could seriously get used to falling asleep next to him and doing mundane tasks like cooking together.

"So James tells me you're a runner?" Gran asks. I crack the eggs into a bowl, and James adds the milk before melting the butter.

"Yes, ma'am. I've been running since I was about eight. I have an invitational coming up in a couple of weeks."

"Maybe I can come cheer you on?" James asks.

"That might be kind of risky," I say, wrinkling my nose. I'm beginning to dislike my dad more each day.

"Don't worry, I'll wear a hat and one of those Groucho Marx glasses." He kisses me on the cheek on the way back from the pantry then adds the cornmeal, flour, and sugar while I whisk the batter.

"Well, you're always welcome over here," Gran says. "You're the first girl James has ever brought over."

"Gran, I've only lived here for a few weeks. But she's right, you are the first girl I've ever brought home." James winks at me and my insides feel like I've taken the whisk to them, too. I put the cornbread in the oven and set the timer.

No pressure, Rachel.

James seems to sense my sudden onset of nerves. "Relax," he whispers in my ear. "You're doing great. Gran loves you." The hairs on the side of my face and neck stand at attention, and goose bumps line my arms. I'm not sure how his mouth isn't illegal, but since I'm still underage, I'm glad it's not. We lock eyes. Being this close to him moments after he said the "L" word—even though he didn't say it *that* way—has my heart racing. But more than anything, I'm surprised at how easy all of this is. The stories I hear in the hallways and locker rooms about mixed signals and immaturity are nothing like what I'm experiencing here. James is just so much... more. The fact that it's *me* he wants here is mind-boggling.

The front door opens and a head full of blond curls walks through the door. "Hey guys, I'm home!" The woman turns to hang her jacket on the hook in the foyer and I see streaks of pink and purple in the back of her hair.

"Hey, Mom," James says.

Her eyes immediately spot me when she enters the kitchen. "Hi, son! Who's your friend?"

HAZEL JAMES

"This is Rachel," Gran answers for him. Her eyes are sort of sparkling and she offers his mom a wink.

"Oh, this is the reason River's been smiling all week."

River?

James leans his head on the counter and groans.

"Mom, you did *not*."

"What, call you by the name I gave you after laboring with you for thirty-two hours? Yes, I did." She pats him on the shoulder on the way to the sink, where she unloads a lunch box. She unties her Healing Touch Massage apron and walks toward me.

"Hi, I'm Sunny, River's mom."

"Hi, nice to meet you. I'm Rachel," I say, biting back a grin. River? Really? It's a good thing he never had a sister. Her name would probably be Stardust or Sage Blossom.

"Alright, let's get this over with." James lifts his head from the counter and looks at me with a pained expression. "My hippie mom named me River, but every *other* person on the planet calls me by my middle name, James, after my grandfather. Because thankfully *his* parents gave him a normal name." He shoots his mom a sidelong glance and rolls his eyes.

"It's not that bad," I say. A giggle slips out, but I cough to cover it up.

"Okay, this is enough embarrassment for one evening. I'm setting the table." James grabs five plates and five bowls from the cabinet.

"Oh, I meant to tell you earlier, Gran. Your pies are delicious," I say. "Why haven't you sold them to local bakeries or restaurants?" This woman could make a killing.

89

"Oh, I've always just enjoyed making them for my family or giving them away. Besides, I don't know the first thing about running a business."

"My best friend's aunt owns the Sweet Pea and her mom manages it. I'm pretty sure they could take care of everything for you."

"Yeah, Gran. You should really think about it. This town needs your pies," James says.

She dismisses his comment with a careless wave and announces dinner is ready. "James, go let your grandpa know it's time to eat."

"Yes ma'am." He takes my hand again (yay!) and we walk outside, step off the wrap-around porch and head toward a greenhouse.

"What's this?"

"Grandpa's working on this year's tobacco crop. The seeds start in the greenhouse before they're transplanted to the seedbeds and then into the fields."

"He's a tobacco farmer?"

"Yup, he's been doing this for more than thirty years." He leads me through the door and I'm greeted with a delicious, earthy aroma.

"That's kind of badass."

"Grandpa is definitely badass," he says with a grin. "Hey Gramps! Gran said to let you know dinner's ready."

"Thanks, boy. Say, who's this here?"

"Grandpa, this is Rachel."

"Ah, I thought you were smiling more." He winks at James and chuckles, then pulls his gloves off and sets them beside small beds of soil. His hands are rough from years of farm work, but the deep laugh lines on his face show he's enjoyed every minute of it.

"Hi, young lady," he says, taking my hand in his. "I'm Jimmy, but you can call me Grandpa."

"It's nice to meet you, Grandpa. I'm beginning to think this guy never smiled before he met me," I say, tipping my head toward James.

"Oh, I smiled plenty, I just never had as good of a reason to," James says. "Come on, let's go eat." He grabs my hand and pulls me toward the door. *Please*, as if I could walk right now. How can something so simple turn me into such goo on the inside?

A few minutes later, we're all settled at the circular table. James' grandpa starts the blessing and takes Gran's hand. She grabs mine, I grab James' and he takes his mom's hand. Sunny completes the circle with Grandpa.

"Lord, bless this food and the people who prepared it. Thank you for family, friends and reasons to smile. In Your name, Amen."

I can't remember the last time my family said grace. Or even sat at the table together. Dad's always working late so it's usually just me and Mom. I look around the table and I'm overwhelmed by the feeling of *family*. Mom and I are obviously related, but there's never been this kind of warmth at our dinner table. Maybe that's why I prefer to be at Avery's?

"Alright, let's see. Who's up for a game of Embarrassing Stories About James?" Grandpa asks, rubbing his hands together.

"That is *not* happening!" James manages to shout with a mouthful of chili.

"Oh, come on! I can't tell the one about you running naked through the grocery store?" his mom teases.

"Abso*lute*ly not," he says, pointing his spoon at her.

"But it was so sweet! You were just starting to read and thought the sign that said 'buy one, get one half off' meant you had to take half of your clothes off."

"Mother!"

"Oh fine. What about the time you cut the hair from your head and tried to tape it on your chest so you'd look older?"

"MOM!"

"Okay, okay. You win. I won't mention anything else. Especially not the story about you shoving whole cloves up your nose."

His spoon clatters into the bowl, and for the second time this evening, James leans his head down and groans. I'm doing my best to not laugh and choke on my dinner, but it's so hard not to.

"River loves Christmas," his mom starts in. Her eyes are twinkling and she lets a giggle slip. "He was around nine and it was the middle of June. He decided he missed the smell of Christmas, so he got two cloves and stuck them in his nose. He starts running through the house yelling 'Christmas is burning my nose!'" She's wiping tears from her eyes now. "It was the funniest thing. We got them out a few minutes later, but he hasn't gone near cloves since."

I've learned so much about James this afternoon. Like exactly how many shades of red he can turn in ten seconds. "Don't worry, I'll be sure to keep you safe from the cloves next Christmas," I say, patting his arm. I don't know what's weirder—the fact that I just mentioned still being together next Christmas, or the fact James didn't seem to be bothered by it.

"That's mighty swell of you," his muffled voice says. He lifts his head and wipes his face. "If you don't mind, I'm going to finish the dinner my favorite female adult cooked and then I'm running away from home."

"You know I love you, River," his mom says, still laughing.

"Yeah, yeah," he says. He rolls his eyes, but he can't hide his smile anymore. "It's a good thing you know how to make chocolate chip cookies. That's the only reason I love you."

"I always knew those cookies would come in handy."

I laugh to myself and finish my dinner while taking in the easy banter at the table. I'm not sure how I'll manage tomorrow at my own house. I'm sort of sad just thinking about it.

"Turn here. Her house is the fourth one on the left." I point to the red brick house with the Audi in the driveway.

"What does 'mahogany' mean?" James asks as we pull in front of the house.

"I'll tell you about it later," I say, laughing as we walk into Avery's house. I haven't knocked in more than a year. Mandy said if I kept asking permission to enter the house, she was gonna start telling me 'no.' Aunt Devin took that one step further and made me a copy of the house key.

"The Tennysons are here!" Avery bounds down the hallway. If I had to cast her in any cartoon role, she'd be Tigger. She's one of the most exuberant people I know. Sometimes it's annoying, but it's mostly sweet.

"Hey, when's Fletcher getting here?" I ask.

"In about ten minutes." She holds up her phone, and points to her call log. "Can you believe it?" she nearly shrieks. Fletcher's name is on the top of the incoming calls list.

"So about hoping Harris would ask you to the movies..." I start.

"Harris? Oh please, Ray. Keep *up*!"

"I know, I know. Who's it gonna be next week?" I tease.

"God willing, Fletcher. And the month after, and the one after that."

"Seriously?"

"Before he left this afternoon, I overheard him asking my mom if he could pick up a few extra shifts this month. Get this, he lives at home so he can help his parents out. His mom was sick a while back and hasn't been able to return to work full time, so he stays there to help with the bills and so he can watch his little sister." Avery sighs. "I already thought he was cute, but that kind of love and dedication to your family? I'm a goner." She pats her heart for effect. This is the first time since Derrick that Avery's mentioned wanting a boyfriend longer than a weekend or two. I'm not surprised that it was Fletcher's family mindedness that put her over the edge. Ever since her parents' divorce, family has been of huge importance to Avery.

"I guess I won't need to take your Saturday shifts from you," James says.

"Not so fast." She pokes him in the chest. "I like Fletcher. The jury's still out on whether he likes *me* or not."

The doorbell rings, and Avery shrieks and runs for her bedroom.

"Why don't you get that, and I'll go pull Avery down from the ceiling," I tell James. After ten solid minutes of outfit changes and me convincing her that she's overreacting, we emerge.

"Wow." Fletcher hops off the couch and takes in Avery's skinny jeans, knee-high boots and red sweater, which makes her mocha skin look even creamier. But she's one of those girls who could wear a potato sack and still look stunning. Me? I'm rocking my favorite pair of Sevens and Toms.

"Mom, we're leaving," Avery shouts toward the kitchen. Mandy comes out wiping her hands on a dishtowel.

"I hope y'all have a good time tonight. Fletcher, take care of my baby. Drive safely and don't do anything reckless. I'm looking at you, Avery."

"We'll be fine, Mom." She stands on her toes to kiss Mandy's cheek.

"I mean it. We're not in New York City."

"Thank you for the quick geography lesson, Mom." We walk outside to our respective vehicles.

"And remember to be safe! I'm too young to be a grandma!" Mandy shouts from the doorway.

"JESUS CHRIST, MOTHER!!"

"Mouth, young lady!" Mandy calls. "You're too young to be using that language."

Avery slams the car door and covers her hands with her face. James laughs as we get in his truck.

"Well at least I'm not the only one being embarrassed by their mom tonight."

"Speaking of embarrassing moms, why'd yours name you River?"

"Remember when I said she left right after high school? Well, she changed her name to Sunshine and decided the hippie life was what she wanted. She met a guy named Arlo Tennyson and she said she fell in love with him while he quoted Alfred, Lord Tennyson. He claimed to be a descendant, but I doubt that."

"That does sound pretty romantic."

"I guess. Anyway, I was their love child and was apparently born near a river in Florida."

"How come they didn't stay together?"

"I don't think she was looking to settle down then. Over the years, she said marriage was too institutionalized for her, but I think that became a defense mechanism when none of her other relationships worked out. I sort of feel bad for her."

"Why's that?"

"Everyone deserves a shot at growing old with the person they love."

He reaches for my left hand, and it's really hard to not read into the timing of his gesture. We pull into the theater parking lot behind Fletcher and Avery. He lets go long enough to put the truck in park and take the keys out of the ignition, but doesn't get out of the truck yet. He reaches over and grabs my hand again.

"Come here," he says. He leans in and he offers a simple, sweet kiss. "I never said thank you, by the way."

"For what?" I ask, lost in his woodsy scent and long lashes.

"For sitting next to me in Economics so we'd be partners."

"You left me no choice. You sat in my seat, and the only other empty desk was next to Smelly Warren." I run my nose along his jawline and lightly kiss the skin below his ear.

"I was in your seat?"

"Yup."

"Well now I'm really glad *I* didn't sit next to Smelly Warren." A tapping at my window interrupts our fit of laughter.

"Let's go, lovebirds!" Avery shouts. "I'm freezing!"

We walk toward the theater when Fletcher's phone chimes. He unlocks it and a tiny face fills the screen. He hits play and the cutest little voice says, "Goodnight Avewy and Fwetcher. I wuv you!"

"Hang on guys," Avery says. She and Fletcher stop to record their own goodnight video.

"Who was that from?" I ask.

"My little sister, Samantha," Fletcher answers, sliding his phone in his back pocket. The smile on his face oozes pride and love. No doubt, this is earning him serious bonus points with Avery.

"We've been sending videos back and forth since we left my house," Avery says. "She's the coolest four-year-old I know. Her favorite color is sparkles, she loves My Little Pony and she wants to be a mommy and a baker when she grows up."

"She's adorable, Fletcher!"

James reaches the ticket booth a step ahead of me, purchases our tickets and hands me mine. "You didn't have to, but thank you," I say.

"I told you, this is an official date. That means I get to kiss you at the end of the night."

"But you've already kissed me today."

"I know." He grins while I roll my eyes and walk in the theater.

Fletcher's phone chimes again in the concession line.

"Fwetcher, I'm scawed. Sing me the monster song."

Instead of ignoring her request, he sings her the monster song. In the middle of the lobby. With people watching. I look over at Avery. Her hands are cupped over her mouth and her eyes brim with tears. "Sorry, I sing her that every night before bed," he says quietly after he sends the video. Avery takes his hand and leans her head on his chest.

"You never have to apologize for being the best big brother on the planet." She wipes her eyes. "Ray, you going for Buncha Crunch or Milk Duds?" she asks, changing the subject. She's such a softy.

"Do you even have to ask? Milk Duds all the way."

We settle into our seats. A few minutes into the movie, I look to my right and see Fletcher and Avery holding hands. Her head's on his shoulder and his head's resting on hers. Looks like James won't be taking her shifts after all.

"Is this the part where I say I had a really nice time with you?" James asks. We're still sitting in The Beast in front of Avery's house. Double dating on the same night I'm sleeping over at her house means both couples would be at the front door and that's just weird.

"Only if you want to."

"I had a really nice time with you," he says softly. He unbuckles my seatbelt and pulls me closer to him.

"Eh, it was okay," I tease.

"Ego. Head. Oven." God, this guy makes me laugh.

"There, there," I say, kissing him on the cheek. He pulls away and stares at me. His face looks puzzled as his eyes search mine.

"How is it possible that I didn't know you last Saturday? I mean, I've started at a new school more times than I can count, but I've never had a week like this." He takes a deep breath. "Maybe that's because I've never met anyone else like you." He traces his finger up and down my left arm, which has come alive with nerve endings. I love every single one of them.

"You mean this isn't all part of your M.O.?" Not that it would matter much. I'd follow him off a cliff like he was the Pied Piper.

"Definitely not," he laughs. "I don't have an M.O. Just a serious crush on a beautiful girl." He presses his lips to mine and for a moment, I forget how to breathe. His hands move to either side of my face and he deepens the kiss. If I could choose one moment in my life to live over and over, it would be this one. "Sorry," he says, his eyes smiling as he pulls away slightly. "I sort of got lost there for a minute."

"No complaints from me." Avery's mom flashes the porch light and we both sigh. Four car doors open and we make our way to Avery's house.

"Have a good night, Mrs. Tennyson." He places a chaste kiss on my lips.

"Have a good night, Mr. Tennyson. I'll see you in class Monday. I'll be the one sitting next to the hot firefighter."

"So I passed the test?"

"Most definitely." I laugh as he pumps a fist in the air. "How many tattoos do you have?"

"Four."

"Looks like I still need to find the other two." I can't help my mischievous look as I drum my fingertips together.

"Anytime, sweetheart." I love it when he grins like that. It makes me want to eat his face off.

"Okay, teenagers, it's final call," Mandy says from the front door.

Fletcher kisses Avery on the cheek. "Can I call you tomorrow?" he asks.

She blushes and tucks an errant curl behind her ear. "I'd like that. Give Sam a goodnight kiss from me, okay?"

"Will do."

Avery and I head to her bedroom after the guys leave. She closes her door and leans against it.

"Ray, I have a problem."

"Uh, oh. What?" I mentally review the evening, but nothing between her and Fletcher jumps out at me.

"I think I'm in love," she sighs.

Yeah. I think I know what you mean.

James

"I got a boogie!" Samantha runs toward me with her right index finger extended. Fletcher intercepts her with a tissue and spares me from being assaulted by her nasal nastiness. Even guys have to draw the line somewhere.

"Slow down, Booger Butt. Let's not scare James away, okay?"

"Sowwy, Fwetcher." She bats her eyelashes and he instantly caves. With eyes and pouty lips like hers, he never stood a chance.

"Good save, bro," I say with an appreciative nod. It's easy to see why Avery instantly fell in love with Sam a couple of weeks ago. The kid is pretty rad, despite her fondness for nose picking. I've only been at Fletcher's for an hour and she's already made me three cups of tea and painted my toenails. I couldn't say no to the last one, therefore I'm sporting a sparkly pink pedicure. I'd like to believe I'm man enough to pull it off. Ray's spending the next week gearing up for her invitational, and Avery's working at the Sweet Pea (I didn't have to take her shifts after all), so I'm playing guitar with Fletcher at his house. It's his parents' monthly date night.

"James, did you know I'm a supwise?"

"No, I definitely didn't know that." I look at Fletcher for translation.

"Yes, you are a surprise, Sammy girl. Now go surprise us with the most spectacular dress up outfit ever." She runs back to her room full of inspiration.

"In case you hadn't noticed the fifteen-year difference between us, Sam wasn't exactly planned. Mom hates it when people say she was an accident, so we've always said Sammy was our surprise baby. She loves it though, since she thinks surprises are the best thing ever."

"Smart kid, that one." I remove the capo from the neck of my guitar and continue strumming.

"What about this one?" he asks. I listen to the easy intro and nod along, picking out harmonies. "Hey, what do you think about playing at the Sweet Pea sometime? I was thinking of asking Mandy and Devin about doing an open mic night kind of thing."

"That could be pretty cool," I say, considering it.

"Well, it sort of leads into the other idea I had. And I kind of wanted your opinion on it."

"Shoot."

"Avery has been dropping hints about prom like crazy so I know she wants me to ask her. The thing is, I can't afford a tux rental and a corsage and dinner at a nice restaurant. If we had a couple of open mic nights and had a small cover fee, maybe we could earn enough money to do a post-prom senior dinner thing at the Pea."

"Wow, you've put a lot of thought into this." Never mind that it's January and Avery's already making prom plans.

"Yeah." He scratches the back of his neck—more in a show of nerves than dry skin, I'm sure. "Avery's really cool, man. These past couple of weeks have been pretty epic. And it's not even been anything big. We talk every night and she came here a few days ago for dinner. I just don't want to give her any reasons to dump me."

"From what I've heard from Ray, I don't think you have anything to worry about. But no doubt, she'll appreciate the gesture. I'm on board, just let me know what you need me to do."

"Just show up with your guitar and sing."

"Consider it done, dude." He exhales a sigh of relief. "I guess that means we should practice some songs, huh?"

"Probably."

We spend the next couple of hours making a set list—five cover songs and one original that we started on. Samantha regularly interrupted us (two games of duck-duck-goose, one ice-cream mishap and an emergency surgery on Mrs. Bear's leg after their dog amputated it). She finally passed out in a sea of stuffed animals and My Little Ponies at 9:30. She's a cute kid, but damn, I'm exhausted.

"Are you tired?" I ask, when Rachel's face fills my screen. I know she's working really hard on her personal record. I kick my shoes off and flop on my bed.

"Yeah, I'm pretty beat."

"Well you've been running through my mind all day." I laugh and she rolls her eyes.

"Very original, Romeo." Her face moves off camera.

"Where'd you go?" I say to her ceiling.

"I just got out of the shower and I'm putting on my pajamas."

"You're naked? Christ, Ray." I groan. "This is sixteen kinds of unfair here."

"Down, boy," she says from across her room.

"Easy for you to say." To retaliate, I remove my shirt and prop my phone up on my footboard, then lean back on my pillows and lace my fingers behind my head. Two can play at this game.

"Okay, I'm back." Her face fills the screen again, just in time for me to see her jaw fall open. "Wait a minute mister," she says, narrowing her eyes and pointing at the phone. "That's not fair. I didn't get naked in front of you."

"I'm not naked. I have pants on. And I promise I wouldn't have complained if you did." I send her my most angelic smile.

"Fine, have it your way." She flips the video around and her face is replaced by her cat, who is currently sprawled on the floor giving his man parts a bath.

"That's disgusting. And I must say, I'm a bit disappointed. I was sort of hoping for a case of tat-for-tit if you know what I mean." I hope she knows by my laugh that I'm just joking.

"Very clever, but dream on. You can watch kitty porn until you put your shirt back on."

"You mean you want me to cover my hot firefighter abs?" I ask in fake shock.

"They distract me, so yes." She can't hide the sound of her

smile. I acquiesce, but only because I'm not in a kinky Animal Planet kind of mood.

"Alright, you win. What are you doing tomorrow?"

"Nothing, it's a rest day. Coach has us scheduled for runs the first four days of next week, then a rest day before our invitational on Saturday."

"Does this mean I can see you tomorrow?" I don't even try to hide the hopefulness in my voice.

"I don't know..."

"You still haven't talked to your dad?"

"No. I'm sorry," she says quietly, and looks down. It's not her fault that her dad's an unrelenting ass. I just need to figure out a way to remove the threat so he doesn't object to me hanging out with her. I've never wished I was a girl before, but I admit having girl parts would help me out in this situation. Not that surgery is in my future anytime soon. But maybe...

"Why are you smiling like that?" She looks suspicious.

"Ray, I'm coming to your house tomorrow," I say confidently.

"I'd rather not get grounded tomorrow."

"You won't get grounded, I promise. You'll see. Just text me your address."

"James, I have no idea what you're up to, but it can't be good."

"You're right, it's not good. It's brilliant. Prepare to be amazed, my dear." She only stares at me. "I miss you, Ray. Only getting to see you for one class and one lunch every day sucks."

She sighs. "I know, I miss you too."

"Okay, then. Tomorrow. I'll see you then. I'll be the desperate one knocking on your front door."

"If you get me in trouble, I'm kicking your ass."

"As much as I'd love your hands anywhere near my ass, you won't get in trouble." I smile reassuringly, and I can see the moment she gives in.

"Good night, Mrs. Tennyson."

"Good night, Mr. Tennyson."

I ring Rachel's doorbell and hear her dad's muffled voice telling her to answer it. I take a deep breath and order my hormones to behave themselves. Staying in character is the only way this will work. She opens the door and clamps her hand over her mouth, taking in my slightly too-tight jeans. I rolled them at the ankles and I'm wearing Converse with no socks. I went to Goodwill this morning and scored a magenta shirt in a women's large. I normally wear a men's large. The result is an extremely tight shirt with a hem that floats just above the top of my jeans. I snuck one of my mom's wigs out of her closet, too. She calls this one her "girlfriend." It's platinum blond and hangs in loose waves past my shoulders. Pink aviator style sunglasses complete my look.

"Hey, girl! Thanks so much for offering to help me with this stupid report." I make an effort to emphasize all of my s's and wave my hands around animatedly. I step into the foyer, where her dad's eyes fall on me. "I mean, what is up with Mr. Jackson's awful assignment? Does anyone *really* care about the courtship rituals of Neanderthals?" I roll my eyes and fake a shudder.

"Yeah, it's pretty dumb," she manages to say without

laughing. Her dad walks over and before Rachel can blow it, I take charge.

"Oh my gosh, you must be Rachel's dad. She's told me so much about you." He glances back and forth between us, trying to figure out what the hell is happening in his entryway. "I'm Jamie, the new girl? Well, sorry," I say with a flourish of my hand. "I know I'm not *exactly* a girl, but I may as well be." I wink at her dad and he takes a few steps back.

"Yeah, Dad," Rachel says, catching on. "Remember I was talking to Jamie a few weeks ago after she moved here? I offered to help her out if she got stuck on any assignments. Unfortunately, Mr. Jackson is a stickler. I told Jamie she could come over today and I'd tutor her since this paper is worth twenty-five percent of her grade." She emphasizes the last part.

Her dad still has no idea what to do. He clears his throat and glances at his watch. "Sure, sure. That sounds fine. I just forgot. I'm supposed to meet your mother at the thing she's at right now."

"The Bingo game?" Rachel asks.

"Yes, the Bingo game. Exactly! So I'm going to do that. I'll be back later. Have fun with your report, uh, Jamie." Her dad extends his hand, then drops it, then extends it again. I shake it with the lightest grip I can offer. "Okay, then. I'll see you later tonight, Rachel. Bye Jamie."

He practically runs out the door. I don't think he cares that he left his coffee cup on the table or that his jacket is still hanging on the coat rack. We wait until he rounds the curve of the driveway before falling apart in a fit of laughter.

"Oh, my God, I can't believe you," she finally manages to say. "What the hell are you *wearing*?"

"I am wearing the victory outfit of a genius." I remove the wig and sunglasses, then pull her into my arms and kiss her. She smells so damn good. Her hands take advantage of my short shirt and slip up my back. I gently bite her lower lip when she rakes her nails across my muscles. If she keeps that up, I'm gonna devour her face.

"Alright, genius. One rule for this afternoon."

"Name it, as long as I'm still allowed to do this." I bury my face in her neck and suck on the skin just below her ear. She mumbles something that sounds like "Christ Almighty" and fists her hands in my hair. Which feels amazing, by the way. Everything she does feels amazing.

"My rule. No sex." She pulls her face away and looks me in the eye to make sure I heard her. I place my hands on either side of her face and kiss the tip of her nose.

"Rachel, I'd never make you do anything you didn't want to do or weren't ready for. If it makes you feel any better, I don't think I'm ready for that, either." She smiles, and I see the relief in her face. "That doesn't mean I don't think about it, but you can't fault me for that. I am a guy, after all."

"I may have thought about it a time... or five, too." Her cheeks flush at her admission, but I'm glad to know I'm not alone.

"You're worth the wait, Ray. Trust me. I'm not going anywhere." I pull her into my arms again, but this time we just hug. We sway silently for several minutes, enjoying the feel of our bodies together. Then she starts laughing.

"What?" I ask, putting an arm's length between us.

"The courtship rituals of Neanderthals? What was that all about?"

"I kept expecting your dad to club me and drag you back into your cave, so I thought it was fitting."

She high fives me. "Well played, James. Well played."

Like usual, I walk toward Economics on Monday morning excited to see Rachel. Even though I got to spend yesterday afternoon with her, it's never enough. Eternity wouldn't be enough time with her. We're caught up on our project so that means we get to hang out for forty-five minutes. I'll take what I can get at this point. At least I'm not wearing a pink shirt and tight pants. The downside is we have to keep all PDA to a bare minimum at school. The last thing we need is her dad getting wind of our relationship (or whatever it is we have). It's mostly okay. I'm just glad I can be near her.

When I step into the classroom, something feels off. Nothing looks out of place, but something's not right. The feeling doesn't go away when Mrs. Mason starts talking about what's coming up this week. It's still there when we break up into groups for our project. Rachel can tell I'm a bit distracted but she doesn't push it.

By the end of the day, I'm getting irritated. The nagging feeling has intensified but hasn't gotten any clearer. Rachel's doing her track thing, and I'm not scheduled to work until Wednesday, so I head home. Everyone's gone, so I grab a piece of pie and go to my room. I turn on my favorite Sunset Sons song and taste Gran's first blackberry pie of the year. Both are good, but I'm not enjoying them as much as I normally do.

I set my plate down, rub my face, and grab my phone. My finger touches the keypad and my heart starts beating faster.

Everything clicks into place. I close my eyes and my fingers dial the ten digits I see flashing in my head. I don't breathe again until she answers.

"Yeah?" I hear water running.

"Gretchen?"

"S'rry, she won't be here 'nymore," she slurs.

"Gretchen, where are you?" I shout into the phone. Ten seconds pass. Twenty.

"Not here." Her voice sounds farther away.

"Gretchen!"

I jump off my bed and run for the house phone in the kitchen. Thank Christ my grandparents still have one. I put my cell phone on speaker and dial 9-1-1 on the house phone.

"9-1-1, what is your emergency?"

"Someone needs help!"

"What's the address?"

Fuck.

"Gretchen, what's your address?" I hear the phone clatter to the floor. Then, a splash of water. Then the call drops.

"I don't know her address, but I have her phone number. Can you use that?" I read off the number on my phone log and fight off the bile rising in the back of my throat.

"What's the nature of the emergency?"

"I don't know exactly. She sounds like she's on something and I hear water. That's all I know."

"Standby, sir."

I watch the kitchen clock. Two minutes and thirty four seconds pass, but it may as well be two hours. My fingernails are nearly gone by the time the operator comes back on the line.

"We have located the address and have sent emergency response personnel to the house. Would you like to leave your phone number if the first responders have any additional questions?" I have no idea how this lady can be so calm. My heart feels like it's going to beat out of my chest.

"Yeah, sure." I tell the operator my number. With nothing else to offer, I end the call.

After an hour of pacing the kitchen, I grab my keys and jacket and head to the hospital. The emergency room is buzzing. I run to the triage desk.

"Can I help you, sir?" I glance around the waiting room, not sure exactly what I'm looking for.

"Was someone brought in here on a stretcher?"

"Yes, we've had eleven today."

"Within the last hour. A girl named Gretchen?"

"Are you family?"

"No."

"I'm sorry, privacy laws prevent me from sharing any information with you." I know she's not trying to be a bitch, but that doesn't help my cause. I move to a chair in the waiting room. I glance around at the faces and wonder if any of them are here for Gretchen.

Probably too old.

Definitely too old.

Probably too young.

None of these people look like her. I lean forward and bring my hands to my forehead, trying to assess what the fuck happened today. I've never predicted anything like this. Never even come close. Whatever it is that I have, has been more of entertainment value than anything, sort of like those fake commercial psychics. I can't even begin to understand what changed today.

"James?" I hear my name so quietly that I wonder if I imagined it. I lift my head and scan the room. My eyes fall on Lainey. She runs to me, throws her arms around my neck and sobs.

"What the fuck is going on, James?"

"I have no idea. When Gretchen answered the phone, she was practically unresponsive. I heard water and I called 9-1-1."

She lets go and we sit in a side-by-side vigil on the world's most uncomfortable chairs.

"I couldn't reach her all day. She sounded weird when we talked yesterday, but she said she'd see me tomorrow and hung up. That was the last time I talked to her. I got worried so I drove to her house and the neighbors said she was taken away in an ambulance."

"She wasn't in school today," I say, picturing the faces in Economics, more of my nagging feeling clicking into place.

"She was supposed to tell her parents last night." It comes out in a whisper, and if I wasn't focused on the sound of her voice, I would have missed it.

"I gather it didn't go well."

Lainey balls her hands into fists. "They're such mother fuckers. I don't get them at all. Would it be too much to ask for them to be accepting of their daughter? Fucking bastards." She lets out a deep sigh. "James, I swear to God if Gretchen lives I'm going to kick her ass into next Tuesday for pulling this shit."

"If she lives, she's going to need a huge support network, and it's obvious she's not getting it at home. What can we do?"

"I'll make her stay with me for a while. She's already eighteen, so her parents can suck it as far as I'm concerned."

"How long have you been in love with her?"

"We've been best friends for about five years. So... about five years." She laughs once before a new round of tears start. I pass her tissues from the box on the end table next to me. "She said she was bi-curious at first, but I knew she was kidding herself. That fuckhead boyfriend of hers was her attempt at being normal for her Bible-thumping parents. They made it quite clear that the college fund they set up for her would only be available if she met their standards. I thought if she was just honest with them, they'd eventually come around. I was the one who pressured her to tell them. This is all my fault." She picks apart the tissue in her hands while tears roll down her cheeks.

"No, this is absolutely not your fault. This situation is entirely of their creation. I hope this is a wake-up call for them."

Lainey and I sit in the waiting room for three more hours. I texted Mom earlier and told her I'd be home late, but I didn't tell her why. I'm not sure how to explain it. At 8:05, a man and woman emerge from the back area of the emergency room. Lainey stiffens in her seat beside me. I stand and walk toward them.

"Are you Gretchen's parents?"

Her mom nods. Their eyes are both red and swollen and it looks like they're bearing the weight of the world on their shoulders. Good. Maybe they can empathize with their daughter for once.

"I'm James, a friend of hers from school. Is she going to be okay?"

"The doctors are... what did they say, Craig?" She looks to her husband.

"They said they're cautiously optimistic," he responds, his voice sounding hollow. "They pumped her stomach."

"What did she take?"

"A bottle of sleeping pills. The paramedics found her in the bathtub. She was unconscious, but her chin never submerged," she says. "She's resting now, and the doctors said she'll be okay. There's nothing more we can do for her tonight, so they advised us to go home and get some rest. We'll be back in the morning before she goes for her psych eval."

"What room is she in? I'd like to come visit tomorrow after school."

"221."

"Come on dear, let's get you home," Craig says. They start walking but Gretchen's mom stops and turns around.

"The paramedics said they acted on a tip from Gretchen's friend. Was that you or Lainey?" I raise my hand.

"Thank you for saving my daughter's life." She turns and they leave the emergency room, taking their wake of guilt with them.

I walk toward Lainey. "Did you hear all of that?" She nods yes. "I guess I'm gonna head home too. You gonna be okay?"

"I think so."

I take her phone and program my number. "Call or text if you need me." I start walking to the exit when she calls my name again. "Yeah?"

"I forgot to ask earlier. How did you know?"

"Know what?" I ask to stall for time.

"How did you know Gretchen needed help?"

I lift my palms in the air and shrug my shoulders. I'd love to know the answer to that myself. I turn and leave before she questions me further.

Rachel

"Thanks again for the mocha frap, Avery. I seriously owe you. I'll be so glad when this invitational is over." I try fighting off another yawn, but it's useless. We grab our backpacks and do the zombie shuffle across the parking lot, my quads protesting the entire way. Thank God for Epsom salt baths. I'd hate to see what they'd be saying if I hadn't soaked for an hour last night.

"No problemo, Beef. I refuse to start my day without coffee. Cheers," she says, clinking her to-go cup with mine.

We navigate the hallway, making every attempt to protect our cups of liquid gold from the never-ending stream of people who seem to be much more awake than we are. A group of jocks walk by, their voices carrying over the din.

"I heard it was Katie Stewart. She tried to slit her wrists but did it in the wrong direction."

"No, it was Anastasia Powell. You know, the girl who sharted in gym class last week? She tried to hang herself."

"That's not what I heard." Their voices trail off when they round the corner.

"What the hell was that about?" Avery asks.

"I have no idea. I had practice yesterday then took a bath and passed out when I got home. I didn't even talk to James last night." Which sort of sucked. I didn't realize how much I enjoyed our evening conversations until I skipped one. Come to think of it, he didn't text me last night either.

"I was working last night but I didn't hear about anyone trying to off themselves."

"Wasn't Fletcher working yesterday? I have a feeling the Rapture could have happened and you wouldn't have noticed." She narrows her eyes and opens her mouth to make a snarky comment, then stops and smiles.

"Yeah, you're probably right."

We turn our attention to our combination locks. It takes me three tries to open my locker, even though I *know* I got the damn numbers right. This happens almost every time, and, as usual, Avery has no problems. We exchange yesterday afternoon's books for the ones we'll need this morning, and she crosses off another day on her birthday countdown calendar. "Twenty-one more days! I still haven't heard anything from my dad about a car. So help me God, he better come through." She applies a splash of body spray and another layer of hairspray.

Principal Rosser's voice comes over the intercom. "May I have your attention please. All students are to report to the gymnasium during first period for an emergency assembly. I repeat, all students are to report to the gymnasium during first period for an emergency assembly. Thank you."

I look at Avery and shrug. I put my first period book back while she expertly coats her lips with Red Vixxen, her favorite lipstick, in her locker mirror. As we walk toward the gym, I text James.

Me: Wanna sit with us during the assembly?
James: Good morning, Captain Obvious.
Me: Haha. I'll wait by the main entrance.

"Well if it isn't the two prettiest girls in the school," James says a few minutes later. He walks between me and Avery and puts his arms over our shoulders.

"James, you're making us look like you're our pimp," Avery jokes.

"Sorry, Avery. You're a means to an end right now. I couldn't keep my hands off Ray, but her dad's sort of a bastard. You're just a part of my cover plan."

"The things I do for you, Rachel Lynn," she sighs. We trudge along toward the gym when James steers us away from a classroom door. Moments later, it swings open.

"Wow, good timing," Avery says, giving him a curious look. "How'd you know that was gonna happen?"

"Your mom never taught you to not walk in front of closed doors?" he counters.

We sit through an assembly on suicide awareness. Apparently, someone tried to overdose on sleeping pills yesterday, though they don't say who. "This is depressing," I whisper.

"For real. I wonder who it was," Avery says.

I look over at James and he's staring off into space. He hasn't been his normal self this morning. "Hey, you okay?" I ask.

"Yeah, sorry. I'm just tired. I didn't sleep well last night." He rubs his hands over his face and I notice his chewed fingernails.

"Must be because I didn't tell you a good night story," I tease, nudging his shoulder. I don't know what's bothering him, but I'd do anything to make him feel better.

"That's exactly it. Don't make that mistake again, Mrs. Tennyson." He smiles, but it doesn't quite reach his eyes.

"I've got track all this week, but I'll make sure to call you when I get done."

"I'm just kidding, Ray. I know you're busy because of your invitational."

"You know, I wouldn't mind it if a certain tall, handsome guy found his way out to the track after school this week."

"I have plans this afternoon, and I'm working Wednesday, but I'll be there Thursday." He turns his attention to the counselor and I use the moment to study his face. He looks exhausted. Shadows line the area under his eyes and he begins chewing on his lower lip.

"I can tell something's wrong, James. You know you can tell me anything."

"I know, Ray. Everything's fine. But thanks." He does that pathetic smile again.

During practice, I can't shake James' expression. I take my place at the starting line and wait for Coach Larson to give the signal. Although we haven't known each other for long, I've never seen James look so... sad. I admit it bugs me that he's not confiding in me. I hope he opens up soon. I'd do anything to help him not look like that.

"Wheaton!" Coach yells from the side of the track. I look up and notice the rest of my team is already off and running. *Shit.* I take off at a sprint to catch up. When we finish, I hear a voice from the sidelines that sends chills up my spine. And not in a good way.

"Young lady, what the hell was that?"

"Sorry, Dad. I got lost in thought for a second."

"I'm so glad you're enjoying your nice, relaxing afternoon on the track." He glares at me. Dad never comes to my practices. I wonder what he's got up his sleeve. He sighs with frustration and rubs his hands over his face. I hate that he makes me feel like I'm five years old and I just got busted with my hand in the cookie jar. "I'll have you know that I called in some personal favors, and the coach of the UNC track program is in the stands watching you. Your future is riding on your performances from here on out. This invitational on Saturday? It's huge. This is the real stuff, Rachel. I don't have time for you to walk around with your head in the clouds. You need to snap back to reality and make sure you're focused on winning. Unless, of course, you don't have a problem with community college?" I don't think he could be more condescending if he tried.

"Sorry, Dad. I'll do better," I say quietly. He stares at me for a few more moments and then walks away. I go through the motions for the rest of practice, but the only running I really want to do is to James' house to help him work through whatever is going on in his head. I normally wait until I'm home and showered before I call him, but I can't wait today. As soon as I get to the locker room, I grab my Bluetooth out of my bag and jog to my car.

"Hey, handsome. How was your afternoon?"

"It was good. How was practice?"

"I've had better, but whatever. What plans did you have this afternoon?"

"Oh, I... um... delivered a pie to the hospital."

"Gran's spreading her culinary cheer, I see."

"Yeah." He still sounds distant. Doubt creeps over me like a cold blanket. Since I've never had a boyfriend, I'm not sure how this break-up thing works. I summon all the courage I can muster.

"James, I need to ask you something but you have to promise to give me an honest answer." He doesn't respond, so I blurt it out. "Do you want to break up with me?"

"Rachel, how can I break up with you if I never asked you out in the first place?" Okay, he makes a good point. But still. Dodging the question isn't answering it.

"Well, are you wanting to end whatever it is that we've been doing these last few weeks?"

"Can we switch to FaceTime?"

"Sure, I guess. Give me a few minutes to get home."

Nothing like delaying the inevitable. Ten agonizing, panic-ridden minutes later, his face fills my screen. "Why FaceTime?" I try to control my breathing. Maybe he's the kind of guy who'd rather break up with someone face-to-face? I imagined all the things he could possibly say on the drive home. None of them were good.

"Because you need to see my face when I tell you this." Oh, God. Here it comes. I hold my breath. "I purposely never asked you out because you're not allowed to have a boyfriend. But this thing we have—whatever you want to call it—is the best thing that's ever happened to me. I've never connected to anyone the way I have with you. It sounds stupid when I say it out loud but when I met you, I felt like I was coming home. Which is interesting, considering I've never really had a home before."

Well I can honestly say I didn't see *that* coming. I let out a sigh of relief.

"You were seriously worried that I didn't want to be with you anymore?"

"Yeah, kinda. Things were fine over the weekend, but you were really distant yesterday and today. It's like you were saying all the right things, but the meaning behind them was missing. I just thought you realized you didn't want to be with me but didn't know how to say it." I hate that I turned so quickly into one of *those* teenage girls. The ones who jump to conclusions and invent entire scenarios without having all the facts. And then wrestle an anxiety attack while driving home, certain they're marching to their dating death.

"I promise everything is fine with us. There's no one I'd rather not be boyfriend and girlfriend with than you." He smiles, but this time his face lights up. And it's beautiful.

"So then, what's up? And don't tell me you're not stressed out about something." I watch his eyes look upward, then fall. His face contorts into an expression I've never seen. His fingers pinch the bridge of his nose, as it whatever he has to say physically pains him. He takes a deep breath, and finally looks at me again.

"So remember when you and Avery were asking about my bucket list that first day at lunch?"

"Yeah?" I don't see what that has to do with anything, but I'll play along.

"What did I say was the top thing on my list?"

"To save someone's life."

"Right. Well, it seems I can check that one off now."

"What? How? When? *Who*?"

"The assembly we had this morning. It's because Gretchen Rawls tried to overdose on sleeping pills and drown herself."

"How do you know that?" He pauses and looks down again. This time he doesn't look back up when he starts talking.

"Because I was on the phone with her right before she got in the bathtub."

"WHAT?"

"I called her and her voice was all slurry and then I heard a big splash. So I called 9-1-1."

I'm trying to connect the dots here, but there are still *a lot* of missing dots. "How did you know to call her?"

"I don't know."

"How did you know her number?"

"I don't know."

"What do you mean you don't know?"

"I mean, I don't know. All day on Monday, I had this really bad feeling. It started when I walked into second period and it didn't go away. When I got home, I felt like I was starting to have a panic attack. Before I knew it, I had my phone in my hand and I was dialing her number."

"So you didn't know why you were calling her or what her number was, but you magically called her anyway?" Great, my first non-boyfriend is psychotic. Just. My. Luck.

"It might help if I explained something else."

What? Like how he broke out of the mental hospital before he moved here?

"Ever since I can remember, I've known things. Before they happen."

"You're psychic?"

"I wouldn't go that far. It's always been just for fun. I'll know what someone's wearing before I see them. Or who's on the phone before I answer."

"James, that's called Caller ID."

"Without looking at the phone, Rachel." He laughs for the first time since we started talking today.

"So you predict things."

"Kind of. It's sort of like having a memory. Only, I have the memory before it happens. It's never been anything important. I've never aced my SATs or won the lottery or anything. It's always just been random things. The first time I had a big premonition was the day you walked in late to class."

"So *that's* why you were acting like a moron." I laugh, remembering our first conversation.

"Exactly. And I'm so glad I left such a good impression on you." He smiles again and shakes his head.

"What about me did you predict?"

"I can't exactly put my finger on it. I didn't see you walking in the room or anything. It was more like a feeling. My heart and my brain were going into overdrive. I didn't know what was going on because nothing like that had ever happened before. But when you walked in the room, I was blown away with your beauty. Except it had nothing to do with how you looked. I just *felt* it. The only way I can describe it is like this intense thing that gripped me from the insides. I knew you were it for me."

Oh my God, that's the most beautiful thing anyone has

ever said to me. I want to get all those words tattooed so they'll be with me always.

"Anyway, I don't ever talk about it because the last time I did, I was labeled a freak. So I've just had my own personal inside joke all these years. Until Monday. I have no idea how it happened. I got home from school, and I had this memory of being at school when they announced that Gretchen killed herself."

"Holy shit, James."

"Yeah, tell me about it."

"But you saved her life. Why do you not seem happy about that?"

"Ray, what would I have done if I was too late? If I didn't figure it out in time?"

"You can't think like that. All that matters is you saved her. Is she the person you went to the hospital to see today?"

"Yeah, I wanted to see how she was doing."

"And?"

"She was sleeping, so I put Gran's pie on her table and left."

"Why did she do it?"

"Because her parents don't agree with her sexual orientation."

"Wait. I thought she was dating a guy."

"She wasn't attracted to him. It was part of her trying to be something she's not to please her parents."

"Wow, that's really sad."

"For real." He pauses, starts to ask a question and then stops. I'm glad he decided to have this conversation over FaceTime. It helps to see his expressions.

"What?"

"Well, now that you know all of this about me, do you still want to be with me? If it's too much weirdness, I understand." Equal amounts of hope and anguish dance across his face.

"You're going to have to try a lot harder than that to get rid of me." He flashes his million dollar smile, and my insides threaten to turn to mush. "But this is fair warning. I expect you to never forget our anniversary."

He holds up his right hand. "I solemnly vow to always remember my anniversary with my first non-girlfriend."

"Thank you." I giggle. "I've gotta shower and eat dinner. I'll see you tomorrow before school?"

"I'll be the handsome guy waiting next to your locker."

Insides. Mush.

"See you tomorrow, Mrs. Tennyson."

"Tomorrow, Mr. Tennyson."

"Hey, Ray?"

"Yeah?"

"You won't say anything, right? About all of this?"

"About all of what?" I say, with a look of feigned innocence. He smiles again. I wish I could kiss those perfect lips. Instead, I settle for blowing a kiss and end the call.

Mom's in the kitchen when I get out of the shower. I can't stop thinking about Gretchen. My heart hurts for her. I can't imagine being in a situation where the best option is to just end it all. Mom and I have never been very close, but I find myself appreciating our relationship a lot more after my phone call with James.

"Hey, you making dinner?"

"Hey, sweetie. We're having lasagna. Want to help?"

"Yeah, I'd like that." I take over chopping vegetables for the salad, and Mom moves to the stove to start browning the ground turkey. She and I look alike—I get my blonde hair and body structure from her. I know she used to be a ballet dancer in college, but I realize there's a lot of other stuff about her I don't know. "Mom, how did you meet Dad?"

"He was my knight in shining armor. Or, at the very least, my knight with a pair of strong arms." She stops stirring, momentarily caught up in the memory. "I was going for a jog around campus and I stepped in a pothole and twisted my ankle. Of course, this was long before we had cell phones, so I was stranded and couldn't walk. I sat there for about an hour and finally saw this handsome fellow walking toward me. When I told him what happened, he scooped me up and took me to the campus clinic. He carried me the whole way."

"Was it love at first sight?"

"For me it was. He was happily single—the typical college guy. But the next semester, he started having trouble in one of his English classes. He asked me to tutor him since that was my major. One night I came to his dorm, but he didn't answer the door. I could hear a lot of commotion inside and what sounded like a fire alarm. I opened the door to find him in the kitchen with a fire extinguisher. He was trying to cook dinner for me, but it backfired terribly." She and I laugh. Dad's never been very comfortable in the kitchen.

"So what'd you guys do?"

"He took me to Genova's instead and we had our tutor session there. He kissed me for the first time that night."

"So that's why you go there every year for your anniversary."

"That's right."

"How'd you know you were in love?" I put the salad in the fridge and move to the other counter to help Mom assemble the lasagna.

"I realized there was no one else I'd rather spend my time with than him. It didn't matter that your dad didn't have a lot of money. He didn't have to buy me gifts or take me to fancy restaurants. I just wanted to be with him, no matter what we were doing."

Well, I know how that feels. "Dad was broke in college?"

"Oh, absolutely. He went to college on a track scholarship. He was the first person in his family to earn a college degree. The reason he was walking when I sprained my ankle was because he didn't have a car. He'd gotten a job at Genova's the week before he took me there, but hadn't gotten a paycheck yet. His manager let him work our meal off by washing dishes for the next three weekends." Mom covers the lasagna and puts it in the oven while I set the timer.

"Wow, that doesn't sound like Dad at all."

"That's why he's worked so hard to get where we are now. So you'd never be without." She says it so matter-of-factly, but it stuns me nonetheless. Here I thought my dad was just a colossal asshole with a bad case of Living Vicariously Through His Child. I think about Gretchen again and nearly break down in tears. It doesn't go unnoticed by Mom.

"Rachel, what's wrong?"

"Nothing really. It's just... this girl in one of my classes tried to kill herself yesterday."

"Oh my goodness, that poor child," Mom says, covering her mouth.

"Yeah. She told her parents she was gay and they flipped out on her." We move to the kitchen table and sit down.

"I can imagine that would be a difficult thing to hear, but I certainly don't agree with their choice to shun their own flesh and blood."

For the first time, I think about my own college plans and what James and I talked about the first day we met.

"Mom, can I tell you something?" She looks at me with wide eyes, then swallows and puts her hand on top of mine.

"Of course, Rachel. There's nothing you can't say to me."

"Don't worry, I'm not gay," I say with a smile, trying to reassure her. Not that that'd be the worst thing in the world. I take a deep breath. I feel like I owe it to Gretchen and James to be honest with my mom. If they had the courage to speak the truth, so can I. "Mom, I don't want to pursue track in college and be an Olympic athlete."

"I thought you loved running."

"I do—the running part, anyway. The competition part takes all the fun away for me. I'd rather be a P.E. teacher instead. There are so many kids who don't have someone like Dad supporting their fitness. I want to be that person."

She squeezes my hand and smiles. "Honey, that sounds very admirable. You know I'll always support you one hundred percent. I just want you to be happy. If that means being a P.E. teacher and not competing in track, then I support you." Just like that, I feel like a weight has been lifted. Well, partially lifted at least.

"Can you help me with one thing?"

"Anything, sweetie."

"Can you help me tell Dad that my invitational on Saturday will be my last race?"

"Oh, boy." She sighs. "Yes, I'll help you. Safety in numbers, right?" I know she's joking, but I can't help but be nervous.

"Thanks, Mom. And thanks for this afternoon. I didn't know how much I needed that."

"Me, either."

I decide to wait to tell her about James. There's only so much truth one person can handle in a day.

James

I didn't mean to tell her. Well, not yet anyway. But hearing her freak out about our relationship and knowing I was the cause of it was too much to bear. She should never question what I feel for her. It's my job to make her feel special and beautiful and amazing, and I failed.

I won't fail her again.

Thankfully, she accepted everything. Not that I really thought she wouldn't. But it was nice to have the reassurance that she still wanted to be with me. I lean against Rachel's locker and check my phone. Knowing Avery, they wouldn't get here for a few more minutes. That girl makes punctual look like a disease.

"Hey, James." A curly brunette named Vivien Tanner saunters toward me. She's curvy in all the right places, I'll give her that. But her breathy greeting and "screw me" smile don't do anything for me. "You look so lonely standing here all by yourself. I'd be happy to keep you company." She tries to touch my chest, but I step back to shift my stance against Ray's locker, this time crossing my arms in front of me. I don't like being rude to girls, but there's no part of me that wants any part of her.

"Not lonely at all, but thanks." I look toward the end of the hall and see Rachel and Avery walking in. A smile overtakes my face and my stomach does some weird judo shit. (Mom's romance book talked about butterflies, but that's way too sissy for me.) "In fact, if you'll excuse me," I say, not bothering to finish my sentence before walking away. I get about five steps down the hall when Rachel looks up and sees me. She smiles, but this one is different. She looks... happier? I wonder what that's all about. I have no control over what premonitions I have, and the Gods of Psychic Abilities have kept me in the dark on this one.

"Hey," I say, when we finally reach each other. Certainly not the most poetic greeting, but whatever.

"Guess what Rachel did last night!" Avery's way too excited. Whatever it is must be huge because she's never this keyed up this early in the morning. I turn my attention back to Rachel.

"I have no idea, but I'm guessing it's a good thing because you're smiling."

"I told my mom I want to be a teacher."

"What?" I pick her up and spin her around before I remember that we're in a hallway full of eyes and mouths that can tell on us. I set her down and take one step back. "Ray, that's awesome! And pretty huge. What made you tell her?"

"After the assembly and our conversation yesterday, I decided it was time for me to tell the truth. I don't want to waste my life doing something that makes everyone happy but myself." She shrugs her shoulder as if it's no big deal, but I know how scary it must have been for her. Especially knowing what Gretchen did because of the way her parents reacted.

"She's gonna be the most kick ass teacher *ever!*" Avery shouts, squeezing Rachel's arm as we reach their lockers.

"What'd your mom say?" I ask, making sure to stand on the other side of Rachel to avoid Avery's cloud of hairspray and perfume. It's a mistake I made exactly once.

"Surprisingly, she was supportive. But I still have to tell my dad." She opens her backpack and quickly hands me a note before swapping her books. I tuck it in my back pocket. I don't think a girl has ever written me a note.

"You absolutely never cease to amaze me." I wish I could touch her face and kiss her and wrap my arms around her. I glance at my phone again. Nine minutes before the first bell. "I just remembered I forgot to grab something in The Beast. Want to walk with me?" I ask Rachel.

"Sure. See you in third period?" she asks Avery.

"Later, Beef!"

Most kids are either already inside or heading that way. We maneuver against the stream and when we get halfway across the parking lot, I take Rachel's hand. It fits perfectly inside mine. I unlock her door first and help her in.

"I thought you said you just needed to grab something in your truck?" she asks, looking confused. I walk around to my side of the truck, open the door and get in.

"I do." And then I grab her and kiss the hell out of her. We enjoy the next several minutes making up for all of the lost time we've had while she's been at practice. Begrudgingly, I look at my phone again.

"Two-minute warning until the first bell."

"Which technically means we have seven minutes before we're late for first period," she says, while nibbling my neck.

We use the next five minutes very wisely.

On the way to lunch, I realize I never read the note Rachel wrote. I spent all of first period thinking of our morning in The Beast and we actually had work to do in second period. I step into the courtyard and pull her note out of my back pocket. She folded into some sort of star shape. Girls are so weird.

Mr. Tennyson,

I can't thank you enough for being you and giving me the courage to tell my mom what I really want to be when I grow up. I thought about our first conversation and how you guessed that I want to be a P.E. teacher. I'm pretty sure that wasn't a guess after all, but that's okay.

I never really gave guys much of a thought, thanks to my dad and Avery's screwed up love life (until Fletcher, anyway). But now I can't imagine my life without you. You've given me hope for the future I want, not the one other people want for me.

Thank you, from the bottom of my heart.

Love,

Mrs. Tennyson

I fold the note (the regular way, not the origami crap she used) and walk to the lunch room thanking God for Economics and projects and my grandparents' address and anything else that led to me sitting next to Rachel that first day.

"How can you eat that shit?" Avery's eating yogurt when I sit down across the table from her. I wonder if I can hold my breath for the duration of lunch.

"Because it's delicious and healthy."

"It's spoiled milk with strawberries in it, and it reeks. I think all that hairspray has finally gotten to your brain." I smile at her to let her know I'm joking. Well, except for the part about it being disgusting. That's the God's honest truth.

"So I take it you don't want to share?" She extends her loaded spoon toward me and it takes all I have to not shove it back at her. Fletcher would kick my ass if he knew I started a food fight with his girl.

"Definitely not." For good measure, I slide my tray over and scoot down one seat. Normally Rachel sits next to Avery, but today she takes my side. Literally.

"Alright you two, let's call a truce. I have an idea." She pulls out a notebook and pen. "I got to thinking about bucket lists last night. James started one, but Avery and I haven't. We should change that."

I raise my eyebrows and mouth "Did you?" while discreetly nodding in Avery's direction. Rachel shakes her head no.

"Oh, I know what I want my first item to be!" Avery says emphatically. "Getting a car for my eighteenth birthday."

"I don't think that's quite how this thing works, Avery. It has to be something *you* do, not something someone else does for you," Rachel says.

"'Kay, give me a minute." She finishes the last bite of her yogurt while she thinks. *Thank God.*

"What about you?" Rachel asks, turning toward me. "I know you already have one thing, but I thought we could each think of three." She's written 'save someone's life' in my top spot and is ready for the next item. I don't need time to think about it. Constantly being stuck in a car on the interstate has given me plenty of time to come up with stuff for my bucket list. I've made a few over the years, but this is a fresh one.

"Promise you won't laugh?"

"Of course!"

"I've always wanted to volunteer at an animal shelter."

"Really?" Avery asks, thoroughly confused. "You'd be willing to let random animals claw and bite you?"

"I was never allowed to have a pet growing up since we moved around so much. So this is like the next best thing." Rachel writes it down.

"What's next?"

"To ride in a helicopter. I remember watching them as a little boy and I've wanted to go in one ever since then."

"That's pretty adorable. What else did you like as a little boy?"

"Scooby Doo and the Avengers. And my favorite snack was grape juice and graham crackers." I love sharing trivial shit with her, but more than that, I love that she actually cares to hear it. She cocks her head to the side and studies me for a moment, then smiles.

"I bet you were a really cute kid."

"Guess you'll have to come over and dig through my mom's photo albums to find out. We moved around more times than I can count, but she always took her camera with her."

"If you tell me I can have some more of Gran's pie, I'm in."

"Deal." We shake hands.

"What's the last item for your list?"

"To perform on stage." The girls have no idea about what I'm working on with Fletcher. But it's either cheat and list something I'm already planning on doing or say "to marry you." I'd rather not scare her away, considering she's only been my non-girlfriend for three weeks, and I haven't even told her I love her yet. Which is getting increasingly harder to keep in, by the way.

"I can definitely see you doing that one day. You have a great voice. I better get a front-row seat to see you perform."

"I wouldn't have it any other way." Having Avery and Rachel in the front row is the most important part of our plan, actually.

"Okay, Avery, you've had some time to think. What's your first item?" Rachel asks.

"To wear the Champagne Foil Splattered Tulle Oscar de la Renta gown for prom."

"You're killing me!"

"What? You said something I want to do. I want to wear that dress."

"It doesn't count! His dresses are at least eight thousand dollars! Who's going to pay for it? It can't be a bucket list item unless it's something you pay for."

"Daddy's said he'd buy me whatever dress I wanted." She pouts while I do my best to not choke on my Salisbury steak. Holy Christ, this girl is willing to spend that much money on a dress? I look at Rachel and she seems to be having the same reaction.

"Avery Jane Murphy, over my dead body will you spend that kind of money on a prom dress. If you wanna be a fashion designer so bad, why don't you make your dress yourself?"

Avery stops chewing her lunch and stares at Rachel. "That's actually a fucking brilliant idea. Why didn't I think of that?"

"Probably because you've been too distracted by a certain short-order cook," Rachel teases.

"Okay, that's my number one. To design my own prom dress," she says, ignoring Rachel's dig.

"Now you're talking." Rachel writes it down. "What's next?" Avery stares at Rachel for a few seconds. Then she taps her fingertips together and smiles.

"To design yours too."

Rachel drops her pen. "I haven't even decided if I want to go to prom yet, Avery. You know that's not my thing." Avery looks at me for help. Spending the evening with Rachel on my arm? Hell yes.

"Rachel, will you go to prom with me?" I tip my head down slightly and use my best puppy dog eyes. "Please? Or do you not wanna go with me?" I fake a pout to complete the look.

"Oh God, not you too." She covers her face with her hands and lets out a frustrated sigh.

"Come on, Beef. It'll be epic! If you let me design your dress, you won't have to go shopping for one. Just think... you'd be saved from a whole day of fitting rooms."

I admit, Avery is pretty brilliant and this may actually work in her favor. Rachel spreads the fingers on her right hand and peeks out.

"You make a good point."

"Of course I do. And this way we know for sure we won't be caught wearing the same dress as someone else. Not that you particularly care about that, but I refuse to commit that fashion sin on such a momentous occasion." Rachel drops her hands and looks back and forth at me and Avery.

"Fine. Whatever. You win." I'm not sure which one of us she was referring to, but I'd like to think we both won. I lift my hand and high five Avery, who's now beaming.

"Thank you, you're the best Beef ever!"

"Calm down before you burst." Rachel begrudgingly writes the second item on Avery's list. "What's your third thing? And it better have nothing to do with playing beauty shop with me." Avery's entire expression changes. She's still excited, but her face is softer.

"I want to take Fletcher and Samantha to New York City."

"Really?" Rachel asks.

"We were talking about the city the other day and Fletcher mentioned how much fun Sam would have in M&M's World in Times Square. They'd never be able to afford it on their own, but I could use Daddy's frequent flyer miles and we'd stay at his condo so it wouldn't cost them anything."

I can't believe Fletcher was ever worried about Avery liking him. "Avery, that's really cool. Like really, really cool. They're gonna love it," I say.

"You think so?" She sounds hesitant. "I know we haven't been dating very long, but he's so different from Derrick. I like Fletcher so much. For the first time, it's not about sex. Aside from kissing me, he hasn't really touched me at all. Which is sort of frustrating to tell you the truth, but really sweet."

Fletcher texted me last night saying he'd had to take a cold shower after he left Avery's house. I know that feeling all too well.

"Avery, you deserve someone who likes you because you're awesome and funny and fiery. Fletcher is the lucky one," Rachel says.

"I gotta talk to my dad about when we can go, but I really want to make this happen."

"I have no doubt that you will," I say. "Alright, Ray. It's your turn. What's your bucket list?"

"Number one is to run a marathon. I may not be training for the Olympics anymore, but I still really want to earn my 26.2 bumper sticker."

"I wonder if I could get one when I put the first 26.2 miles on my car," Avery says, earning her a poke in the shoulder from Rachel.

"Not unless you're pushing it the whole way," she says, laughing. "Okay, number two. I want to see Lake Street Dive in concert." She looks at me and my heart skips a few beats. Rachel and Rachael in the same room? I might implode.

"So you like Lake Street Dive, huh?" I ask.

"Yeah, this really cute guy sort of turned me on. To them, I mean." She facepalms and I throw my head back with laughter. I hear Avery joining in across the table.

"Freudian slip, much?" I ask when I can breathe again.

"That was pretty funny, Ray," Avery says in my defense.

"Are you both finished laughing at me?" She looks a little embarrassed. Without thinking, I give her a quick kiss. She takes a deep breath and focuses on her notebook again.

"Moving along. My third bucket list item is to get a tattoo."

"Clearly, I've inspired you," I say, winking at her.

"Yeah, well..." she waves her hand in a gesture of nonchalance but I'm not buying it.

"It's okay, Ray. You inspire me too," I whisper.

"What do you want to get?" Avery asks.

"I'm not exactly sure yet. Nothing too big since I'll have to hide it from my dad."

"Nah, I think you should go for a full sleeve. That would be super hot." I briefly indulge myself in the mental image of an inked Rachel.

"That's never gonna happen, so keep dreaming buddy."

I collect our trays and take them to the conveyor belt as the bell rings. "Can I walk you to your next class?" I ask Rachel when I return to our table.

"Won't that make you late for yours?"

"It'll be worth it. I won't see you this afternoon since I have to go straight to the Sweet Pea." We follow the crowd out of the cafeteria. We squeeze through the doorway, and I feel someone grab my ass. I spin my head to the left toward Rachel, but she's waving bye to Avery. I look to my right as Vivien grabs my arm.

"Hey there, handsome. I've been meaning to catch you for a few days now. Why don't you sit with me tomorrow at lunch? I'm having a party soon, and I want you to come." She looks up at me through doe eyes and maneuvers her mouth into a perfect pout. I'm sure this works on every other guy at Edison, but she's wasting her time. I extract my arm from her grip and make a mental note to rub some Purell on it later. No telling who or what she's had her hands on today. Rachel's walking a half step behind me. I grab her hand so I don't lose her.

"No thanks, Vivien. My lunch seat is the best in school,

and I have plans so I can't come to your party." We turn down the main hallway and Vivien stops.

"But I didn't even tell you when it was!"

"Doesn't matter. I have plans."

Vivien's raising her voice, which means people are starting to look at us. I drop Rachel's hand so we don't get caught, but take a step closer to her to make up for the lack of contact.

"With who?" She puts her hands on her hips and juts her boobs and chin out. Desperation really isn't very becoming on her, or anyone. I don't think she's used to guys telling her no.

"My friend Rachel." I point my thumb in her direction, then abruptly spin around and continue down the hallway before she can respond. "Sorry about that. Vivien sort of scares me," I say, linking fingers with Rachel again. I don't want her to think for one second that I'd entertain Vivien's offer. "Anyway, I just wanted to say thank you for the note and tell you that I'm really proud of you. Telling your mom took guts. I guess I was just too distracted earlier to remember to tell you that."

She smiles, obviously remembering this morning like I am. "Thanks. Hopefully my dad doesn't blow a gasket when we tell him tonight." We stop outside her class. I stand a little closer to her than I should, but the power of her sunshine and vanilla is strong.

"I get off at seven tonight. Text me when you're done talking to him?"

"If I'm still alive."

Fletcher and I walk in the front door after our shift. Rachel texted me earlier saying her dad wasn't going to get home until later tonight because of some business deal. She didn't want me to worry about not hearing from her. Mandy and Devin gave us the official thumbs-up for our open mic night, so Fletch and I figured it'd be a good time to practice. We round the corner from the foyer and see Gran and Grandpa at the kitchen table with a bunch of papers scattered around them. Their expressions are a mix of confusion and amusement.

"Good evening, my favorite old fogies," I say, kissing each of them on the cheek. "What's all this?"

"Hello, son," Gran pats my hand. "Who's your friend?"

"Oh, this is Fletcher. I work with him at the Sweet Pea and he's dating Rachel's best friend, Avery."

"And here I thought you were bringing home a handsome young fellow for me," she teases. "Would you boys like some pie?"

"I've been hearing about this pie for a few weeks," Fletcher says, rubbing his hands together. He's practically drooling.

"Well, I can't let growing boys like y'all starve, now can I?" We follow her into the kitchen and get our plates while she slices the pie.

"What kind do you have tonight?" I ask.

"Apple and pecan."

Fletcher and I high five each other. "What's all that paperwork, Gran?"

"Oh, your Grandpa got some documents delivered about the farm. He's been thinking about retiring for a while, and I think he's finally going to do it."

"This is gonna be your last crop, Grandpa?"

"I think it might be," he says from the table, engrossed in what looks like a contract.

"What're you gonna do with all that spare time?"

"I have no idea, boy. I reckon I can find something to do though."

Fletcher grabs his guitar case and I take our plates back to my room. We decide to work on our original song first. We finished most of the song the night we were at his house. He's covering the vocals on this one since it's his song to Avery.

"I've been thinking about the lead up to the chorus after the second verse. I think we should have more guitar there," he says.

"Sure thing, bro. Did you figure out the lyrics to the third verse yet?"

"I think so. Let's run through the whole song so we can see if they work."

Thirty minutes later, he's happy with the song. Most of what we're playing is from the 80s and early 90s. It's the music we both grew up listening to and it's so much better than most of the shit on the radio these days. Even though my song for Rachel isn't an original one, I hope she likes it just the same.

"Alright, we need to finalize the order. Do you want to start with *She Talks to Angels* or *Don't Stop Believin'*?" he asks.

"Let's do *Don't Stop Believin'* and then *Faithfully*. And maybe *She Talks to Angels* and *Hotel California* after that?"

"That works. Do you want to finish with your song or mine?"

"Let's finish with yours. I don't think Avery's gonna be able to keep herself from molesting you after hearing it. That might get awkward if we still have to sing mine."

"You've got a good point," he laughs. "I should probably head out though. I told Sammy she could stay up late tonight so we could have story time together when I get back." He stands up and puts his guitar in his case. I look at him for a minute, remembering what Avery said at the theater about Fletcher being the best big brother on the planet. She wasn't quite right about that one, I just didn't pick up on it then.

"Sam's a lucky girl, you know."

"Why's that?"

"She has a great dad. I didn't have one growing up and I always wish I did." Fletcher freezes for a moment, but makes a quick recovery. He clears his throat and snaps the case shut.

"Yeah, well my dad's the lucky one. He always wanted a daughter."

"Sure," I say, giving him a knowing glance. My phone chimes with a text from Rachel.

Rachel: I told him.

"Go ahead," Fletcher says, pointing to my phone. "I'll let myself out. Tell Ray I said hi."

"Will do. See ya, bro."

Me: Can I FaceTime you?
Rachel: Sure. Be warned. I look like shit.

Her eyes are red and swollen when she answers. "Didn't go well?" I ask.

145

"Not exactly. He acted like the way a three-year-old does when he finds out there's no Santa Claus or Easter Bunny."

"What do you *mean* there's no Santa or Easter Bunny?" I ask, trying to inject some humor into the conversation. I hate that she's so upset.

"Very funny." She attempts a pathetic smile.

"What'd he say?"

"That he couldn't believe I was throwing my life away to be a P.E. teacher. I asked him what he thought I was supposed to do after going to the Olympics, but he just started talking about sponsors and contracts and money. I don't care about that stuff."

"Give him a few days and I'm sure he'll come around."

"I doubt that. He may not have said he was disappointed in me, but I know he is. Our relationship was already strained because of how hard he pushes me, but he's still my dad. He just got up off the couch and walked away. That really hurt." She blows her nose and flops on her bed. She doesn't know her dad is sitting in his room crying too.

"Rachel, trust me on this one." Her eyes snap up and search mine.

"What do you mean?"

"I mean, he's not upset with you. He's upset with himself." I'll let him tell her the rest of the story. It'd mean more coming from him anyway.

"Are you sure?" Her lip quivers and a new round of tears spill down her cheeks.

"I promise you're not a disappointment to him. If anything, you just opened his eyes. Give him a while to get used to his new view."

"Thank you. I feel like you're always coming to my rescue."

"There's nothing in the world I love doing more than rescuing you. Besides, you make a pretty hot damsel in distress." She laughs finally. I give myself a mental pat on the back.

"I should go. Tomorrow's our last practice before the invitational and I'm pretty beat."

"Sleep well, Mrs. Tennyson."

She pauses, then quietly says, "I love you, James."

My heart, brain and ears do one of those elaborate handshake-high-five-fist-bump maneuvers while my stomach does the equivalent of an epic touchdown dance. When the first "I love you" happened in Mom's romance book, it was when the dude drove to the chick's house after an argument. It was raining and he swung himself off his motorcycle and pounded on her front door. She opened it and gawked at the way his wet shirt clung to his muscles and watched the water drip off his perfectly wet hair. Then there was lots of kissing. (I can't believe chicks buy into this shit.)

But this moment is nothing like that one. This moment is real. The truth is, I've loved Rachel before I saw even saw her. When she walked in second period on my first day at Edison High, my heart stopped beating for me and started beating for her.

"I love you too, Ray. More than you'll ever know." I don't bother fighting the grin on my face. She just made my day. Year. Life.

Rachel

I toss my bag in a locker and re-tighten my shoelaces. My race is in two hours and I really wish we didn't have to get up at the ass crack of dawn to get here so early. I could have killed for some extra sleep. Mom and I stayed up last night talking, which was nice. Odd, but nice. She assured me Dad doesn't hate my guts and that he'll come around (which I already knew, but I was glad to hear it again). She even confessed that she's been distant with me these last few years because she didn't have a great relationship with her mom and therefore didn't know how to have one with me.

Talk about shocking.

The ride to the invitational was really awkward. Mom kept trying to make small talk to fill in for the fact that Dad and I weren't really speaking. He's been busy all week with some business deal with a farm, though I suspect my career change had something to do with him coming home late these last two nights. Normally, he'd go over the strategy the night before my race and give me pointers about my competitors on the drive to the track. This time, he didn't even tell me to buckle up.

I walk outside and pull out my phone to text James. Mom and Dad went to find their seats so I have an hour to myself before I have to warm up.

Me: I'm here.
James: Good morning, beautiful.
Me: What time does your shift at the Pea start?
James: Not for a while. Did you talk to your mom about the movie tonight?
Me: She said yes. ☺
James: Hell yeah. Can't wait to see you. I'll be the one next to the hot running champion.
Me: She said I could stay at Avery's house tonight too.
James: YESSSSSSSSSS.
Me: Hahahaha. Good to know you're excited.
James: BRB A hot girl caught my attention.
Me: Ummm...that better be a joke.
James: Nope. She's seriously hot.
Me: NOT FUNNY.

A pair of strong arms come up from behind and wrap around me, making me drop my phone in the grass. Two seconds before I unleash a blood-curdling scream, I smell a familiar woodsy scent.

"See, I told you a hot girl caught my attention."

"What the hell are you doing here?" I turn and give him a quick kiss before backing out of his grip. The last thing I need is my dad catching us together.

"You seriously think I'd miss your last invitational?"

"You drove an hour away to watch me run one stupid race?"

"Wrong. I drove an hour away to watch the love of my life kick some serious ass in the 1600 meter."

Well. When you put it that way.

"Aren't you going to be late for work?"

"I lied. I don't work today," he says, grinning mischievously. "How much free time do you have before your race?"

"It doesn't start until nine but my warm up's at eight."

James checks his phone. "Looks like we have about forty-five minutes. Wanna come with me to The Beast?"

"As tempting as that sounds, I can't afford to get all hot and bothered right now. There's a one hundred percent chance I'd miss the race altogether."

"Thanks for the ego boost, but that's not quite what I had in mind." He smiles and kisses me on the cheek. "Come on, I promise I'll be a perfect gentleman." As usual, he helps me into my side of the cab when we reach his truck.

"I see you didn't travel alone." I run my hand over his guitar case.

"Lucy always helps me relax, and I thought she could help you too."

I've heard him sing, but this is the first time I've seen him do it. The phone doesn't do him justice at all. His voice is slightly raspy in all the right ways. I want to close my eyes and lose myself in his music, but then I'd be missing out on the spectacular show that his mouth and hands are putting on. After several songs, he sets his guitar to the side and pulls me to him.

"You're really talented. I can't believe you haven't started your own YouTube channel or something. How'd you learn to play?" I lace my fingers with his. I love the way our hands fit together.

"Mom dated a bunch of musicians over the years, so I just picked it up from watching them play."

"Well thanks for the private concert." I turn toward him. My face is close to his neck and I can see his heartbeat right below one of my favorite nibbling spots. I squeeze his hand and watch it flutter a bit faster. "Do you have any predictions right now?" I know that I said I couldn't afford to get hot and bothered, but I'm okay with warm and slightly unsettled. Waste not, want not.

"Hmmm. Yes, I can see it now. You are about to be kissed by an extremely good-looking man."

I lean up and kiss him first. "Wrong! God, you suck at this game." We both laugh before he makes his prediction come true.

"So tell me more about your predictions. Do you know most of what's going to happen? Or only some things?" I lean against him and take his hand again.

"Definitely not most things. I rarely knew we were moving ahead of time, but once Mom told me I usually got memories of my new school or where we'd live." He rubs his forehead. "On the other hand, I had no problem with stupid shit like knowing what the cafeteria was serving. Without looking at the menu," he adds with a sidelong glance. "I also had an advantage when it came to girls."

He smiles but I'm not sure I really want to know the story. "Please, *please* tell me you didn't use your psychic abilities to have sex."

"That's impossible. I've never had sex."

Oh, yeah.

"But when we lived in Birmingham, there a girl named Stacey who really wanted to change that. She tried to get me to go out with her for months, but I knew she was off her rocker. She had huge daddy issues and was just looking to get pregnant."

"Did she? Get pregnant?"

"Yeah, she got her way with some drunk football player. The rumor was the condom failed. The truth was she poked holes in it."

"Wow, that's really sad."

"Tell me about it. Just another reason I was glad to never have had a girlfriend."

I sit up and look at him. "What about now? Do you still wish you didn't have a girlfriend?"

"I *don't* have a girlfriend," he says, kissing the tip of my nose. "But I hope to change that soon. I don't like sneaking around your parents. I want to be able to pick you up and take you home and enjoy goodnight kisses on the front porch."

"Yeah, I need to figure out a way to tell my dad. I feel bad for all the bombshells I'm dropping on him." I look down and twist my hands together. "Anyway, sorry for the moment of insecurity. Sometimes I'm afraid that you'll get tired of being tied to one person since you never were before."

"That's because I didn't want to be. I hadn't met you yet." He frames my face in his hands and kisses me with a sweet intensity that sends my heart to my toes and back again. We both sigh when he pulls away.

"Come on, Flo Jo. It's time to get you back to the track." He puts his guitar back in the case and we get out of the truck.

"I can't believe this is my last race."

"You nervous?"

"No, surprisingly. I'm sort of just at peace with it. I'm more nervous about my acceptance letters from UNC and State. They should be coming in soon."

"What if you get accepted to both?"

"I might have to go to a sudden-death eeny, meeny, miney moe." I still want to intercept the envelopes. Dad doesn't know I applied to State and at this point, I'd rather tell him about James than I would about his rival college. "Have you thought more about applying to colleges?"

"I applied to some a couple of weeks ago."

"Really? Which ones?"

"State and UNC." He laughs when I look at him. "What? You can't fault me. It was peer pressure."

"And just who was pressuring you?" I tease.

"This hot blonde girl in my second period class. Man, she's brutal. She threatened to give me a wedgie if I didn't apply to the same colleges she did. I'm sort of scared of her."

"She sounds nuts." We stop outside the locker room.

"I like nuts. Wait. Not *those* nuts. I mean—shit." He facepalms and groans while I collapse against the building in a fit of laughter. He joins in, and it takes us a few minutes to compose ourselves.

153

"Now that I'm done making an ass of myself, I'm heading to the stands to cheer you on."

"Just don't get caught by my dad."

"What are you talking about?" he asks, pulling Groucho Marx glasses out of his back pocket. "I'll be the one in disguise." He puts them on and my laughter returns in full force.

"You've lost your mind, James." I fight back another round of giggles and walk into the locker room.

I make my way to the starting line. I should be more focused, envisioning each lap and my eventual win. Instead, I'm thinking about going to the movies and spending the evening with my most favorite people. This race is so different from all the other ones. For the first time, I feel like I'm running it for *me*. No matter what my time is, I know this one will be my best race ever.

"RACHEL!" I look over at the fence at the edge of the track. My dad signals me over. Oh God, this can't be good. If he saw me with James, I'm beyond dead.

"Hey, Dad, what's up?" I ask, trying to keep my nerves at bay. He looks a little uncomfortable.

"Watch number twelve. I saw her out her earlier and I think she's gonna be your biggest competition. And remember to wait until the final lap to push it, no matter how tempting it'll be before then. Let everyone else burn themselves out while you're draft off them. The final 400 meters is all you."

I fight tears as I suck in a breath. I definitely wasn't expecting that. "I will. Thanks, Dad." *Don't cry. Don't cry. Don't cry.*

"Come here." He opens his arms and we hug over the barricade. "I love you and I'm proud of you."

A few tears escape, despite my attempts to contain them. "I love you, too. I gotta get to the starting line." I let go and start to walk away when he calls my name again. I look back at him, and this time he's grinning.

"Have fun."

I smile in return and jog back to the track to take my place in lane four. I didn't realize how much I needed to hear those words until now. He might be uptight and demanding, but he's still my dad. I slide my toe behind the starting line. When the gun cracks, I bolt forward and immediately head for lane one. My legs find their rhythm and I settle into a comfortable pace with four girls in front of me. I focus on my form: elbows at 90 degree angles and arms pumping in line with the track. After the first lap, one girl drops behind me. I ease up very slightly to conserve my energy but remain in third place. Lauren, the girl my dad warned me about, is in second. My breaths are still holding steady as I round turn four and focus on the third lap.

Coming around the first turn, I drop back to fourth as a girl overtakes me just outside lane one. I remember my dad's words and keep my pace steady. In turn two, Lauren moves to first place. I move from fourth to third in turn three and watch Lauren. She's already starting her surge, which means she'll start fatiguing in the final lap. At the start of lap four, I kick up my pace. One hundred meters in, I take second place. Lauren's about ten meters ahead of me. At turn two, I increase my speed again. I make sure to keep my feet light and bring up my knees. The distance between me and Lauren decreases. I see her straining as we hit turn three. I approach her on the right and complete my pass just before the last turn.

Hugging the inside line of lane one, I open my stride and use my arms to propel my body in the final surge. Everything I've trained for has come down to this moment. With the finish line in my sight, I concentrate on moving every muscle in my body. My lungs suck in air and my heart pumps at a frenzied rate. Three hundred meters left. I know I won the race. Two hundred meters left. I hope I can set a new personal record. One hundred meters left. I see James at the end of the track jumping up and down like a maniac. With adrenaline and love coursing through my body, I cross the finish line.

My legs slow to a stop and I gasp for breaths.

"Rachel Wheaton takes first with an unofficial time of four minutes, forty-nine seconds," I hear over the loudspeakers. God, I need more air. That can't be right. When I ran earlier in the week, I only got to five minutes, two seconds. On the way back to the locker room, my dad hops the barricade and runs toward me.

"Four forty-nine!" he shouts before picking me up in a bear hug. We spin around and he's laughing, and I realize I am too. "That was amazing, Rachel! You shattered your record!" He sets me down and hugs me again before taking a step back. We've had a lot of touchy-feely moments today, and I think we just hit tomorrow's quota too.

"Thanks, Dad!" I still can't believe it. I wish I could high five my feet. "I'm gonna go grab my stuff. I'll meet you by the car, okay?" I need to get away before he launches into a tirade about how I'm throwing my career away and how some people were born with no legs and would love nothing more than to run track and blah blah blah. On the way to the locker room, I scan the crowd for James. I wish more than anything that I could run into his arms, too. I grab my phone out of my bag and see a text waiting for me. Make that a lot of texts.

> **James: Holy shit, that was hot.**
> **James: Your legs are amazing.**
> **James: I'm going to pretend your smile was because you saw me and that it had nothing to do with you knowing you won.**
> **James: Also, I'm ignoring the fact that your mile time kicks my mile time's ass.**
> **James: I can't wait to see you tonight.**
> **James: Track's over now. Does that mean you can be my girlfriend?**
> **James: I don't like the word girlfriend. It just doesn't... contain everything.**
> **James: Not that you need to be contained.**
> **James: I'm not a chauvinist or anything.**
> **James: Oh God. Why can't I delete texts I've already sent?**
> **James: I'm gonna go now.**
> **James: Call me later.**
> **James: Love you.**

His texts make me laugh, but picturing his expressions as he wrote them makes me laugh even harder. As I walk to the car, I try to think of ways to bring up the subject of having a boyfriend to my parents. With my vast experience in this arena, you'd think I'd be bursting with ideas. Which actually does give me an idea. I open my text messages and click on Avery's name.

Me: Yo, Jenny from the Block. I need your help.

Avery: Sorry, Jenny's not here. She ran off to Cancun with the hot short-order cook.

Me: You wish.

Avery: Totally. What's up?

Me: Track's over. Which means no more distractions from boys.

Avery: Well hot damn! It's time to get you a MAN.

Me: How do we tell my dad?

Avery: We?

Me: Come on. You're supposed to be my wingwoman or something.

Avery: Fine, fine. Let me think about it.

Me: Hurry up.

Avery: Impatient?

Me: It's like having a chocolate cake in front of you and not being able to eat it.

Avery: Are you saying you want James' cake?

Me: AVERY. Get your mind out of the gutter.

Avery: Hey, this mastermind is going to help you tell your dad, remember? Maybe the gutter helps me think better.

Me: Oh God. I'm scared now.

Avery: Don't worry, I'll make sure whatever idea I come up with doesn't involve a pregnancy or STD.

Me: Avery Jane Murphy! I will kill you.
Avery: Calm your tits, Ray. I'll come up with something. Gotta go for now though. I'll pick you up this afternoon.

I glance down at my uni-boob (I should really invest in some more flattering sports bras) and confirm that my tits are, indeed, calm.

Me: All's quiet on the Northern Front. See you later.

A few seconds later, I text her again.

Me: Oh yeah, forgot to tell you. I won.
Avery: DUH. Congrats, Beef!

"Rachel!" I turn and see Mom half-jogging toward me. "I'm so proud of you!" she says, as we hug. I think I've touched my parents more in the last week than I have in several months. It's weird. I thank her and sink into the backseat when Dad unlocks the car.

"I'm gonna put in my earbuds, okay?" I say, not waiting for their response. I spend the next hour flipping through photos of James on my phone, wondering when I won't have to keep him as my secret anymore.

I toss my deodorant and toothbrush into my overnight bag and survey my closet. I reach for a black sweater, leggings and Toms, wishing for the first time that I was slightly more fashionable. I've seen the way other girls at school look at James. Girls like Vivien with big boobs, nice outfits and faces full of perfect makeup. Essentially the exact opposite of me. I pull my sweater on and hear the doorbell ring.

"Mom, can you get that? I'm getting dressed," I shout from my room. Once my clothes are on, I fix my hair into a ponytail and rub some Coppertone sunblock onto my hands. I read an article in one of Avery's magazines about beating the winter blues that said the smell of sunblock has positive effects on a person's mood. The article probably wasn't very scientific, but the scent makes me think of the sunshine and that definitely makes me happy. I splash my neck with Warm Vanilla Sugar body spray from Bath and Body Works and declare myself ready. Avery hasn't made her way to my room yet, and I hope that doesn't mean that Mom's holding her hostage in the living room. I open my door to investigate and see Mom walking toward me.

"Rachel, you have company." She's smiling, and I'm not sure if I should be alarmed.

"Just tell Avery to come on back. I'm almost ready."

"It's not just Avery."

"What do you mean?"

"She brought a fellow with her." Mom wiggles her eyebrows.

"Fletcher?"

"Nope." Mom heads back toward the living room without elaborating. I give myself a once-over in my mirror and follow her down the hall wondering what in the hell Avery is up to.

"Hey, Beef!" Avery shouts from sofa. "You know James." She gestures to the person next to her and gives me a look that says "just play along."

"Uh, yeah. He's in my second period class, and I think he works with you at the Sweet Pea, right?"

"He does. He and I have chatted a bit at work, and it turns out James has a bit of a crush on you." She pats him on the shoulder. He smiles and scratches the back of his head with a look of slight embarrassment. Oh, my gosh, he's adorable. "I told him that your dad didn't allow you to date because of your track obligations."

"That's true," I said, wondering where she's going with this.

"Well, when I went to the Pea this afternoon to pick my mom up, James overheard me tell her that you won your last race. So..." She trails off, looking at James. I know he wasn't working today, but Mom doesn't.

"Hi, Rachel," he says, nervously. "Since track is over, I was wondering if you'd like to be my date for the movie tonight? That is, if your mom says it's okay."

"Don't worry, Mrs. W. Fletcher and I are going too, so it's a group thing," Avery adds, obviously trying to sway the odds in my favor. Mom turns to me and puts her hands on her hips.

"Well, your father's not here and it's his rule. But track *is* over, so I don't see what harm is in letting you go." She smiles at me again before turning to James. "It was nice to meet you, young man. I hope we'll be seeing more of you."

"Nice to meet you. And yes, ma'am, I hope so too. Thanks so much for letting Rachel go." Mom loves the ma'am stuff. I wonder if that's something James knows already.

"Come on, Beef. Get your stuff and let's go!" I turn and jog back to my room to get my bag. When I return to the living room, I give Mom an awkward side hug and kiss her cheek.

"See you tomorrow, Mom. Love you!"

We walk to Mandy's car, and James opens the front passenger door for me. I smile at him and briefly look toward the living room window. Mom's watching us from behind the blinds, no doubt taking note of James' manners, as he takes his place in the seat behind me. Avery pulls out of the driveway like a calm, rational person and makes it about a half mile from my house before cheering and doing a happy dance in the driver's seat.

"Rachel, that was epic! It worked like a charm!" she shouts. I'm in the middle of a high-five with James when I remember that I forgot to check the mail. I meant to earlier, but ended up taking a nap instead.

"Avery, turn around! Today's the thirty-first! Just make sure to stay behind the trees so Mom doesn't see the car." She makes a U-turn and I jump out when she reaches the mailbox. I sort through a stack of bills and typical housewife magazines and see an envelope from UNC tucked between Better Homes and Gardens and Southern Living.

It's the big one.

I replace the mail and rush back to the car. Avery sees my expression and her eyes bulge.

"What does it say?" she shouts, as I open the door. My hands are shaking, causing me to fumble with my seat belt.

Once I hear the click, Avery pulls back onto the road and I tear open the top edge of the envelope.

"Dear Rachel, congratulations on your acceptance to The University of North Carolina at Ch—"

"WOOO!" she shouts, before I can even finish the sentence. "That's my Beef!" I scan the rest of the letter before tucking it back into the envelope.

"Congrats, my little Tarheel," James says from the backseat. I turn to blow him a kiss and decide he looks lonely, so I undo my seatbelt and climb over the console to join him.

"Thanks! I didn't see an envelope from State, which means I'm still on mailbox watch."

"Are you happy about getting into UNC?" he asks.

"Sure, it's a great school."

"But..." he prompts.

"But I don't know if I want to go there because that's what my dad wants or because it's what I want."

He pulls me into his arms and kisses me on the side of my head. "Don't worry, Ray. Everything's gonna work out." I push away from him to look in his eyes. If he's holding out on me, I might hurt him.

"Wait, do you know what college I'm going to?"

"No, I just see you at college and you're happy."

"Do you happen to see me wearing red or blue?" I know it's a long shot, but it doesn't hurt to ask. He just laughs and pulls me close again.

James

"Avery did what?" Rachel and I hold hands across the school parking lot on the way to her car. I could really get used to this touching her in public thing.

"She told Mrs. Atkins to refuse delivery of any more flowers if they were addressed to her."

"Who's Mrs. Atkins?"

"You know, the really high-strung secretary in the front office?"

"Ah, yes—Caffeinated Secretary. So what did she do with today's bouquet?"

She laughs at my nickname for Mrs. Atkins then continues her story. "She stormed down to the field past the Agriculture building and fed it to the goats."

"Leave it to her to use goats for vengeance." The image of Avery hauling a dozen roses across campus in a rage makes me laugh. However, the thought of Derrick sending her flowers makes me uneasy. I try to ignore the feeling in the bottom of my stomach. When we reach Rachel's car, I open her door and then walk to the passenger side. She may be driving, but manners are manners. "Thanks for the ride, by the way. Grandpa said he'd have The Beast fixed by this evening."

"I'm just glad your truck waited until after my final track meet to break." She pulls out of the parking lot and heads toward my house. Fletcher is coming over later to practice for the open mic night tomorrow night, but I hope to spend some time with Rachel first.

"Hey, are you sure you and Avery are okay with Gretchen sitting with us at lunch now? I know I kind of sprung it on y'all today but I really feel bad for her. I figure she's dealing with enough shit in her life. She shouldn't have to worry about lunchtime drama, you know?" Gretchen is finally back in school and seems to be doing alright, all things considered. Yesterday, I caught her sitting in the courtyard by herself during lunch since she was ostracized from her ex-boyfriend's table. She said she's still living with Lainey and started counseling last week. I haven't talked to either of them much about my well-timed phone call, which is fine by me. I still don't have any answers for them. Well, none that I feel like sharing with them anyway.

"It's perfectly fine. She seems really cool, and, unlike Vivien, at least I know Gretchen's not trying to hit on you," she says, smiling.

"It wouldn't matter if she did. You're it for me, Rachel." She glances at me. Her expression is at least half disbelief. "Why are you surprised to hear me say that?"

"I just don't understand why," she says with a shoulder shrug. "Today at lunch, I watched Vivien and her minions ogle you and they definitely have a lot more to offer in the looks department than I do."

"And I watched one girl. The blonde with the killer legs sitting across from me." For as smart as Rachel is, she's acting pretty dumb right now.

"Just promise me that if you decide I'm not what you want that you'll break up with me first." She turns off the street and we bump along the dirt road leading to my house.

"Rachel, you've officially been my girlfriend for a week. Why are you talking about breaking up?" She furrows her brow and sighs but doesn't answer until she parks in front of the house.

"I don't mean that I want to break up, I just mean that I want you to break up with me instead of cheat on me if you realize you don't have feelings for me anymore."

I grab her hand to keep her from picking at her nails. "That is the most ridiculous thing I've ever heard."

"Maybe now, but Avery didn't think Derrick would ever cheat on her."

"First, Derrick was always cheating on Avery. Second, have you forgotten that I've spent my life traveling around the country? I've seen just about every type of girl there is. No one ever made me feel the way I do with you. Not one single person."

"But *why*?"

"What happened to the confident Rachel I met one month and one day ago?"

"That was before."

"Before what?"

"Before I had all these *feelings*." The way she said "feelings" makes it sound like a bad word. "We're seventeen. Maybe that means our feelings for each other aren't real. Love doesn't happen this fast."

I cup her face in my hands and bring my mouth to hers. My tongue gently grazes her bottom lip before slipping past it. She angles her head slightly and deepens the kiss while gripping the back of my head. I can't help the moan that escapes my mouth. I catch her tongue between my teeth and playfully bite the tip before pulling away. I take a second to catch my breath.

"Did that feel real?" I ask. I take her hand, which has slipped down to my neck, and place it over my pounding heart. "Does this feel real?"

"Yes," she whispers, her eyes locked with mine.

"Because it is. Screw timelines and rules about love being for adults only. If anything, ours is more real because we're not jaded by all the bullshit and distractions they deal with every day. You say it's crazy to fall in love with me after a few weeks, but don't forget that I knew I loved you before I ever saw you. Before you, I never had a reason to think about the future and now, I can't picture it without you in it. So I could care less if the entire lineup of Victoria's Secret Angels walked through the cafeteria. You are the only person I'd see."

Her eyes well with tears and she bites the side of her bottom lip. Through her damp lashes, I see a look of hopefulness. "So this is all real?"

"All of it. Don't worry about falling for me, Ray. I'll spend the rest of my life catching you." I pull her toward me and kiss her forehead. "Now, come inside and have some pie before Fletcher comes over and eats it all."

The next morning, I wake up covered in sweat. Something's tied around my legs and my heart's pounding like a jackhammer on crack. I open my eyes, but that doesn't do much good since my room is almost pitch black. I reach to the nightstand for my phone and feel a searing pain on the right side of my torso. It's only 5:49. I flick on the lamp and run my hand down my side to investigate the source of my pain. Nothing seems out of place and there's no blood, though I have a metallic taste in my mouth. I manage to free my legs from the sheets and then lie back down to figure out what in the hell happened. The edges of a dream float in my mind. The last thing I remember is dancing with Rachel, then feeling like my soul was being ripped out of my body.

My mouth is dry and still tastes of metal, so I head to the kitchen for a drink of water. I stop at the bathroom on the way and check the mirror. Apparently, I bit the shit out of my tongue. I sit at the table with my water and try to piece together any remaining bits of my dream. Rachel was wearing a blue dress, and her hair was up, exposing the wondrous flesh on her neck and shoulders. Everything on her was soft, and she smelled like sunshine. Then, everything turned black and the pain came. I know it was just a dream, but the residual ache in my side worries me. I shut my eyes in an attempt to remember anything else, but everything is beyond the reach of my memory.

Since my brain and body won't calm down, I give up and change into running clothes. The sky is clear and the sun, while still an hour or so away from rising, paints the lowest portion of the horizon in a light glow of orange. Inspired by the scenery, I fit my earbuds into my ears, put my phone into my armband and take off at a jog toward the sunrise. My breath sends warm bursts of steam into the crisp air, and the pain from my dream finally eases. I prefer to take the trail toward the lake when I run eastward, but I'm compelled to bypass the turnoff and head toward the main road instead.

Since it's still not daylight yet, I put an extra five feet of space between me and the road. Headlights in the distance illuminate an animal at the edge of the treeline. It's probably a deer, and the last thing I want to do is spook it and send it directly into the path of the car. I slow my jog to a walk and hope the deer runs back into the forest. The car's high beams turn on for a few seconds, probably because the driver sees the deer too, and then zooms past me. Once the spots clear from my eyes, I resume my jog. I make it about a hundred feet before I see a mass lying in the road.

I turn my music off and switch on the flashlight feature on my phone. Roadkill is quite possibly the last thing I wanted to experience during my run, but I don't want anyone else to get in a car accident because they hit a deer carcass. I approach slowly and discover it's not a deer, but a dog. Which makes the whole situation infinitely worse.

"Hey buddy, you're gonna be okay," I assure him. He looks to be some sort of shepherd mix. His eyes are closed, but I see a faint rise and fall in his chest. I have no idea how to take a dog's pulse. He doesn't appear to be bleeding, so I bend down and lift him up. I carry him the half mile back to the house and gently lay him on the front porch while I run back inside.

I scribble a note letting Mom know I'm heading to the animal hospital and grab an old blanket from the linen closet since I'm not sure whether dogs can go into shock. He's right where I left him on the porch, still showing no additional signs of life or death. As I load the dog into the cab, I make a mental note to thank Grandpa again for fixing The Beast last evening.

Ten minutes later, I reach the animal hospital.

"Can I help you?" a lady behind the counter asks, taking a swig of Red Bull.

"I was jogging this morning and I think this guy got run over."

"What kind of animal is it?"

I almost respond with a smart-ass remark but then I realize I've bundled him too well and she can't see him. "He's a dog."

"Okay, come back to exam room three." She starts walking and I follow her. "Did you see the accident?"

"No, the car's lights were too bright. I just saw him lying on the road after the car passed. He wasn't moving or anything." My hands are subconsciously patting the dog's side through the blanket. I stop when I realize I could be contributing to his internal damage.

"Did he yelp?" She folds down an exam table and gestures for me to lay him down.

"I don't know. I had my earbuds in."

"Any bleeding?"

"Not that I can see." I unwrap the blanket and pet the dog's face. "It's okay, buddy. You're in good hands now." He opens his eyes and blinks at me. That's a good sign, right?

The tech takes his vitals and does a basic assessment. "He actually looks to be in pretty good shape, so that's promising.

Hang tight and I'll go get the vet." She opens the door to the back area and suddenly the dog springs up, jumps down and skitters past her. She snaps her attention back to me. "Are you trying to pull something here? Dogs who got ran over don't do that," she says, pointing to the commotion in the back. I hear something clattering and a few people shout and chase after the dog.

I hold both hands up as if I'm under arrest. "I swear to God he was lying in the road. That's the most movement I've seen since I found him." I push past her to help capture the dog, considering it's my fault he's here.

"He went back down the hallway!"

"Block him in that corner!"

He's surprisingly light on his feet and makes darting through legs look like an Olympic sport. I try to contain my laughter as he knocks over a mop bucket, sending bubbles and dirty water across the floor. When he starts sniffing the counters and cabinets, I finally know what to do. Carefully stepping through the mess, I take a bowl from a cabinet and open the mini-refrigerator. The dog sits excitedly at my feet, his tail splattering soapy water up and down my legs. I remove a chunk of dog food from a tube and cut it into smaller pieces. It smells like bacon and fish. Why he wants to eat this shit is beyond me, but it's gone about ten seconds after I put the bowl on the floor.

I stand up to assess the room and see two techs and the veterinarian staring at me. The vet speaks first.

"I'm impressed. How did you know he was after food?"

I shrug my shoulders, my standard response when I don't want to discuss my perceptive abilities. "He was sniffing around. I thought that might mean he was hungry."

She bends down and calls him over with a kissy noise. He lopes toward her and goes belly-up at her feet. I can tell she's irritated with the mess, but her soft spot for animals doesn't allow her to scold the dog. "I didn't expect to see you again so soon, little doggy."

"What do you mean, 'see you again?'" I ask.

"This is the third time this guy's been in here," she says, still scratching his belly. "We adopted him out twice. The first time, he ran away and was back here in a few days. We found another family for him about two weeks later. He ran away the first night. We contacted the new family and they picked him up again. We agreed to give him some more time to adjust. That was two days ago."

The dog walks back toward me and plunks his haunches down in the water. "I think he's only coming back for the food," I say, laughing, though I know I'm right.

"Food or not, he can't stay here. We're a veterinary clinic, not a boarding facility. I'll call the family who adopted him in a while. It's still pretty early for a Saturday." She crosses the room and reaches out to shake my hand. "I'm Jennifer Brooks, by the way."

"James Tennyson." I survey the room. "Do you need any help cleaning this place up? I feel sort of bad for all the damage Lazarus has done."

"Lazarus?"

I nudge the dog. "Well, he did come back from the dead," I say, with air quotes around the last word. "Do you think it's possible he knew exactly what he was doing?"

"I once had a dog who couldn't reach the counter where we kept the bread. She learned to drag a chair to the counter. Then we started putting the bread in a breadbox, and she figured out how to open that up. So we moved the bread into the top shelf of the pantry. The first day we fooled her. She dragged the chair to the pantry but couldn't open the doors. The next day she figured out she had to open the pantry doors first, then drag the chair over. So yes, I'd say anything's possible."

"That's epic. What was your dog's name?"

"Sara Lee."

I stare at her for several seconds before bursting into laughter. "You're kidding, right?"

"No, I'm not." She stares at me blankly. "Her dad was named General Lee after the car from Dukes of Hazzard."

"Her name was Sara Lee. And she was a bread thief." She still doesn't get it. "Sara Lee is a company that makes pastries and bread." Her eyes finally light up, and then she facepalms.

"I can't believe I went through eight years of schooling to become a veterinarian and I never made that connection," she says, laughing.

I spend the next several hours cleaning up the back area and chatting with Dr. Brooks and the techs in between patients. Just after ten o'clock, I call the family who adopted Lazarus.

"Hi, this is James from Tarheel Veterinary Clinic and Animal Hospital. Is this Mrs. Olson?"

"Yes, this is she."

"Good morning, ma'am. I'm calling to let you know we have the dog you adopted." I scan the folder in front of me for his name. "Albert was brought in this morning as a stray." Really? Who names their dog Albert?

"That mutt got out again?"

"Yes ma'am. When would you like to pick him up?"

"Never."

"Excuse me?"

"You keep him. We don't want him anymore." Then she hangs up.

I repeat the conversation to Dr. Brooks, who pinches the bridge of her nose. "Alright, I've got a folder on my desk with other applicants. Go through those and see if any of them want to adopt him."

I make it ten feet toward her office and turn around.

"Dr. Brooks? Maybe I could take him. We've been hanging out all morning and we get along great. I could take him home, and I promise to buy the same food y'all stock here." I offer my best smile and fold my hands into a praying position. She puts her hands on her hips and turns to Lazarus, who's napping in a borrowed dog bed in the corner.

"What do you think, buddy? Do you want to go home with James?" He stands up, shakes off, farts and flops on the bed again. "I'll take that as a yes?" She giggles and turns to me. "Alright, we'll try it. But if it doesn't work out, you have to promise me to bring him back here. I don't want him running around out there."

"Promise! Come on, Lazarus. Let's go home, buddy." He pops his head up and stretches, then joins me at my side. "Hey, Dr. Brooks? I actually had a lot of fun this morning. Do you think I could volunteer here for a few hours a week?" It's not an animal shelter, but it's close enough for my bucket list.

"I'm always happy to find free child labor." She pulls a card out of her pocket. "Come by in a few days and I'll introduce you to the other vet. If you're real lucky, you can start by taking stool samples." She grins and hands me her card.

"I can hardly wait," I say, making a thumbs-up. I walk to the front of the clinic and open the door. Lazarus runs toward the truck and sits at the passenger door as if he has everything figured out. We stop at the pet store to get more of the food he likes and I toss a few toys in the shopping cart too. He sticks his head out the window on the drive down the dirt road to the house. I swear he looks like he's smiling. When I pull up to the house, I park The Beast and walk around the cab to let him out.

"Come on, Laz. It's time to go home."

Fletcher and I set up our equipment as more people filter into the Sweet Pea. We spent the last hour helping Mandy and Devin rearrange the dining room so the girls could get ready. Stanley, one of the waiters, is at the door collecting the five-dollar cover charge. From the looks of the room, we've made about two hundred bucks so far. The girls still aren't here, but that's no surprise. Avery's probably holding Rachel hostage over high heels or some shit. The door jingles again and when I look up, I see Gretchen and Lainey walk in, followed by a set of twin boys who look to be about eight years old. Gretchen smiles and offers a small wave. "Hey y'all! Glad you could make it!" Before sitting down, Lainey gives me a hug.

"Hey there, hero," she says against my shoulder. "That night was super crazy for me and I can't remember if I said thanks. So, thanks." She squeezes my arm and steps back.

"You're welcome."

"Oh, I hope it's okay that I brought my brothers with me."

"Absolutely, it's a family event. Fletcher and I promise to keep all sexual references and curse words to a minimum." I give her a cheesy smile and bend down. "Hey guys, what are your names?"

"I'm Judd. I'm eight and I'm the older one." His brother nudges him.

"I'm Jefferson and I'm the stronger one." He flexes his muscles as proof.

"Well it's nice to meet you both," I say, offering fist bumps to both of them. "I hope y'all have fun tonight. You're probably too young to know the words to the songs we're gonna play, but you're welcome to dance. Just no moshing," I add, pointing at them. "Y'all be sure to have some of my gran's pie. It's a special on the menu." I pick one up and hand it to Gretchen. "You can't go wrong, no matter what you pick."

My phone chimes with a text from Rachel.

Rachel: Be there in 5. You better save us some seats in the front row.

I look over at the chairs we've tossed our jackets onto.

Me: You have prime access to the hot guys on stage, I promise.

I pocket my phone and take the makeshift stage. Fletcher and I look over the set list one more time and check our connections when his phone rings.

"Hey, Sammy girl. Just one sec." He flicks the mic off, holds up one finger to me and steps off stage. A few minutes later, he returns. "Sorry, dude. Sammy wanted to hear the monster song before bed."

"No prob." He should really tell Avery the truth, but now's not the time to discuss it. The front door jingles again and the girls walk in just as Fletcher comes back and climbs onto stage with me.

"Good evening, ladies and gents. I'm James and the guy to my right is Fletcher. Thanks so much for coming out on our experimental open mic night. This year the Sweet Pea's doing something pretty awesome for prom, so we appreciate your support," I say. "We're going old school this evening. Fletcher and I hope you don't mind going on a little Journey." We start with *Don't Stop Believin'*. The crowd seems to enjoy it, and at least half of them sing along. Perhaps there's hope for this generation after all.

Fletcher switches out his acoustic for his electric and we start the intro for *Faithfully*. He's singing this one, which means Avery is beside herself in the front row. It's pretty cute to watch, actually. God knows she needs someone good in her life after all the bullshit she's been through. When Fletcher gets to the "whoa" part of the song, he really opens up and Avery leans her head against Rachel's shoulder. I see Mandy off to the side wiping at the corners of her eyes.

"Well, now that Fletcher's done showing off, let's move into the next song shall we?" I say as I smile in his direction. Fletcher throws a towel at me when he picks up his acoustic and the crowd laughs. I play the beginning of *She Talks to Angels* and get an enthusiastic "Yeah!" from the back of the room. I don't want to brag, but I'm pretty sure Fletch and I made Chris Robinson proud. We fist bump after strumming the final chord and move right into *Hotel California*. Fletcher taps out the percussion on his acoustic while I play the intro, and then he joins in for the chords as I play the melody. Most of the crowd sings along and we have a proper jam session before hitting the four final beats to end the song.

"Hell yeah!" I shout into the mic. "We're gonna take it down a few notches for this next song. Most of you know me as the new guy, but what you may not know is I've never lived in a place longer than six months. I was always up for the adventure, but that kind of lifestyle made it hard to settle down with someone." I readjust myself on the stool and softly strum the four chords to the next song as I gather my thoughts. "Sometimes I'd wonder when I'd meet that one person, or if it'd even be possible. When I moved here, I'd seen and done a lot of things, but I'd never fallen for anyone. Rachel, all of that changed when I met you. I've traveled across the United States and back again, but I managed to find love right here. This song is for you."

I play Ed Sheeran's *Thinking Out Loud* without taking my eyes off her. She sways from side to side and gently taps the beat over her heart. I pour all of my feelings into the words I sing to her, changing the part about falling to "seventeen" instead. At the end of the song, I whisper, "I love you" into the mic. She mouths the words back to me and blows me a kiss. I feel a small lump in the back of my throat, so I'm grateful for Fletcher's interruption.

"Yeah, yeah, yeah," he jokes. "We want to say thanks for hanging out with us tonight. We had a lot of fun and we hope to do this again next month. This is our last song of the night, and it's an original so we hope you like it. And if you don't, just pretend and clap anyway, okay?" The audience laughs. "I had a wonderful muse for this song, and she's sitting in the front row. Avery, when I drove you home from our first date, we talked about wishing for something more. I've been wishing for you for a long time and that finally came true. Here's to the future and our something more."

Fletcher closes his eyes and plays the intro, and Avery's already tearing up. She clamps her hand over her mouth as he moves into the first and second verse. By the time he reaches the chorus, she's sobbing.

Something More

My future's looking brighter
Than it ever has before
For the first time I'm not afraid
I want to wish for something more
The real world is scary
I've been out there on my own
Tired of thinkin,' believin'
That I'm better off alone
So now it's time for something more
I've watched you
I've wanted you
Please say you'll be mine
Give me your hand
And I'll make you understand
This is our time
For something more
I'll be your one
I'll be your only

I'll Be The *One*

I'll be the reason
You'll never be lonely
It's our time, it's our time, it's our time
For something more

"Thanks again, everyone. We'll see you next time," I say. I flick the mic off and high five Fletcher. As expected, Avery launches herself at him. I hop off the stage and pull Rachel into a hug.

"If I wasn't head over heels in love with you already, I definitely would be after tonight," she says against my chest. "Thank you for playing that song for me."

"We didn't have a song yet, and I thought that one was pretty fitting. We may be seventeen, but there's no way my heart will ever beat for anyone else."

"That's good. I'd hate to pull an Avery and shank a bitch."

I laugh and press a kiss on the side of her head. "You really have a way with words, Ray."

Rachel

Avery finishes the rundown of today's plans as she buckles up in the back of Mom's car.

"You've gotta be kidding me. I thought you said the whole point of you designing my prom dress is so I don't have to be held hostage in a fitting room." She's lost her damn mind if she thinks I'm spending all day playing dress up. "Mom, tell Avery she's being unfair." This was supposed to be a female bonding experience. From the looks of it, I'm in for a day of torture instead and we haven't even left Avery's driveway.

"Relax, Ray. I just need you to try on two different styles. I have ideas for both, but I need to see which one looks best on you and which one you're more comfortable in," Avery says.

"That's easy. Neither."

"Mrs. W, how have you put up with this girl for seventeen years? I know she didn't get her fashion sense from you." Avery gestures to Mom's ensemble. She's always been good at being put-together. I'm perfectly comfortable in my track pants, thank you very much.

"Rachel never wanted to play dress up, even as a little girl. She used to play Flo Jo instead. And call me Gina. I decided Mrs. W sounds too stuffy. Where are we heading to first, Avery?"

I look back at Avery and our mouths drop in unison. "Mom, are you feeling okay?" She swats my hand away when I check her forehead for a fever.

"I'm quite fine, thank you."

"Why the change in names?" Avery asks.

"I turn forty-five this summer and I feel old. It's time for me to cut loose a bit." She grins and wiggles her eyebrows as she merges onto the highway.

"That's what I'm talking about, Gina! Oh, and head to the mall first. We'll go to the fabric store after that."

"Oh, did you post that hashtag yet?" I have the perfect birthday present for James. My only fear is that whatever psychic thing he's got going on will ruin the surprise. The fact that I have a boyfriend is weird. The fact that I have one who can predict the future... kind of... is even weirder.

"Yup, I did it right after Fletcher dropped me off so I wouldn't forget."

"What's a hashtag?" Mom asks.

"It's something we use on Twitter and Instagram. I bought tickets to a Lake Street Dive concert for the day after our birthday. Avery suggested using a 'LakeStreetBirthday' hashtag so they would give James a birthday shoutout at the concert. We figured it might take a while, so we wanted to start now."

"What's Tweeter and Instagram?"

"Twitter, Mom. It's social media. You post stuff in 140 characters or less. And Instagram is for sharing pictures."

"Hmm. Maybe I should get on social media. Three younger ladies in my book club talk about their Kinder app. I think that's where they set up playdates for their kids. They seem to really like it."

"You sure it isn't Tinder?" Avery asks.

"Yeah, Mom. I've never heard of Kinder. Besides, their kids are all school age and no one has playdates once they're out of diapers." She can't possibly be this naïve.

"It could be," she says, shrugging her shoulders. "I'll have to pay closer attention when we meet next week."

"Just promise me you won't make any social media profiles without my help. There are a ton of sickos out there and I don't want you getting taken advantage of." The last thing I need is my mother's face on the wrong app.

"That sounds like something I should be saying to *you*." She parks the car and claps her hands. "Let's get started!" Avery squeals from the back seat and jumps out while I say a silent prayer for strength or patience...8 or the ability to speed up time to get this afternoon over with. It's too bad I'm too young to drink. I haven't even made it five feet from the car when Avery starts in.

"Hey, while we're here maybe we could—"

"No."

"What about—"

"No."

"Oh, come on. Just—"

"I agreed to try on two dresses *after* you promised me I wouldn't be subjected to an afternoon of fitting rooms. Don't push your luck, Murphy." I give her my sternest look for about five seconds before sticking my tongue out at her. We link arms and continue across the parking lot. "Come on, Vera Wang. Let's do this."

Avery's on a first-name basis with half of the sales staff, which isn't the least bit surprising.

"What's a fitting suite?" I ask, following an associate named Della. Her hair is huge. She makes me think of the phrase "the higher the hair, the closer to God." Turns out a fitting suite has a seating area for guests and a phone that calls the sales counter if you need help. She hangs both dresses in the fitting room.

"Miss Avery says to start with this one. Do you need help with the zipper?"

"No, I'll be fine." It's just a dress. How hard can it be? There's a table in the corner of the room that I'm sure is meant to hold my clothes, but I drop them on the floor anyway. I undo the side zipper and step into the dress. It's a strapless but I'm small enough that I don't need a bra. The zipper goes up halfway and sticks. I try a few jump-and-tugs, but that doesn't work. Neither do twist-and-tugs. I try unzipping it, but it doesn't budge in that direction either. I have just enough hips and boobs to prevent me from sliding it down or lifting it over my head. I'm officially held hostage by fabric and metal, but I refuse to let this dress defeat me. I try the jump-and-tug again, but catch sight of my B cups flopping around in the mirror. I look like a cross between a New Age dancer and a dolphin.

"How are you doing in there, Beef?"

"Fine! Just fine. I'll be out in a sec." Or an hour. Possibly next Thursday. I grab the dress with my right hand and yank the zipper with my left hand as hard as I can. The metal cuts into my finger, but it finally goes up. After making sure my boobs are where they're supposed to be, I open the door.

"Don't you just look lovely!" Mom's grinning, but Avery just cocks her head to the side.

"Turn."

I do a one-eighty with my finger in my mouth to keep blood from dripping on the dress. I don't care what Avery says, I'm not wearing anything with a zipper to prom.

"Okay, you can change."

"That's it? That's all you're gonna say?" I did *not* just endure torture at the hands of a dress for a "turn" and "you can change."

"I saw what I needed to see. Go try on the second one." I roll my eyes and go back into the room. I manage to get the dress off without ripping anything or causing more bodily harm and return it to the hanger. The second one is mocking me from the hook, but at least it doesn't have any zippers.

"Rachel, honey, let me know if you need help. I used to powder your little behind, so I've seen it all before."

"Thanks for the unwanted visual, Mom." This one is completely different from the first. It's a halter, and the dress closes like a robe with hidden buttons instead of a sash. I can work with buttons. When I open the door, Mom gasps and Avery's hands fly to her mouth.

"Yes! That's it!" Avery does a happy dance and brings me down to the three-way mirror. "I'm going to use this bodice but the straps will be different. And this color palette is all wrong for you, but I'll fix that too. What do you think about a slit running up your left leg?" She has a faraway look in her eyes that's both inspiring and scary.

"Sounds great. Now let me get out of this thing."

Ten minutes later, I'm back in my clothes on the way to the food court.

"I think a salad sounds great, what do you think?" Mom, ever the picture of Southern charm, is out of her mind if she thinks I'm eating a salad right now.

"You have fun with that. I'm going to Buck's Burgers. This girl needs some fries and a large Diet Coke after that experience." I get in line and Avery joins me. Her phone starts singing "YMCA" by the Village People, which means her dad is calling. She has such a twisted sense of humor.

"What's up, Pops? No, I'm off until after my birthday. Really? Sweet! Thanks!"

"Was that about your birthday car?" I ask after she hangs up.

"Nope. He booked three round-trip flights with his rewards so I can take Fletcher and Sam to the city this weekend!" She doesn't quit smiling as she dials her phone. "Hey, Mom! Can you make sure Fletcher is off Saturday and Sunday? Dad's flying us up. 'Kay, lemme know. Love you too."

It's our turn, but Avery's already dialing her phone again so I order for us both. Judging by her facial expression, she's talking to Fletcher now. I grab our bags and lead the way to Mom's booth.

"It looks like you're going to finish your bucket list by the end of the school year," I say with a mouth full of fries a few minutes later.

"What bucket list?" Mom asks.

"Avery, James and I made a bucket list a few weeks ago. Avery's was to design our prom dresses and take Fletcher and Sam to the city. James wanted to work with animals and perform on stage, which he's done, so all he has left to do is ride in a helicopter."

"What about yours?" Mom asks.

"Mine is to run a marathon, see Lake Street Dive in concert and get a tattoo."

"I'll pretend I didn't hear the word 'tattoo.' I heard your father talking about running a marathon next month in Durham. He finished up that last contract, so he'll have more free time to train. Maybe you can sign up for that one too?"

"Maybe. I don't think I'm that out of shape yet, so I should be able to do it."

We finish our lunch and head over to the fabric store. Thankfully, that experience wasn't as painful as the fitting suite. Avery ended up choosing fire engine red for her dress, which isn't at all surprising, and a variegated blue for mine. It sort of made me feel like a mermaid, but I refuse to admit that I'm excited to see what she comes up with. I'll take that secret to the grave.

Later that evening, I flop on my bed to start my favorite part of the day. "What's up Mr. Tennyson?" James' face fills my screen, causing my heart and stomach to dance the tango.

"Not much. How was your girls' afternoon?"

"I survived."

"That good, huh?"

"It wasn't bad. It was actually pretty fun, but don't tell Avery or Mom that. I have a reputation to uphold and all."

"Scout's honor," he says, holding up two fingers.

"So I think I'm gonna run in a marathon next month. Mom told me about it at lunch."

187

"That's awesome! I'll start working on my inspirational signs now. Mile one can be 'Smile if you just peed a little.' I guess I better hit the Internet for twenty-five more ideas," he says, rubbing his chin in thought.

"You make a pretty awesome cheerleader. Just make sure they're not too risqué. I'm gonna run with my dad and I'd like to keep my boyfriend after the race is over." I smile at the word "boyfriend." Hearing that word will never get old.

"Father-daughter marathoning, huh? That's pretty cool."

"Yeah, Mom said he finished up his last contract and will have time to train." James closes his eyes for a moment and a look of pain flashes across his face. "You okay?"

"Yeah, I think so. That was weird." He rubs the side of his face and lets out a breath.

"What happened?"

"I'm not sure. Just a bad feeling."

"Is it gone now?" I try to keep the concern out of my voice, but I can't. The last time he said he had a bad feeling, Gretchen ended up trying to kill herself.

"Not really. It's okay, though. I'm sure it's nothing."

"What triggered it?"

"When you said your dad finished the contract. I don't have any memories flashing in my head, it's just a weird feeling in my chest. That's new."

"Well as far as I know, Dad doesn't work with the mob so hopefully it's just a fluke." He smiles and yawns.

"Can I pick you up tomorrow morning? I don't want to wait until school starts to see you."

I grin and roll my eyes. "Can't wait an extra twenty minutes, huh? I guess I'll be the one next to the impatient guy tomorrow. Goodnight, Mr. Tennyson."

"Goodnight, love."

I toss my phone on the bed and try to not dwell on James' bad feeling. Today was actually pretty good, and him picking me up in the morning means he has to take me home too. That's like winning twice in one day.

"This is so good I could cry." I lean back in my chair, savoring the last bite of Gran's cherry pie. Technically speaking, you're not supposed to have dessert before dinner but I'm willing to break the rules. "I need to find out a way to make her bake pies for me when I leave for college."

I still haven't heard from State, which worries me. It's not that I particularly want to go—I've pretty much decided that a bachelor's degree in exercise and sports science from UNC is what I want. I just really don't want to piss off my dad. He's been reluctant about me dating James, but he hasn't said no to me spending time with him and I'd like to keep it that way.

"You better get in line, Mrs. Tennyson. I'm her favorite grandson."

"You're her only grandson. That means you're her favorite by default. Speaking of, where is everyone?" I take the plate to the sink, stepping over Lazarus who's taken up permanent residence in the kitchen. He lifts his head to scan the floor for crumbs but settles for some scratching behind his ear. He ranks in the top five ugliest dogs I've ever seen, but he's super sweet.

"Mom's at work. I think Gran and Grandpa are in Durham. They mentioned a meeting or something. They should be home soon though."

"Hey, let's get a head start on our Economics homework so we don't have to worry about it for the rest of the week. Besides, I'll feel less guilty about coming over to work on our project if we actually work on our project." James crosses the kitchen and grabs my waist from behind. He runs his fingertips up my spine and brings his mouth to my neck. Goose bumps sprout along both arms, and I grip the counter to prevent me from keeling over right here in the kitchen.

"How 'bout we go back in my bedroom and make out for a little while instead?" He nips at my left earlobe and places kisses from the edge of my jaw down to my collarbone. I think I know why old folks call it "necking" now.

"Very tempting, Mr. Tennyson, but I'd rather your family didn't walk in on me in a compromising position."

"That's what my door is for." I don't have to see him to hear the smile in his voice. He turns me around and takes me in his arms. I indulge myself with a kiss before backing away. This boy is seriously distracting.

"Maybe next time, Casanova. You and I have a date with homework now." I walk back to the table and reach in my backpack for the packet Mrs. Mason gave us at the end of class.

"What are we doing this week?"

I scan through the first few pages. "Do you want the good news or the bad news first?"

"Bad news. Better to get it out of the way."

"The county budget wasn't approved, and you got laid off."

"I guess that means I'm not a hot firefighter anymore. What's the good news?"

"We're having another baby."

"Really? Sweet! So what do we need to do?"

"Our revised budgets are due on Friday. Students who were laid off this week are expected to report on the unemployment process and discuss where they're applying to."

"Sounds easy enough." We spend the next half hour filling in our charts, including what our medical co-pays will be for the new baby. "How many kids do you want to have?" he asks, looking up from our homework.

"I dunno. Two or three, probably. I hate being an only kid. What about you?"

"Definitely at least two. I never felt like an only child since we usually lived with people who had kids. This is actually the first time in about ten years that I've been the only kid in the house."

"That sounds like a really strange way to grow up." James puts our finished homework in my backpack and leads me to the couch. Lazarus follows and flops down at our feet. He may be ugly, but he makes a great ottoman.

"I didn't know any different, so it was normal to me. It wasn't until I was around seven that I realized most people didn't move around like we did."

"Do you ever wish you grew up like me? In the same house and school district, I mean?"

"Not for one second." He takes my hand and traces his finger along the lines of my palm.

"Why not?"

"Because I wouldn't have met you." He presses a kiss into my palm and goes back to tracing the lines. "Besides, I had a pretty fun childhood and I got to see a lot of the country."

"Where was your favorite place to live?"

"Actually, it was right here. Gran and Grandpa's house is where I always felt the most at peace. I used to walk through the fields with Grandpa and help with the planting or harvest. Gran tried to let me help with her pies, but I kept eating the fruit, so she shooed me out of the kitchen and made me the Official Taste Tester instead." He laughs softly at the memory. "You know, all these questions made me remember that you still haven't asked me question twenty."

"Huh. I forgot all about that. I can't believe I made an ass of myself that day in the cafeteria." I wrinkle my nose just thinking about it.

"Nah, you were pretty adorable. Besides, there is no beating my epic display of stupid in Economics that first day. I'm really surprised you voluntarily spoke to me after that."

"It was just because I felt bad for you," I say, teasingly. "I still can't believe you felt all of that stuff the minute you saw me. Instant feelings still seem... I don't know... like the garbage in romance novels."

"Have you ever read a romance novel?"

"Ummm, no. Romance novels are for losers. They're all the same anyway. Boy meets girl. Boy seduces girl. Boy hurts girl. Boy gets girl back. The end."

"That may be true, but that doesn't mean instant connections don't happen or that they're doomed for failure."

Lazarus jumps up and runs to the front door. Several seconds later, Gran, Grandpa and Sunny walk in, talking animatedly.

"Dad, I better not catch you in a Speedo, that's all I'm saying," Sunny says.

"Oh, come on. I'll blend in with all the other old farts on the beach!"

"I can't wait to make my first gooseberry pie. Or maybe

strawberry pie. You know, they have festivals every year for that!" Gran's grinning from ear to ear.

James sits up on the couch. "What's all the fuss about?"

"Well hey there, son! I wasn't sure if you were working this afternoon. I'm glad we don't have to wait to share the good news," Sunny says.

"What good news?"

"I sold the farm, boy! We're moving to Florida!" Grandpa spins Gran by the arm, then dips her backward and kisses her. Sunny does what I assume is her version of a happy dance. It's eerily similar to those solar powered hula dancers that people have on their car dashboards.

"What do you mean we're moving? When you mentioned selling the farm before, you never said we were moving."

"The land developer bought everything. In about five years, this will be a whole new community, and they don't need the farm or the house. If I'm not mistaken, this house is the site of a future elementary school. You think they'll name it after us, dear?" He turns to Gran and winks at her.

"But what about me and Mom?"

"We're going with them, River. The package is more than enough to buy some property with a separate cottage for us." Sunny looks at James as if he sprouted two heads.

"It's *James*! And I'm in the middle of my senior year!"

"You're a pro at moving, kid. And this will be the last time." Her smile begins to falter. The news obviously isn't going the way she thought it would. I'm still trying to get my brain to catch up with all of this.

"That's what you said when we moved here." James leaps off the couch. "This is all about money?" He snatches the folder out of Grandpa's hands.

"No, this is about your gran and me enjoying our retirement years." James flips the folder open and I see the top of the contract. My hand flies to my mouth as I realize the severity of the situation. James immediately walks toward me and hugs me over the back of the couch.

"It's okay, baby. I'm gonna figure something out."

"You don't understand. That's my father's logo. Wheaton Properties bought Grandpa's farm." Cherry flavored bile threatens to make an appearance on Gran's worn rug. James comes around to my side of the couch as I sink back and concentrate on taking deep breaths. Grandpa's voice carries over the sound of my heart breaking.

"I know you don't understand our decision, but this was too good of a deal to pass up."

"What about the crew who helps you? They're just out of a job now?" He rubs small circles on my back.

"No, that was part of the contract too. They'll be paid through the summer."

"When?" I ask. It comes out in a whisper, but it's still loud enough for James to hear. He relays the question.

"A month or so. We're not going to move until we have a property lined up down there."

"I can't believe you did this without asking me." James' voice is a mixture of defeat and betrayal. His eyes shoot daggers at his mom.

"River, don't talk to your grandpa in that tone of voice."

"What the hell, Mom? Can you honestly stand there and think everything's okay? That I'd be happy about this?"

"You're going to college soon, and you've never been upset about us moving before. Why would now be any different?" She puts her hands on her hips and huffs with exasperation.

"Because I've never had *her* before," he says, pointing to me. He stands up and gets my backpack, then walks me to the front door. "For someone who spent her entire adult life chasing love, I can't believe you are so willing to take me away from mine." He slams the door behind us and helps me into The Beast. The engine rumbles to life, but he pulls me to him before we drive away.

"Rachel, I swear I'm going to find a way to fix this. I'm not going to Florida with them." I buckle up and he drives toward the main road.

"You don't have a choice. You're not eighteen yet." I wipe more tears from my cheeks. "Is this what your bad feeling was about yesterday?"

"No, I still have it so it's gotta be about something else. Don't worry. It's going to be alright," he says, squeezing my hand. "And we still have a month to figure something out."

Those words should be reassuring, but they're not. I don't want to figure something out. I want everything from the last thirty minutes to go away. A month ago, James was nowhere on my radar. Now, I feel like something is being surgically removed from my heart. Whoever said "It's better to have loved and lost" needs to be junk punched.

"Great, another month for me to make memories with you? To fall more in love with you? To make it even harder to say goodbye?" I remove my hand from his and lean against the door.

"Why are you acting like you're mad at me?"

"Because I am. You promised we'd be together, and in a month we're gonna be ripped apart and you're going to find someone new and I'll be left here trying to put back the pieces of my heart." A new round of tears spill out of my eyes. Truth be told, I'm madder at myself than I am him. He is a habitual nomad, after all.

"Ray, it's Florida, not Mars. And if I *do* have to go, it'll only be until the end of the school year. Then I'll be back up here to start college."

"We're seventeen, James. Long-distance relationships don't last. Just ask Derrick and Avery."

"Don't *ever* compare what we have to Derrick and Avery. That fucktwat doesn't deserve the air he breathes. And me moving has nothing to do with my feelings for you."

"Just wait until Florida's version of Vivien comes waltzing your way." The thought of another girl rubbing all over him makes me wanna hurl. I crack the window to chase the feeling away. Garth Brooks' *Shameless* comes on the radio, which makes me think of my dream on the day James first kissed me. God, that feels like a million years ago.

"Ray, I'm not the bad guy here. I'm not sure why you're blowing up at me."

"You should have known this would happen, Mr. 'I know things!' For someone who is supposed to know what happens in the future, you really suck at it. I could drive into downtown Durham and find a handful of phony psychics who are better than you. My Magic 8 Ball could probably do a better job."

"Well I'm sorry my psychic radar isn't as in-tune as you want it to be. So what if I would have known I was moving? What difference would that have made?"

I hold up my fingers and start counting the reasons. "I would have asked for a new Economics partner because I'm pretty sure my grade's gonna suffer now. I wouldn't have told

Avery I'd go to prom and get her hopes up. I wouldn't have quit track. I wouldn't have fallen in love with you."

I cross my arms and return to leaning against the window. James physically jerks in reaction to my words. I know I'm being harsh, and probably irrational, but I'm a teenage girl. These things happen. Besides, it's true. If I would have known he wasn't staying, there's no way in hell I would have ever given him the time of day. I'm not sure that all the good stuff was worth feeling like this. And I probably shouldn't have thrown track in his face, seeing as I'm the one who wanted to quit anyway, but I just don't have time for that kind of logic right now.

"I can't believe you just said that."

"What am I supposed to say? That everything's gonna be fine? That the person who first said 'Out of sight, out of mind' was wrong?" Adrenaline courses through my veins. I guess this is what they meant by a "fight or flight" response. We're fighting because he's leaving.

"What about 'Absence makes the heart grow fonder'?" His voice is laced with desperation, something I've never heard coming from him. I hate it. He pulls into my driveway and puts the truck in park. "Rachel, please don't shut me out."

"I'm sorry. I just don't see how this is going to work."

I grab my backpack and slam the truck door without a second glance at James. Seeing his face would only cause another round of tears. I open the front door and focus on getting to my bedroom where I can have a breakdown in relative privacy.

"Not so fast Rachel Lynn." Dad's voice is stern and it's the last thing I want to hear right now. I forgot on the drive home that technically *he's* the one responsible for all of this. I hate him so hard right now.

"What?"

"What the hell is this?" I look over at him and he's holding an envelope from State. A big envelope.

Fuck.

It looks like it's seen better days—crumpled, one corner is ripped off and there are black streaks across the front of it.

"Would you mind explaining why this envelope came in the mail today and why it has your name on it?

"Would you mind explaining why you bought the Glenn farm without telling me?" I counter. His eyebrows draw together, and for a moment, confusion replaces the anger on his face.

"What does the Glenn deal have anything to do with you?

"I'm dating their grandson." Was dating. Whatever. I don't even know anymore. "That deal means they're moving and taking James with them."

"That deal got me a thirty-five thousand dollar bonus, which I thought would be handy considering my only child is starting college this year. Which brings me back to this." He thrusts the envelope toward me. "How could you do this to me?"

"Relax. It's just an acceptance letter. I thought it'd be good to have some options."

"Is this where James is going to school? Is that why you applied there?"

"Actually, I applied before I met James." I cross my arms. He will not talk to me like I'm a love-struck fool who's incapable of making her own decisions. Even though that shoe fits a little better than I'd like it to.

"Well, if you're this upset about some teenage fling moving away, I'm glad he's leaving. You're entirely too young to be this worked up over a boy."

I manage to keep from screaming out loud, but internally it's a different story. I can't do this right now. I reach over and snatch the envelope out of his hand and stomp down the hall to my bedroom. Deciding to skip dinner, I put on pajamas and crawl into bed. This morning, I woke up with a boyfriend. Tonight I'm going to bed with a broken heart, and I have no idea how to fix it. Or even if it can be.

James

The movers are everywhere. There's a rhythm to their movements, and from a choreographer's point of view, it's actually quite beautiful.

Reach, remove, wrap, pack. Reach, remove, wrap, pack.

One guy walks down the hallway toward the kitchen carrying Lucy. The sleeves of his light gray hoodie are pushed up, and there's a grease stain next to his embroidered name. Instead of "Carl," it looks like his name is "Carly."

"Hey man, check this out," he says to another mover. "Didn't you say you were looking for a new one?" He holds Lucy out for inspection. The other guy picks her up and strums a few chords.

"Yeah, this one's pretty nice. Put it in the cab of the truck, will ya?"

"No prob." He steps toward the front door. I have no idea what's going on, but Carly better back the fuck off of my guitar.

"Hey, asshole, that's mine!" It doesn't come out nearly as loud or authoritative as I intended. Carly keeps walking. I run toward him, but my feet won't move. What the actual fuck? I scan the room for Gran, Grandpa, or Mom, but they're not here. It's just me and a bunch of thieves. Another guy walks out the front door with an opened box full of my stuff. From here, I can see my speakers and my amp. He smiles and nods at the guy in the kitchen packing up Gran's dishes.

"You look like a repo man!"

He shifts the box up to his shoulder and uses his free hand to point toward my bedroom. "It's like Christmas back there, dude. You'd better take a look before all the good shit's gone."

"They're not taking any of that stuff?" He sets down a cup – my blue cup – and heads to my bedroom.

"Nope. The kid's gone, and they don't want his shit anymore." The speaking thief passes Mom and Grandpa on his way outside. They sit on the couch, which has been shrink wrapped, and Mom props her feet up on a stack of boxes. She looks tired.

"It'll be good to get a fresh start," Grandpa says.

"Yeah, it will. Besides, the sunshine always makes everything better."

"Is that why you changed your name when you left home?"

"I suppose so. Thanks again for all the help with River's life insurance paperwork. I'm just glad that's all done with." Mom rubs her hands over her face and sighs.

"It's the least I could do. I was working on your mother's at the same time so it only made sense to take care of his, too." He pats Mom on the knee. Is it me, or is his hair grayer? His face has more lines in it, and for the first time he looks every bit of his age.

"I'm gonna fall asleep if I keep sitting here." Mom stands up and walks into the kitchen. "Want any coffee, Dad?"

I bolt upright, my heart hammering in my chest. Lazarus lifts his head and thumps his tail against the covers.

I flip the edge of my curtain back and see the colors of an early morning sunrise. This is the second one I've watched since I dropped Rachel off at her house. She hasn't spoken to me since then. She was out of school yesterday and didn't answer any of my phone calls or texts. I admit that I'm mad at the way she flipped out on me. She knows there's no rhyme or reason to what I predict, so I don't know why she's making this my fault. But mostly, I miss her. If this is what two days feels like, I'm not sure I can make it three months.

There's no chance of me going back to sleep, so I head to the kitchen and start the coffee pot. Lazarus runs to his food bowl and exchanges glances between me and the refrigerator.

"You know the rules, dude. Pee first, then food." I take him to the front door so he can do his business. I haven't had him that long, but he's already made himself home. His favorite place, besides the kitchen, is underneath the pine tree off the corner of the house. He'd lay there for hours if I let him. Gran, ever the early riser, pads down the hallway as I fill my blue cup with coffee. Without needing to ask, I start her teakettle.

"What has you up so early?" She moves past me and takes the waffle iron out of the bottom cabinet. Gran's a fantastic pastry chef, but she makes a mean Belgian waffle too. I don't anticipate having a great day, but at least I know breakfast will be awesome.

"Bad dream."

"Wanna tell me about it?"

"We were moving, only I apparently died and y'all told the movers they could have all of my stuff." I decide to leave out the part about her being dead too. With that thought, I rub the ache that flares in my chest. It's the same feeling I had on the phone with Rachel the other day, and the one I've carried with me since then. I take a minute to watch Gran as she makes the waffles, wondering if she's the cause of this feeling. She looks like she's lost a little bit of weight, and she doesn't move as fast as she used to, though that part could be attributed to the general aging process.

"Well, you'd better make sure you've updated your will so we know who gets what." Her laughter mixes in with the sound of the teakettle, and I try my best to commit the sound to memory. I fix her cup and set it on the counter next to her.

"Do you have a will?"

"Sure, all of us old fogies do." She plates a waffle and passes me the maple syrup before turning back to the waffle iron. "Don't you worry, I'll make sure you get your blue cup."

"Gran, why are you and Grandpa really moving to Florida?" From my seat at the table, I watch her purses her lips briefly.

"It's time for us to relax. Your grandpa has worked very hard and we feel like we need a break."

"But why Florida? Why not stay here?"

"Florida has a lot to offer us. You'll see. Maybe you can check out the colleges down there too. I hear Spring Break is pretty good." She turns and wiggles her eyebrows at me. I suppose I should be mildly grossed out that my grandma is making an off-color comment, but I learned all of my best dirty jokes from her.

"I want to get back up here as quickly as possible. Florida doesn't have Rachel, and that's all I care about."

"I didn't realize it was quite that serious with you two."

"Neither does anyone else in this family." It comes out more bitter than I intended, but it's true. "And please don't give me the bit about my age. I know I'm young and I have my whole life ahead of me, blah, blah, blah."

"You *are* young. But like I told you before, the heart knows what it wants. It's everything else that gets in the way."

"Yeah, like grandparents who sell their farm." I give her a sidelong glance as I take another bite. "I just hope Rachel's in school today. She was out yesterday and won't answer my phone calls."

"Did y'all get in a fight after you left here?"

"I guess somewhere between our house and hers, she decided she didn't want to spend another month together. She said it would make it harder to say goodbye. If she's not in school today, I wanna stop by her house before I go to the Sweet Pea. You think I can make it in time?"

"Where does she live?"

"In that big blue house on Kestwick past Andrews Street." Gran puts the last waffle in the pan and stows it in the microwave, away from Lazarus' reach.

"What time does your shift start?"

"Three-thirty."

"Hmm. That might be cutting it awfully close. I'd say skip it and try talking to her tomorrow."

I was afraid she was going to say that. "Thanks for the waffles, Gran." I stand to clear my plate and cross the kitchen to give her a hug on the way to the sink. The minute my arm circles her shoulder, the pain in my chest explodes. My plate crashes to the floor and shatters. I hear her hollering at Lazarus to stay away before a whoosh of ringing floods my ears. Each beat of my heart feels harder than the last, and memories of Gran flash through my mind.

When I was four, she bought me a kids' shaving set so I could be just like my grandpa. She hung an eight-by-ten picture of my shaving cream beard in the living room. For my tenth birthday, she bought me a pair of rollerblades. I wore them every day until my feet grew out of them. When we visited two summers ago, she pulled me aside and gave me a new wallet. That night I found twenty dollars and a condom tucked inside. I never had to use it, but I appreciated the gesture all the same. The last image, the one that brings me to my knees on the kitchen floor, is of me, Mom and Grandpa on a beach spreading Gran's ashes. Mom still has pink and purple streaks in her hair.

Mom never leaves her hair the same way for longer than six months.

No.

No!

NO!

Gran leads me back to the kitchen table as sobs take over my body. She makes calming noises, and her fingertips trace a soothing pattern over my face. She used to do this when I was sick. I swear it was medicinal, because I always ended up feeling better. Not this time. Mom would be freaking out right now, wondering what's wrong with me, but Gran's always been good about letting me speak when I'm ready. We sit like this for a while, me losing my shit, and her trying to patch me back together.

"H-how long have you been sick?" I manage to say once my breathing has returned to a more normal state.

"Off and on for about three years." Her voice is calm, which I find impossible given the situation.

"How bad is it now?"

"Terminal."

"How long?"

"They said six months to a year." The noise that comes from my mouth is what I imagine a bear that slammed his paw in a car door would make. No matter where we lived, Gran has always been around. I can't imagine waking up one day and not having her here with me. The thought brings a new round of sobs from me and Gran's calming noises and soothing fingertips.

"How'd you know?" she asks several minutes later.

I take a deep breath. I need a moment to figure out how to tell her without getting into the psychic stuff. "When I gave you a hug, I remembered more of the dream that woke me up. You died too. And now all the signs make sense. Your hair's thinner. You haven't been eating much. I noticed a few weeks ago that you look frailer, but I thought that was just because you're old."

"Watch it, buck-o. This old lady had great sex last night. My age doesn't stop me from living, and neither does this disease."

"God, Gran! There are some things I just do *not* need to know." I can't help but laugh, though, and I'm sure that was her point. I pick my head off the table and wipe my face.

"There now. That's better." She pats my cheek and brings me my blue cup with fresh coffee.

"You said it's been off and on for a few years. Why didn't you tell me or Mom? And what do you have, anyway?"

"Colon cancer. The doctors were optimistic when I first went in, so your grandpa and I felt that we didn't need to worry y'all. I had a little bit of chemo and things looked good for a while. I had a relapse a couple of years ago and had surgery. Last fall, I had another relapse. Turns out, it spread to my liver. We told your mom, and she said she'd move home as soon as I wanted her to."

"So that's why we came here right before Christmas?"

"It is."

"Why didn't you tell me that it might be our last one together?"

"I didn't see any sense in having people cry in their turkey and stuffing. Knowing about my cancer doesn't change anything. It just makes people sad."

"Why do you not seem more upset by all of this?"

"What's to be upset about? We're all gonna die, James. Some just do it faster than others."

"I may not have grown up in this house, but this has always been the most 'home' that I've ever had. Now, everything's being taken away. You. This house. Your pies." I offer a small smile.

"The folks at the hospital are gonna miss my pies too," she laughs.

"Is that why you always take pies to the hospital? Because you had appointments?"

"I decided I wanted to be remembered for something greater than cancer at the hospital. And it worked, too. I'd walk through the door and their tongues would start wagging."

"How does Grandpa feel about all those tongues wagging for you?" I wink at her over my coffee cup.

"He doesn't mind since he knows his tongue is the one I care the most about. In fact, it was wagging pretty good last night."

"Gross, Gran!" I dig my fingers in my ears, but the damage has already been done. "You aren't gonna let me be sad about this, are you?"

"Not if I can help it. I'm blessed, James. Nothing in life is more humbling than sitting in a chemo room. I was there with toddlers and teenagers. Young mothers and fathers. Folks who should have been enjoying the prime of their life, not fighting for it. I sat there hooked up, feeling guilty."

"Why guilty?"

"Because I'm an old woman. I've lived my life. My time's coming to an end, cancer or not." She pauses for a sip of tea. "The chemo room is always filled with books and magazines and ways to pass the time so you're not sitting there thinking of the poison going in your body. One day, there was a bright orange book sitting on the table. I started reading it, and I'll be damned if it didn't change my life."

"What was it about?"

"A girl who embraced the hell out of life, even though hers was coming to an end."

"Did she have cancer too?"

"She did. But she didn't sit there bellyachin' about it. She went to college. She listened to loud music. She fell in love. She *lived*, James. And that's what I'm gonna do until the very end. I might struggle, but I'm gonna struggle with joy. Besides, old people shit themselves all the time. At least I'll have a better excuse!"

With that, she winks at me, downs the last of her tea and

gets the dustpan from underneath the sink. There's no way she's cleaning up the plate I broke.

"Go sit down, I'll get this." I sweep chards of ceramic off the floor and run a damp paper towel over the area for good measure. "So what's really in Florida?"

"Besides the sunshine and your grandpa on the beach in a speedo?" She grins and wiggles her eyebrows again. "There's a cancer hospital in Tampa that I'm transferring to. They'll help with all the shitty stuff—pun intended—before I ride the big elevator to the QVC in the sky."

"Are you scared?" I dump the contents of the dustpan in the trash and return to the table.

"Not in the least. I know exactly where I'm going." She offers a reassuring smile and glances at the clock over the stove. "You'd better get a move on so you're not late for school."

"I'm okay with hanging out with you a little bit longer. Trigonometry won't miss me, I promise."

"Well in that case, let's use our time wisely. Go get my clippers, boy. You need a trim. You look like one of those youngins on the cover of those teeny bopper magazines."

"Yes ma'am."

Caffeinated Secretary—I mean Mrs. Atkins—eyes my note over her cup of coffee. "Family emergency?"

"Yes, but everything's fine now." Well, not really, but whatever.

"Give this late slip to your second period teacher."

I walk in to Economics a few minutes before the dismissal bell rings. Rachel's seat is empty, but that's no surprise.

Gretchen waves at me, and I lift my chin in response. It's nice to see her smiling again. Really smiling. Her ex-boyfriend seems to have moved on with the buxom brunette Mrs. Mason partnered him with. I wonder if she did that on purpose.

When the bell rings, I move to the front of the class. "Excuse me, Mrs. Mason?" She looks up from her desk and smiles.

"Yes?"

"In a few weeks, I'm going to be moving. I'm concerned about how that will affect Rachel's grade for our project." I know I told her I'd find a way to stay, but I don't see how that's possible now that I know about Gran. The best I can do now is make sure her GPA won't suffer.

"I'm sorry to hear that, James. I've enjoyed your time in class. We don't have a lot of kids who move away, but you aren't the first. The best thing about this project is that it focuses on real-life situations. Sometimes that means people leave. Don't worry about her grade. I can work around this circumstance for the remainder of the semester."

"Thanks."

The rest of the day passed in a fog. Vivien kept staring at me during lunch, no doubt wondering where Ray was. She even licked her lips, and it had nothing to do with what she was eating. So gross. Pulling a four-hour shift at the Sweet Pea is the last thing I want to do tonight, but a job's a job. At least Fletcher and Avery are working with me. Besides, it's a Wednesday so it should be pretty slow.

"What's up, dude?" Fletcher says over the radio. "Did you hear Avery is taking me and Sammy to The Big Apple this weekend? I'm so freakin' stoked!"

"That's awesome, Fletch. Has Sam been on an airplane before?"

"Nope, it's her first time. I haven't told her yet. I wanna surprise her on the way to the airport. After our shift ends, Avery and I are going shopping for a little backpack to fill with stuff to do on the plane."

"Sounds like a fun time." Avery's rolling silverware at the hostess station, and the only table I have just cleared out. I plop down on a stool just inside the kitchen so I can watch for new customers. Fletcher eyes me. I know what's coming next.

"Avery said you and Rachel had a bit of a falling out. Wanna talk about it?"

"Not much to talk about. I'm moving to Florida because my gran's sick and she freaked out. Said she can't bear to be my girlfriend while I'm still here, and she's convinced herself that a long-distance relationship won't work. The horror stories of Derrick and Avery have left their mark." I shrug a shoulder in defeat. "How am I supposed to overcome that?"

"That's tough, man. I won't lie." He peeks his head through the window before continuing. "Avery still gets weird on me because of shit Derrick did or said. I hate being compared to him, but that's the last relationship she had. It sucks, but I can see why she does it. Hopefully, Ray will come around soon. What you two have seems legit."

"Yeah it is. For me at least. I thought it was for her too, but now she's acting like a damn girl about it." I rub my hands over my face. You'd think for a guy who had semi-psychic abilities, I'd know what in the hell to do. Instead I feel more like a baby elephant learning to control its trunk: sometimes it goes well, and sometimes I look like a bumbling idiot.

"You need a plan, dude."

"Fine, you got one?"

"Let me think on it some." He grins when Avery slides a ticket over the counter.

"Well if it isn't the prettiest girl in North Carolina."

"Yeah, yeah." She may act blasé, but I know inside she's eating that shit up. She turns to me with a sad puppy eyes before plastering a fake smile on her face. "Hey James! How are ya?"

Seriously?

"About as great as I was at lunch, Avery."

"Still haven't talked to her?"

"Nope. She's not going to have a choice tomorrow, though. If she stays home again, I'm skipping and going to her house."

"You didn't hear it from me, but she's a mess. You may have been the reason she fell apart, but I think you're the only one who can put her back together."

I straighten a bit in my stool. That's the best news I've heard in the longest two days of my life. "You got any tips for me? I could use all the help I can get." She studies me for a moment, then breaks out in a smile. A real one, this time.

"She loved open mic night. Can you write her a song?"

I glance over at Fletcher, who nods his head.

"Done. Lucy's in The Beast. You think it's okay if I go grab her and work on it between customers?" On that note, Mandy walks out of the manager's office and into the kitchen.

"Mom, James is moving because his gran is sick. Rachel freaked out and broke up with him because she's stupid. Is it okay if James hangs out in the back room to work on a song so he can win her back?" Leave it up to Avery to sum up the state of my life in three sentences. Mandy's eyes dart between me, Fletcher and Avery before settling back on me with a sigh.

"I don't care, as long as my customers and restaurant are tended to. If the two of you can carry his load tonight, that's fine by me. Just don't make a practice out of it."

"Thanks, Mandy. And God willing, this is the last time I'll ever have to win Ray back."

"That girl has all but lived at my house for the last couple of years, and I've never seen her the way she is with you. I don't think you'll have to try too hard." She returns to the office muttering to herself. The only thing I catch is something about "mahogany." With a surge of song lyrics filling my head, I run to the truck for Lucy.

For the second time today, I'm filled with hope.

Rachel

Boys suck.

Dads suck.

Florida sucks.

Okay. Florida *itself* doesn't suck. But the five hundred miles separating it from North Carolina do.

I lift my arm for a pit-check. I haven't showered since Monday morning before school. It's Wednesday afternoon and by the smell of it, Secret is spilling all the dirt she has on me.

Mom bought my story of a headache and sore throat and let me stay home from school yesterday and today. Despite her recent attempts to be a more active participant in my life, she's still not a very good nurse. Her idea of caring for me when I'm sick is to leave a few cans of chicken noodle soup on the counter and half of CVS's decongestants in the bathroom. Not that I actually need them.

I just can't bear to see James yet. How I'm supposed to make it through the next few weeks before he leaves is beyond me. How I'm supposed to survive once he's gone is even more unbearable.

Boys suck.

Mom texted me earlier—yes, she actually texted me from inside the house—to let me know she was going to a Bingo committee meeting. I never knew there was such a thing. I raided the freezer after hearing the front door shut, polishing off the last of the Ben and Jerry's and then starting on the Häagen Dazs. Dad hid his stash of sherbet behind a bag of lima beans, and I'm gonna eat that too. Serves him right.

But, remembering the status of my pit-check, I should probably shower first. I'm starting to gross myself out, and Avery would seriously kick my ass if she saw me. Her version of post-breakup attire involved red lipstick, skinny jeans and stilettos. So basically, it was business as usual. I pass Dad's office on the way to the kitchen and flip off the door. Juvenile as it may be, it makes me feel better. I load my ice cream bowl in the dishwasher and head for the bathroom when I hear knocking at the front door. For a moment, I wonder if this is one of those daytime burglary attempts I heard about on the news and grab the phone off the kitchen counter just in case. I creep to the peephole and equal amounts of relief and confusion hit me. *What the hell is Gran doing here?*

"I'm standing on the front porch waiting for you to open the door," her muffled voice says through the door.

Guess I said that out loud.

"Hey, Gran. Um. Won't you come in?" I gesture to the living room and hold the door open for her. She's not carrying pie, which is a damn shame.

"Thank you, dear." She walks into the foyer and gives me a once-over. "It's great to see you, but I have to say, you look like shit." She pats me on the shoulder on her way to the couch.

Well then.

"Can I do something for you, Gran?" I still have no idea why she's here. Or how she knew *I* was here. Or how she knew where *here* is. Damn, I should have paid better attention to that burglary story. How many victims actually knew their burglars? I can see the headline now: 'Local Teen Robbed by Ex-Boyfriend's Granny.' I clutch the phone tighter, sit down on the chair opposite the couch and pull my knees up to my chest. Gran opens and closes her mouth a few times like she wants to say something but doesn't know where to start.

"Rachel, you're a lovely young lady."

"Thank you."

"You're also stupid."

Wait, what? Before I can even respond, she continues.

"But that's okay, because there's still time to fix it."

"Fix what, exactly?"

"You and James."

"*He* sent you here?" Getting your grandma to do your bidding is... I dunno. Creepy? Sweet? I set the phone down on the coffee table and rub my face.

"He has no idea I'm here."

"So why are you here?"

"I know our moving came out of nowhere, but I honestly think it was an answer to a prayer."

That's my dad, answering prayers and ruining my life faster than a speeding checkbook. I don't bother hiding my eye roll.

"Don't you go getting mad at your daddy. He's just doing his job. But now you kids are caught up in the middle of it, and you decided to cut and run. When you're a teenager, it's hard to see the big picture. It's hard to look beyond what's happening right now."

"Gran, I actually have no problem seeing the big picture. That's why I told James it wouldn't work between us. For as much as I'd like to believe we could have a long-distance relationship, there are grown adults who can't manage it. We're seventeen, and the odds are stacked against us. Who am I to—"

Gran holds up a hand to shush me.

"All the things you're fussing about? That's what's happening *right now*. You're still missing the big picture."

It's official. I have no idea what this woman is talking about. She may be more senile than I thought. "I'm sorry. You lost me."

"James said you never had a boyfriend because your daddy wouldn't let you."

"Right."

"Wrong. You never had a boyfriend because no one was worth gettin' your daddy's feathers ruffled." She look she gives me says 'I dare you to tell me I'm wrong.' Which I can't. I never really thought about it that way, but she sort of makes sense.

"Moving on. James has never had a girlfriend until you."

"He said it was because he moved around too much."

"That's partially true. Watching his mama chase men from coast to coast taught him more about disappointment than it did about love. He always said having a girlfriend wasn't worth all that trouble."

"What does that have to do with the big picture?"

"It's the choice. That's the difference between you and Sunny and all those other people whose relationships didn't work out. It's a matter of choosing whether that other person is worth it, but you each have to choose 'yes.' You had to choose between track and James. Which did you pick?"

I don't respond, because she already knows the answer. She stares at me for several seconds before raising her eyebrow. Apparently, I'm in a pissing contest with a lady in her seventies.

"James," I say with a sigh.

"Exactly. And he chose you. For as much as Sunny said she was settling down here, I don't think that girl has a committed bone in her body. There was always a risk that she'd want to move again. But this time, James decided you were worth the trouble. *That's* the big picture. Everything else is just what's happening right now."

"But what's happening right now sucks. Having a boyfriend in high school is hard enough, let alone having one that's five hundred miles away." That came out a bit more petulant than I planned, but whatever. It's still true.

"I never said it was going to be easy." She gives me a pointed look, and all I can do is nod in response. "And furthermore, you need to let go of whatever checklist you've got in that head of yours."

"Checklist?"

"Love doesn't have pre-requisites. You don't *have* to experience heartbreak and all that other mess you kids keep posting about on your smartphones. Love will find you, but you have to be smart enough to catch it when it does. The biggest heartbreak in your life shouldn't be the one who got away. It should be the *thought* of him getting away."

Why do I feel like I should grab the notepad off the refrigerator so I can write this stuff down?

"Now, there's just one more thing."

Oh, God. There's more? I just want to shower, eat Dad's sherbet, and figure out a way to skip school tomorrow without Mom dragging me to the doctor. "Yes?" I ask with as much enthusiasm as I can muster. Which isn't much. My brain is too overloaded with ice cream and sage advice.

"Giving up track for James was stupid."

"What? But you just said—"

She shushes me again. "I know what I said. I'm old, not stupid. Relationships are about compromise. Give and take. But don't give up something you love for someone you love. That's a sure way to lose your identity."

"I quit track because I didn't want to be an Olympic athlete. That's my dad's dream for me, not mine."

"Would you have quit if James had never moved here?" She raises her eyebrow again. I don't answer for several seconds, trying to figure out the right way to say what I want to say.

"My entire life, I've done what my dad has asked me to do. I love running. Dedicating myself to track wasn't hard, but it's not the only thing I want in my life. When James moved here, I finally felt like my opinion counted for something. That my plans for my future were just as valid as my dad's. So yes. I quit track because of James, but that doesn't mean what you think it means. I quit because he gave me the courage to."

"Just because you quit track doesn't mean you have to quit running. Just remember that."

"Yes ma'am," I say with a sigh. I'm so exhausted. Once Gran leaves, which is hopefully soon, I'm gonna take a nap. I've done more conversing and emoting in the last ten minutes than I have in the past two days.

"Okay, then. Now that we got all that stuff out of the way, I have some good news." She rubs her hands together and her face brightens. I'm sort of afraid to ask. "There's a pie on the front seat of my car. Why don't you run out there and get it?"

Yes! The promise of sugar, fruit, and flaky crust instantly banishes my exhaustion. I hope it's cherry. Or blueberry. Or apple. Who am I kidding? It doesn't matter. I run to the car and retrieve the dish from her passenger seat. The warmth from the bottom tells me it's fresh out of the oven, and I'm drooling before I make it back onto the front porch. "Thanks, Gran. You didn't have to, but I'm glad you did." I manage to hold in my happy dance when I get to the kitchen. Foregoing all manners, I immediately cut a slice and take a bite. Mom would be so ashamed of me right now. "You wah shum?" I ask around a mouthful.

"No, thank you. I just figured some wisdom and a slice of triple berry pie could do you some good today." I return to my spot in the couch to devour the rest of my plate. "James wanted to stop by after school today but he'd have been late to work," Gran continues. "He didn't look so great this morning."

Guilt stabs at me. How am I supposed to respond to that? I'd use a cop-out excuse like "It's not my fault," but it totally is. He called me a couple of times yesterday and today, but I couldn't bring myself to answer. I wanted to—don't get me wrong. I just didn't know what to say.

"Is he sick?"

"A little lovesick is all. Nothing a conversation and a makeup kiss can't fix."

Ew. I'm not talking about kissing with Gran.

"Thanks, I'll keep that in mind."

"Don't mention it. Now, if you'll excuse me I have a doctor's appointment to get to." She shuffles to the front door, and I set my plate on the counter so I can properly see her out. See? I have manners after all.

"I'm gonna share a quote with you before I go: *Distance does to love what wind does to fire. It extinguishes the weak and feeds the strong.* It's up to you to figure out what kind of fire you have." She smiles and gives me a hug.

"Thanks again, Gran." She really is a sweet old lady. It's easy to see why James loves her so much.

"I'll see you soon, I'm sure." She pats my shoulder again and starts to leave but stops just across the threshold. "Rachel?"

"Yes, Gran?"

"You really need a shower. Your hair looks as greasy as the inside of a tub of Crisco."

"I appreciate the observation. On my way." I can't help but laugh as I shut and lock the door behind her.

An hour and fifteen sweaty minutes later, I step out of the shower and dry off. I was too worked up to stay inside after Gran left, so I decided to go for a run. I forgot how nice it felt to pop in my earbuds and go. No GPS. No stopwatch. No overbearing dad. Just me, my shoes, and my music.

Somewhere around mile four I decided to surprise James at his house tonight after his shift. I owe him an apology at the very least. Then we need to have a conversation about how to make everything work while he's in Florida. And then, God willing, some kissing. It's been two days. My lips are jonesing, or rather... Jamesing.

Revenge-eating Dad's sherbet doesn't sound very appealing anymore, so I opt for a Diet Coke instead. I still have about two hours before James is done at the Pea. To kill the time, I flop on my bed and look up marathon training programs on Pinterest. I have six weeks and three days until race day. It'll make for a pretty intense regimen, but I'm not a beginner so I should be fine. I'm actually really looking forward to crossing off one of my bucket list items. Hopefully James can come back up here for our birthday weekend so I can surprise him with the Lake Street Dive concert and cross that one off too. And since we'll both officially be eighteen, that means we can get our tattoos and I'll be three for three. I have an idea of what I want, but open a new Pinterest window to see if anyone else has gotten something similar. A knock on my door stops me mid-scroll.

"Come in."

Dad pokes his head in my room and looks around before opening the door all the way.

"You busy?"

"Nope. What's up?" This is the first time we've spoken since I blew up on him Monday night. It's awkward, to say the least.

"I, uh, just had something for you. You're growing up. That's hard for me to come to terms with." He shuffles his feet in the doorway. "I'm sure you'll understand what I mean when you become a parent. Anyway."

He takes something from his back pocket and walks across the room to hand it to me.

"You got me a little State flag?"

"It wasn't easy, I'll tell you that." He gives a half-laugh and sits on the bed beside me. "I've made it no secret that I want you to go to UNC. But I was reminded that you're almost a legal adult, which means you can make your own decisions."

"Who reminded you of that?"

"Your mom." For a brief moment, he looks like a kid who got in trouble. I can't help but laugh. "But, she's right. So if you want to go to State, I'll support you."

"Wow." I wave the small scrap of red back and forth. "That means a lot to me, Dad. But I don't need this flag." I set it on my bed and open my desk drawer to remove my UNC envelope. "I'm gonna be a Tarheel." I pass the acceptance letter to him. His smile grows as he scans the page.

"How long have you had this?"

"A few weeks."

"You didn't want to share the good news with me and your mom?"

I put the letter back in the envelope and return it to the drawer. "I wanted to see what State said before I made any decisions."

"Are you choosing UNC because that's where I want you go to?"

"No, I'm choosing it because they have the program I want. I'm getting a bachelor's in exercise and sports science. Apparently, they're going to be building new schools where James' grandparents' house is. Maybe I'll apply to be a P.E. teacher there once I graduate," I say with fake optimism.

"You may not believe it, but I really am sorry that he's leaving. Mom told me he's your first love. That's a special thing."

"Was Mom your first love?"

He takes a deep breath and rubs his forehead. "No, she wasn't. My first love was my high school sweetheart. Her name was Patti Dolan, and I'd never seen anything as beautiful as her. I had a track scholarship in college, and I was well on my way to the Olympic trials. Everything changed when Patti got pregnant." His voice thickens, and he winces as if the memory is causing him physical pain. I gasp and grip his arm with my right hand. "Neither of our parents were happy. To tell you the truth, I wasn't very happy either. That wasn't a part of my plan. She insisted we could make everything work, but her dad threatened to tell my coach I raped her if she didn't have an abortion."

My left hand flies to my mouth. I can't believe I didn't know any of this. "God, Dad. You must have been so scared."

"Yeah, I was scared of a lot of things. My parents couldn't afford college, which is why I worked so hard at track in the first place. If I had rape charges brought against me, I would have lost my scholarship. If I told Patti I wanted her to get an abortion, I would have lost her. None of my options were very good."

"What did you do?"

"I called Patti's dorm and told her I'd pick her up so we could talk. Figure out what our options were and all that. It was a beautiful summer day, so she said she wanted to go to the park. We were on our way when a pickup truck slammed into the passenger side of my car and totaled it. I was bruised and shaken up. Patti had a broken arm and a concussion. She lost the baby." His head hangs down, and he quickly wipes his eyes. I do the same.

"That must have been so awful." I can't imagine what I would have done in that situation.

"That's the thing. I was more relieved than anything. She didn't have to get an abortion, and I got to keep my scholarship. It was the best of both worlds. Except she didn't quite see it that way and we got in a huge fight. We broke up the next day, and she dropped out of school."

"Did you see her after that?"

"Once, about six months later. I was at a bar with some of the guys from the track team, and she was there with some of her friends. She looked good. Her arm was healed and she was smiling."

"Did you try to talk to her?"

"No. I didn't want to stir up old memories for either of us. I was happy being able to focus on track. I didn't even think about girls at all until I saw your mom on the side of the road with a twisted ankle. I helped her to the clinic, but I couldn't get her out of my head. The next semester, I pretended to be failing English so she'd tutor me." For the first time since he started telling me this story, he smiles.

"You pretended to fail? Does Mom know that?" I can't believe he'd make up something like that just to have a chance to talk to Mom.

"No, I don't reckon I ever shared that with her." He chuckles softly and the darkness in his eyes starts to clear.

"So that's why you didn't want me dating anyone?"

"A father's job is to protect his daughter. I never wanted

you to experience what I did. To have to choose between the lesser of two evils. To be relieved about a miscarriage."

I don't know what to say, so we sit in silence for a few minutes. "Thanks for telling me that story, Dad. I know it was hard. It helps me understand you better though. I just hope one day you understand why I want to be a P.E. teacher. That you don't think it's a wasted career."

"So long as that's what you want—that it's not something you're settling for—I'm happy for you, Rachel. You're a smart, talented young lady. You'll be an amazing teacher."

"With a degree from UNC," I add, which makes both of us laugh.

"Does that mean I can burn this?" he asks, picking up the State flag.

"You have my blessing." He hugs me, and when we separate, he wipes his eyes again.

"Come on, let's go tell Mom I'm gonna be a Tarheel," I say, pulling him off the bed and down the hallway. "Oh, is it okay if I run that marathon next month with you?"

"Sounds good to me. Just be prepared to be smoked by your dad."

"Whatever. I'm gonna run circles around you, old man."

"Why don't you get your shoes on and we'll settle this 'old man' thing right now," he laughs.

My heart is threatening to beat right out of my chest—more excitement than nerves, I think. There's still about thirty minutes before James' shift is over, but I can't wait anymore.

It's time to end my self-inflicted hiatus. I calculate how long it'll take me to reach his house as I back down the driveway. It normally takes me about fifteen minutes, and it'll take him about ten to get home from the Sweet Pea. That means I'll have to drive around like a stalker for about twenty minutes.

Totally doable.

When I started driving, Dad put solar-powered lamp posts along the driveway since it's a long one. I never really thought how helpful they are until I look in the rearview mirror and realize the last four or five are out. Instead, I pull back up to the house, do a three-point turn in front of the garage and drive out the proper way. I make it halfway down when a car pulls in, blocking me from getting to the road. I can't see who it is because the headlights are shining right in my eyes. *Jesus, Mary and Joseph.* With a huff, I put my car into reverse—again—and return to the top of the driveway where it widens so I have room to go around it. The vehicle with the blinding headlights follows me. Who the hell is coming to my house at seven o'clock on a Wednesday night? Just as I try to shift past it, the door opens and my foot slams on the brake.

James.

I throw open my door and run to The Beast.

"What are you doing here?" I ask, my heart pounding even harder than it was before.

"I came to see you. But apparently you had plans?" He looks me up and down, taking in my outfit—soft-as-butter leggings, a long shirt that Avery calls a tunic and some ankle boots. It's something she got me for Christmas that I finally decided to wear. I figured it would make for a great groveling ensemble.

"I was driving to your house. To apologize." God, he's gorgeous. My first instinct is to reach out and touch him, but I don't know if that's what he wants. The shot of confidence Gran gave me earlier is fading fast. His face is void of all expression, and the shadows from our headlights prevent me from seeing his eyes clearly. For all I know, he decided breaking up was a good idea and came here to tell me just that. At least he didn't do it at school. I should thank him for that. "Anyway, I'm sorry for Monday night. None of that was your fault. I just overreacted."

I turn to my car to shut it off when he grabs my arm. "Where are you going?"

"Uh. Inside. I'll let you get back to whatever it is you were doing," I say, gesturing at The Beast. I turn toward my car again, but he tightens his grip.

"You don't want to hear what I have to say?"

"It's okay. I totally understand." I can't bear to look at him. I thought not being with him would be the best thing, but now that he's so close, I've changed my mind. I wish I could take back everything I said Monday night in his truck. He steps closer and lets go of my arm.

"Are you done?"

"With what?"

"Being a dumb girl. Because I'd really like to kiss you now, Mrs. Tennyson." Before I can finish gasping, his lips are on mine, stealing my breath and swallowing my cry of relief. I'm vaguely aware that my parents are inside about a hundred feet away, but I don't care. His kisses are frantic. He cups my face with his hands and pulls me even closer. We use our lips and tongues and teeth to hold an entire conversation without saying a word. Gentle nips and sweet strokes replace everything I meant to say, which is good because I don't think I could form a complete sentence if I tried. The only thing that breaks the moment is my need for air. Stupid lungs. We stand in the driveway bathed in headlights, gulping in the cool evening air. He brings his forehead to mine, then tips his head to the side and kisses me on the cheek.

"We good now?"

I laugh and kiss him in response.

"I'll take that as a yes. You sort of stole my thunder, you know."

"How'd I do that?"

"I came over here with Lucy. I was gonna sing you a song I wrote tonight to win you back."

"You wrote me a song at work?"

"Yeah, I was pretty worthless. Mandy took pity on me."

"I still wanna hear it. Will you still play it for me? Please?" I offer up my best puppy dog eyes and clasp my hands below my chin.

"Fine, fine. Have it your way," he says, grinning. We both turn off our vehicles and he returns with his guitar. "Is your dad home?"

"Yeah, why?"

"Well, the last time I was here, I was dressed as Jamie. I just hope my disguise was good enough."

"I don't think you have anything to worry about." I open the front door and pull James inside.

"Mom? Dad?"

"In the living room!" Mom calls. "Are you back already?"

"Sort of," I say, as we round the corner. "Apparently James

and I had the same idea. You remember James, right Mom?" She jumps off the chaise lounge.

"Hi! It's good to see you again." She hugs him and winks at me over his shoulder. I didn't even know Mom knew how to wink. Dad closes the recliner and walks over to us.

"Dad, this is James." I search for any hint of recognition in my Dad's eyes as they shake hands, but everything seems okay.

"Please call me Stan. It's nice to meet you, son."

"Likewise, sir."

"Is it all right if James and I go to my room? I promise to keep my door open." I expect a silent standoff, but surprisingly Dad's the one to respond.

"As long as it stays open, that's fine. If you'll excuse me, I've got some Walking Dead to catch up on."

"Thanks, Dad!" I grab James' hand and walk toward my bedroom when Avery's face flashes on my phone. I push the "end" button, but five steps later, she calls again. I let out a frustrated sigh and swipe to answer it.

"What's up?" She's hysterical, and I can't make out anything she's saying. "You need to calm down. I can't understand you." James comes up to my side and rubs my back. I shrug my shoulders and mouth, "I don't know" as Avery launches into another round of tears. "Avery. Calm down. Take a deep breath. Good. Take another. What's going on?"

"I n-need you to come g-get me f-from the h-hospital," she chokes out.

"Is everything okay?"

"F-Fletcher's mom r-rushed Sam here because she swallowed a p-penny. Sh-she was breathing, b-but it wouldn't c-come out. We m-met them in the emergency r-room and I helped F-fletcher do the p-paperwork. That's his d-daughter, Ray. *Daughter*." She loses it again, and I know getting anything else out of her is pointless.

"Okay, stay there. I'm on my way." I turn to James to apologize for cutting the evening short, but he stops me before I can say anything.

"My truck's blocking your car. I'll drive."

I quickly explain what's going on to Mom then hop in The Beast after James opens the door.

"So I guess Fletcher's a dad?"

"Yup."

"You knew?"

He exhales. "Yup."

"Why didn't you tell me?"

"It wasn't my place to." He grabs my hand and kisses it. "Please don't be mad at me."

"I don't think I'm mad. Just shocked. Dude. Fletcher has a kid?"

James

I buckle my seatbelt certain of two things: I'm gonna have an epic weekend, and I have a one in eleven million chance of dying before that happens. Statistically, I'm safer in a plane than in a car, but I don't see how that's possible. Cars don't drive seven miles above the ground.

I didn't really give the fear of flying much thought when I agreed to come to New York City with Avery and Rachel. After we took her home Wednesday night, she asked her dad to update the tickets. I guess it's cheaper to switch the names than it was to cancel them. Avery said she needed to take a break and process the fact that Fletcher is a dad instead of a big brother. I get that. Ray asked me if I knew what was gonna happen between them. I don't, but I'm hoping I can talk with Avery this weekend and give her Fletcher's perspective.

As far as the trip goes, I was surprised that Rachel's parents said okay, even after they heard I was going too. Avery pulled out all the stops—tears, her breakup and the eighteenth birthday card—and Ray had to promise to FaceTime her parents every night.

"You gonna be okay, James?" Avery asks from the window seat. She called dibs on that before we even got to the airport. Rachel took the middle, and I sat in the aisle seat. That's fine by me. I'd rather not stare out at the ground the whole flight.

I give her a thumbs up between deep breaths. Rachel rests her hand on my knee, which I hadn't realized was bouncing so hard. Combined with my sweating and pounding heart, I must look like an addict on a comedown. I search the seat back in front of me for a tiny parachute, but only find a sticky Sky Mall magazine and an empty candy wrapper.

"Are you always this nervous before you fly?" Rachel asks.

"I couldn't tell you. This is my first flight." I reach for the bottle of water in my backpack as the flight attendants start their spiel with all the ways we could die. If we crash over water, some yellow inflatable life preserver is supposed to help us. I'm pretty sure that's just to make the bodies more visible for the search teams. *"Affirmative, I have a positive visual on the rubber duckies in the wreckage."* Do sharks like the color yellow? Are they colorblind? Are we even going to fly over water?

"But you've spent your whole life moving around. How have you never flown?"

"Easy. It's called cars. Except for the one time we took a train."

"Wow, that's something I never expected to hear."

"Mom was a hippie. How can we appreciate traveling through the country if we couldn't roll down the windows and breathe in the scenery? Plus, gas was cheaper than plane tickets."

"I guess that makes sense. Don't worry though, we'll be just fine. The flight's only an hour and a half. We'll be there before you know it."

Or, we could be dead before we know it. My grip on the armrest increases as we taxi away from the terminal. *Fuck*, I'm too young to die.

"Ladies and gentlemen, we're cleared for takeoff. Please make sure your seatbelts are buckled." If my seatbelt was any tighter, I'd cut off circulation to the lower half of my body.

"This is my favorite part!" Avery squeals.

"Yes, hurdling into the air and hoping the principles of physics hold are my favorite parts too," I say, trying to not whimper like a little bitch. Rachel laughs and gives a squeal herself, then looks over at me.

"Hey." She cups my face in her hand as the pilot increases the speed. The nose lifts off the ground and her lips meet mine. By the time our tongues tangle, my stomach feels like it's on a roller coaster—glued to the seat one moment, and then lodged somewhere between my ears the next. Logically, I know that's because we're airborne now, but I'm giving Rachel all the credit anyway.

She's a damn good kisser.

Ever the thoughtful girlfriend, she keeps me distracted for most of the flight. I might be sporting a case of blue balls for the rest of the night, but I consider it a small price to pay.

"We're making our final descent into New York LaGuardia. The flight attendants will come through one more time to collect any remaining trash and to ensure your seatbelts are buckled."

"Eeek! This is my favorite part!"

"That's what you said about takeoff," Rachel says.

"No. Look." She opens the sunshades—there are two windows in our row—and instead of seeing my impending death below, I'm greeted by city lights. The sun must have set while Rachel and I were inspecting each other's mouths. I've seen pictures of Manhattan, sure, but nothing compares to the sight of a million lights shining from its skyscrapers.

"Holy shit." I crane my neck to see as much as possible. The pilot banks to the right, which brings more lights into view. "That's incredible."

"Looks like you're not so scared anymore." Rachel smirks and gives me a kiss on the cheek.

"Nah, I'm feeling nice and loose. Well, most of me anyway." I wink and adjust my pants just a bit before looking out the window again. Rachel rolls her eyes and facepalms.

An hour later, we're in front of Avery's dad's condo on the Upper West Side.

"Don't worry about your luggage, I'll have those up just shortly."

"Thanks, Jensen!" Avery high fives the driver who greeted us at baggage claim. Rachel mentioned Mr. Murphy being some rich business dude, but she didn't elaborate. I'm beginning to realize that having a driver is the tip of the iceberg.

"Hey, Moe! Good to see you again!" Avery hugs the gray-haired doorman before we enter the lobby.

"Miss Avery, how you doin'?"

"Now that I've seen you, I'm excellent. Heading up to see the old man now. See you tomorrow?"

"Sure thing, sweets."

"So you have a thing for older guys, huh?" Rachel jokes

as we step into the elevator. Avery punches the button for the twenty-fourth floor.

"Moe has been the doorman in this building since I was in elementary school. I used to sit outside with him after school and eat candy. When I became a teenager, he'd interview any boyfriend who came over and mention his connections to the Mafia." She giggles at the memory.

"Moe's in the Mafia?" I can't help but ask.

"No, dummy. It was all for fun. He loved messing with their heads."

The elevator stops and within ten seconds, I'm speechless. Avery's dad isn't just rich. He's fucking *loaded*.

"Hey Pops, we're here." She leads us through the foyer into a living room twice the size of the one at Rachel's house, which is huge to begin with. The ceilings have to be at least twenty feet high. The walls feature art and opulent drapes and there's even a baby grand piano in the corner.

"Hey, glad you made it!" He hugs her and shakes our hands. "I'm Todd Murphy, it's nice to meet you." We meet almost eye-to-eye, though it looks like I have about an inch on him. His skin is quite a bit darker than Avery's. She definitely has his smile, though.

"Hi, Mr. Murphy. Thanks for the flight and for letting us stay here," I say.

"Please, call me Todd. And don't mention it. I had some rewards points that were going to expire, so you actually did me a favor. Now those damn credit card people will quit hounding me." He smiles and gestures to the couch. "Would you like to have a seat, or are you hungry?"

Avery wrinkles her nose. "Who cooked—you or Hannah?"

"Does it look like the building burned down?" he says with a laugh. "Hannah cooked, of course. She left some plates in the fridge for you."

"Yes! Come on, y'all are about to be impressed." We follow her into the kitchen, where she pulls out three plates of chicken parmesan.

"Has Hannah worked here since you were in elementary school too?" Rachel asks.

"No, she came after we left. Dad can't cook to save his life. If it wasn't for Mom, and now Hannah, he'd starve."

Avery was right about being impressed. The food was phenomenal, and just what I needed since I didn't eat much before the flight. I glance at my watch and realize it's already ten p.m. Judging by the amount of adrenaline I've dealt with today and the size of the meal I just ate, it won't be long until I pass out.

"Hey, what room am I staying in? I think I'm gonna hit the sack after a quick shower to wash the plane off of me."

"I'm pretty beat too. I'll give y'all a quick tour." She grabs Rachel's hand and leads us through the sprawling condo. It's a three bedroom, five bathroom. I'll never understand why people need more toilets than beds, but whatever. I'm not here to judge. Her dad's room is across the house, and the other two bedrooms are on the Central Park side of the building. She opens the door to her room, which is tastefully decorated in a Parisian theme. Go figure. Her suitcases—because the girl can't just pack one for the weekend—are sitting just inside the door.

"Is Jensen a ninja or something? I didn't even see him come inside," Rachel says, laughing. She angles her head into the room. "Hey, where's my suitcase?"

"It's down here," Avery says, leading us to the opposite end of the short hallway. She opens the door and flips on the light. As promised, Rachel's suitcase is there. Right next to mine.

"Um. Avery?" Rachel points to our luggage. "Why is James' suitcase in here too?"

"I may have left out that detail when we were talking to your parents." A devilish grin creeps over her face. "You and James are rooming together this weekend. My bed is a twin and Dad doesn't believe in air mattresses. Hannah will make us a big breakfast tomorrow, so I hope you're hungry. Oh! This will be y'all's bathroom." She points to the door we're standing in front of before turning back toward her bedroom. "Goodnight!"

Rachel and I stare at each other in the hallway, neither of us making a move. *Sweet baby Jesus.* "I promise I had no idea this was going to happen," I say, holding my hands up in surrender. The last thing I want her to think is that I only came because I knew about the sleeping arrangements. Not that I'm remotely sad about the news. I am a dude, after all.

"I believe you. Uh. Should we get ready for bed, then?" She peeks at the doorway, then back to me. Redness creeps over her cheeks and a giggle slips past her lips.

"You don't need to be nervous, you know."

"Why's that? Is this the part where you tell me you'll be a perfect gentleman?"

"No, it's the part where I remind you this isn't our first time sleeping together." I wiggle my eyebrows, then enter the room and flop down on the bed. The very spacious bed. It's gotta be a king, or maybe even a California king. "Dibs on this side!"

"Um. You're in the middle." She's standing at the foot of the bed with her hands on her hips. I admit, I'm jealous of her hands.

"Hey, it's not my fault you didn't call dibs first," I offer with an innocent shrug.

"Fine. I call dibs on the first shower."

"I could help you with that, you know," I say, rubbing my hands together.

"Nice try, Romeo." She grabs her toiletries and pajamas out of her suitcase and disappears down the hallway. I spend the next ten minutes fantasizing about what's going on beyond that door. Now I'm glad she decided to shower first, because I'm gonna need a few extra minutes to... relax... when it's my turn.

Like I said. I'm a dude.

She comes back into the bedroom in a cloud of vanilla, and I have to restrain myself from biting her. I'm pretty sure that smell could wake me from a coma. "You better have left me hot water, Mrs. Tennyson."

"I could have showered for six hours and there'd still be hot water."

The bathroom is ridiculous. There's no other word to describe it. It's half the size of my bedroom, and the shower is sectioned off by a wall of glass bricks that curve around like a shell. It features six different jets along a wall of natural tile and one that pours water from the ceiling. Rachel left her body wash on the shelf, and I decide it's exactly what I need to help me... unwind.

A few minutes later, I'm clean and ready for bed. My eyelids are heavy by the time we both peel back the covers.

"Are you sure you're okay with this?" I ask with a yawn. I don't want her feeling uncomfortable. "I'm sure there are about eleven different couches I could crash on."

"No, it's fine."

I sleep in just boxer briefs at home, but I've upgraded to boxer shorts on top of them for tonight. My shirt's gotta go, though. I lift my eyebrow when Rachel sucks in a breath. "Still okay?" She looks me up and down, and her cheeks redden for the second time tonight.

"Yeah. Just don't get mad at me if I stare. And don't get any big ideas." She points her finger at me for emphasis.

"I'll even put a pillow between us if that will make you feel better." I place one of the gigantic shams in the middle of the bed and settle in. "Good night, Mrs. Tennyson."

"Usually you're FaceTiming me when you say that," she says with a soft giggle. Her hand finds mine over the pillow. "Good night, Mr. Tennyson."

Yes, this is the single greatest night of my life.

"James?" she whispers a few minutes later.

"Hrmh?"

"Do you think we could ditch the pillow?"

"That can definitely be arranged." With one quick motion, the pillow is on the floor and Rachel's in my arms. I don't know what feels better—the soft cotton of her tank top or her long hair trailing across my chest. I kiss the top of her head and close my eyes, enjoying the sound of our breathing and the beating of our hearts.

"James?"

"Hmmph?"

"Why do you smell like vanilla?"

You'd think falling asleep next to the girl of my dreams would mean I'd actually dream about her. Sadly, I was wrong. I've had some messed up dreams lately and at least this one didn't fall into that category. Instead it was just... weird. It was about my volunteer shift at the animal hospital on Thursday—the day after Rachel and I made up and Avery found out about Fletcher. Dr. Brooks had me working the front desk because the receptionist was out. About an hour before my shift ended, Vivien Tanner and her mom came in with an ancient cat. He'd had a few seizures and they were there to put him down.

Dr. Brooks took Mrs. Tanner and Roscoe to the back while Vivien filled out the paperwork. I had to give her credit though. For as much as she tried to get my attention in school, she seemed to be behaving herself that night. She returned the clipboard and paid for the visit, then went back to the waiting area and played on her phone, never making eye contact with me. I heard her sniffling as I finished re-filing the day's charts, but ignored them. Vivien struck me as the kind of girl to take a mile when you give her an inch, you know? When they persisted, I felt like an ass, so I walked over to the chair next to her.

"I'm sorry about your loss." I had no idea what she was going through because I'd never had a pet before Laz. I'd be pretty bummed if something happened to him.

"We've had that cat since I was two." She whimpered again, so I grabbed some Kleenex off the bookshelf and passed it to her. She dabbed her eyes and fiddled with her phone a bit more. "I really appreciate your kindness. I know I must look like a mess right now. When you see me at school, just pretend like you never saw me with mascara running down my face, okay?"

"You have nothing to worry about, Vivien. You're a beautiful girl." Against my better judgment, I offered her a quick hug then stood to return to the front desk.

"Thanks James. That means so much to me."

"Any time."

Brushing my weird dream aside, I turn my attention to the feeling of Rachel's body next to mine. Part of me wishes I could ditch our plans for the day—whatever they are—and stay just like this. We still need to sit down and figure out our schedules for the next few months. Mom said I could fly up here once a month to see Rachel (thank you, extra money from selling the farm), and I'm pretty sure Fletcher will let me crash at his house. It's not the most ideal solution, but it's the best one I have at the moment. I realize that I never had a chance to sing the song I wrote for her and make a mental note to do that when we get home. Technically, I don't need to since we're back together, but I'd like her to know how I felt when we weren't.

"What's that you're humming?" Her breath is huskier than normal, and the sound travels straight to my groin. I hadn't given much thought to that morning issue guys deal with, but it's becoming more pronounced as each second passes.

"Humming?" I release her body and shift to my side to stare her. And also to put some distance between my midsection and hers. Boxers can only hide so much.

"Yeah, I woke up to you humming. What was it?"

"The song I wrote for you. I didn't get a chance to play it for you yet."

"Well then, we'll have to fix that."

She kisses me on the cheek then sits up to stretch, revealing the design on her pajamas—polar bears and ice cream bars. "I meant to compliment you on your choice of nighttime apparel. Very cute."

"What would *you* do for a Klondike bar, Mr. Tennyson?" she asks with a wicked grin.

"I plead the fifth." I need some space before I embarrass us both, so I decide it's a good time to get out of bed. I rummage through my suitcase on the way to the bathroom when Rachel leaps off the bed and kneels down in front of me. I suck in a breath and will all of my appendages to behave themselves.

"Um. Can I help you?"

"I can't believe I forgot about your other two tattoos. This is gorgeous." She traces her finger over a tattoo of a compass and treasure map that wraps around my left calf.

"Why does the banner say 'Home Sweet Home'?"

"With as much as we moved, I figured I could use all the help I could get to find my home."

"And did it work?"

"It did. I found you. My home and my treasure all in one. And *God*, that sounded a lot less corny in my head." I facepalm as we both laugh.

"And this is tattoo number four?" she asks, tapping the top of my left foot.

"Yup. It's the Braille word for faith."

"What's the story behind that one?"

"This was actually the last one I got. I was talking to Gran about my map and compass tattoo and I mentioned being worried that I'd never figure out where I was supposed be. What if I never found the 'X' on my map, you know? She said I needed to keep the faith, even when I couldn't see it. So, blind faith."

"Leave it to Gran to have simple answers to life's problems." Rachel shifts over to her luggage. "Did she tell you she came to see me on Wednesday?"

"No, I had no idea."

"Yeah, she talked some sense into me. Which included her calling me stupid a few times." She laughs and pulls an outfit from her suitcase. "It was a nice visit though. We talked about y'all's move and what that means for us."

"Gran reminds me of that girl from Peanuts that sets up the sign that says 'Psychiatric help, five cents. God, I'm gonna miss her." I'm trying to adapt her "struggle with joy" mentality, but it's not always easy. I pull my clothes from my suitcase and look up to see Rachel's eyebrows drawn together.

"Why would you miss her? You're moving to Florida, right?"

"Right. I didn't want to, but that changed when I found out about her cancer."

"Gran has *cancer*?" Her hand flies to her mouth and tears well in her eyes.

"She didn't tell you?" *Shit.* I drop the clothes in my hand and pull Rachel into my arms. "I'm so sorry, Ray. I haven't had a chance to talk to you about it yet. I found out Wednesday morning. When you said she came to your house, I figured she told you too. She's dealt with it off and on for the last several years, but it's back and it's not going away."

"How can someone as amazing as Gran have such a horrible disease?" she asks between sobs.

"Fuck if I know. I still can't believe it either." We sit on the bed as I fill her in on everything Gran told me, complete with her dirty jokes. Thankfully, they did their job, and Rachel finally smiles.

"You know what this means, right?" she asks, wiping her face.

"What?"

"We're gonna need all of her pie recipes."

Avery didn't skimp on the NYC tourism plans. So far, we've covered Jane's Carousel and Battery Park with a lot of ogling in between. Rachel made us walk across the Brooklyn Bridge on the way back and took no less than four hundred pictures along the way. She decided she wants to decorate her dorm room with a mosaic of our pictures, including a photo of our hands making a heart at every place we've stopped. I like to tease her about it, but I don't mind.

"James, wait! I wanna get one of us kissing with the Statue of Liberty in the background!"

"Babe, you took that about five minutes ago. I know, because you texted it to me right after." I lift my phone as proof. "See? Liberty in love. *And* you got the one of our heart hands. I'm starving and Avery promised us Chinese. Why don't I get a photo of you hailing your first taxi?" A guy across the street catches my attention as I snap the picture. He's well-dressed in dark jeans and a black jacket, yet he doesn't look out of place in the middle of the runners and families visiting Battery Park. His dark hair is cropped short, giving him the appearance of a clean-cut guy. He's too far away for me to get a better look at his face, though. Aviator sunglasses block his eyes, but I can still feel him staring at me. It's one of those movie moments where everything fades away except you and the person watching you. Except this feels more like a scene from a horror movie than a chick flick. Instinctively, I grab Rachel's hand and lead her into the taxi. I keep eye contact—well, sunglasses contact—until the last possible minute. I don't know who he is, but I don't like him.

"Hey, do you know that guy?" I ask Avery when she shuts the door.

"What guy?"

"The one over there." I point, but the spot he was standing on is now empty.

"Why would you think I know a random dude on the street in the middle of New York City?" She shakes her head and laughs at me, then gives the cabbie the address to the restaurant.

"Wait." I pull up the photo on my phone and zoom in to show her, but I guess I caught him as he hailed his own cab because his hand is blocking his face.

"Yup, I totally know him. That's the kid who sat next to me in fifth grade. *Seriously*, James?" She gives me another headshake and turns her attention to her own phone.

"You okay?" Rachel asks quietly, eyeing me.

I look out the back windshield one last time as the cabbie eases into traffic. "Yeah, I think so. Something about that guy gives me the willies. He was probably a director for a porno movie looking for his next star. Too bad you're only seventeen," I say, trying to lighten the mood. The last thing I want is her worrying over nothing.

At least I hope it's nothing.

The cab ride was short and didn't end with any major whiplash, so I consider it a victory. Avery's dad gave us his credit card for an all-expenses paid day in the city so taxis and food are covered. I'm glad she had the sense to take us to an all-you-can-eat buffet in Chinatown because I'm finishing my third plate. "What did you say your dad does again? I couldn't imagine forking over my credit card to my teenager and her friends," I ask around a mouth full of chicken fried rice.

"He's a hedge fund manager."

"What is that?"

"I have no idea. When I was little, I told my teacher he took care of the landscaping at banks." She laughs and spears another pork dumpling.

"Do you miss living in the city?" Rachel asks.

"Sometimes, but he and Mom were so unhappy that I was glad when we moved to North Carolina. The city is an amazing place, but I wouldn't want to raise my kids here."

"Why not?" I ask.

"It's hard to explain." She pauses for another bite of lo mein. "It's like the city forces you to grow up too fast. I mean, y'all saw the kids on the train by themselves this morning. Nine and ten years old, and it's perfectly normal. Just try to imagine Sammy riding the train by herself five years from now." She frowns and twirls more noodles around her fork. "I miss her." She hasn't talked much about Fletcher since Wednesday night, but she's obviously still upset. "Anyway, enough of that." She signals for the check. "I have more to show y'all and the day's not getting any younger."

When the waiter comes, she scribbles her dad's name and passes out our fortune cookies.

"You go first, James," Ray says.

I break the cookie and take a bite before I read the fortune. "When you're lying on black and white, make sure your choice is right." For a split second, my body feels twice as heavy and goose bumps erupt all over my body. I plaster a smile on my face and slip my jacket on before anyone notices.

"Lying is never the right choice," Avery says with an eye roll.

"Avery, it wasn't like he was lying to just you," Rachel says quietly. "He was doing what he thought was best for Sam."

"Well, what's best for Avery is no lying. After everything I told him about Derrick, he should have known better." She cracks open her fortune cookie. "A man with brown eyes has a surprise for you. Just what I fucking need." She rolls her eyes again.

"Okay, Mrs. Tennyson. Your turn," I say, trying to ease the tension around the table.

"You will be hungry again in thirty minutes. James, I think I got yours by mistake." She sticks her tongue out at me. On the way out, I slide my fortune into my wallet. I need to figure out what it means and why I reacted the way I did.

"Where to next, Beef?" Rachel asks.

"It's time to see the city from the top. We're going to the Empire State Building." Her smile's back, which is good. We can save the serious discussion about Fletcher for later. Avery leads us through crowded streets to the subway. I have no idea how far underground we are, but I'm pretty sure we'd survive the zombie apocalypse down here. The girls take a slew of selfies on the way, and Avery snaps a not-so-discrete picture of the guy next to me. Apparently there's a thing on Instagram called Hot Dudes Reading. Who knew?

The doors open to music at the 34th Street and Herald Square station, so we walk toward it. Four guys have set up a makeshift stage and we catch the last few seconds of a song. "Is it always like this?" I ask Avery.

"What, random shit in the subway?"

"Yeah."

"Always," she says with a laugh. "We could probably go a few stops up and see a man with a dancing dog."

When they start into the next song, I grab Rachel's hand and start dancing with her. If there's such a thing as perfect moments in the universe, this is one.

"What song is this?"

"It's called *Cold Night* by You Me at Six." I don't bother telling her any more than that and sing to her instead. I've always loved this song, but after the news about Florida, it's even more fitting.

"Thanks, everyone! We'll be back in a few." The lead singer steps down and walks into the men's room.

"That was pretty badass, dude," I tell the guitarist.

"Thanks man! We're just out here havin' some fun and makin' a few bucks." He takes a hit off an e-cigarette and tunes his guitar. "If you like what you heard, we've got a couple of CDs for sale."

"Arizona Grace, huh?" I ask, picking up a disc. "Y'all ever been out there?"

"Nope," he laughs, but doesn't elaborate.

"You should. The scenery is worth the trip." I take a ten out of my wallet to pay for the CD and turn to Rachel. "Can you put this in your purse?"

"Sure thing, Mr. Tennyson." The look on her face tells me she's up to something.

"Excuse me, what's your name?" she asks the guitarist.

"Lenny."

"Hi, Lenny." She flashes a grin at him. "I have a request. Would you mind if my boyfriend borrowed your guitar?"

"What?" we both ask in unison.

"He wrote a song for me a few days ago, but hasn't had a chance to play it yet. I figured he could keep the crowd warmed up while your other guy is in the bathroom."

Lenny and I look at each other, then back at Rachel.

"Uh. I guess?" He looks about as confused as I do but lifts the strap off his shoulder and holds it out toward me.

"A little warning next time, Ray?" I smile and shake my head. I can't believe she's doing this to me.

"You shouldn't need any warning," she says with a smirk. "A good musician is always ready, right?"

"Whatever you say." I take the stage and adjust the mic. "Okay, Ray. Technically, I don't *need* to sing it to you, but here's your song. This is *Be With Me*."

Rachel

He winks at me, then strums the opening chord.

Be With Me
When you walked in that room
My heart started beating for you
I know it's nuts to say stuff like this
But you have to know that it's true
Yes, we're only seventeen
Would it be better if we were thirty-three?
Would age break down the barrier
You've set between you and me?
Some people spend their whole lives
Looking for a love that's not there
Why are you so willing to throw away
This gift that's ours to share?
I want to spend my life with you
This isn't just some game

I could be old and gray, or I could die today
I'd use my last breath to say your name
We can beat the challenges
I know that it's possible
If you'd just keep your head
From being my obstacle
Forget all the shit
And just focus on me
Shut down your fears
And let your heart be
With me

Every other time I've watched him sing, he's kept his eyes open. I think he enjoys taking it all in when he's performing. But this time he keeps them closed. The smirk that played at his lips when he took the guitar is replaced with a seriousness that I've never seen. He sings with his eyebrows drawn together, almost as if the lyrics physically pain him. He lets the last note hang in the air for several beats, then snaps out of his lyrical trance and passes the guitar back to Lenny with a smile.

"Thanks, dude."

"Uh, yeah. No problem, man."

"Well, shit. If you ain't gonna go up there and show that young man some lovin', I sure as hell will. You're goddamn skippy right I will." I turn behind me to see a forty-something-year-old bag lady giving my boyfriend bedroom eyes. She runs her tongue over her thin, dry lips and I flash back to seeing Vivien do the same thing last week at lunch—though Vivien's lips were unfortunately in much better condition.

"I've got it covered, thanks." I hope I don't have to get physical with this woman. How the hell am I supposed to

FaceTime my parents from jail for an assault charge on a homeless person after my boyfriend serenaded me on a subway platform?

"Well, did my song woo you back?" James asks, rescuing me from my overactive imagination. I look back at the bag lady, but she's already shuffling away from the crowd.

"Consider me officially wooed, Mr. Tennyson." I stand on my tip-toes and wrap my arms around his neck. "I'm sorry I put you through that, but thank you for the song. It was beautiful."

"I told you she loves open mic night." Avery says. She wipes tears from her eyes and gives James the middle finger. "Come on, let's get going." She takes my arm to push our way out of the small crowd, but the lead singer of Arizona Grace stops us before we can leave.

"Hey, Hootie!"

"Close! It's James." He laughs as he turns back to the stage. "Thanks for letting me borrow your mic, Toad the Wet Sprocket."

"Only my mom calls me that. My friends call me Roth. And no sweat. That was pretty good! You live around here?" he asks in a thick New York accent.

"Nah, just visiting."

"We're playing tonight at Labyrinth if you wanna come."

"What's Labyrinth?" I ask Avery.

"Oh man, I haven't been there in *ages*! Yeah, we'll be there!" she says, answering for the three of us.

"Awesome. Our set starts at nine. Let me know if you're up for singing some more tonight. I like the way you sound."

Avery and I shriek in unison, sending out an echo that

could kill a colony of bats. "James, you're gonna be famous!" I grab his arm and jump up and down.

"Calm down, Goldilocks. It's just Labyrinth," Roth says with a smile. "Be there an hour early and we'll go over the set list. We start with some covers that you'll probably know before we do our original stuff."

"Will do." James shakes his hand, then leans in and whispers something in Roth's ear. They both do some nodding and exchange numbers.

"Catch ya later, Blind Melon!" Roth says.

"Later, Pearl Jam!" James leads us through the crowd and up the stairs. "Well, Mrs. Tennyson. It looks like you got me a gig in NYC. I should've put that on my bucket list so I could cross it off. Fletcher's gonna freak when he hears."

"What was all that whispering?"

"Let's just say a man with green eyes has a surprise for you."

"Does this mean I get to be your groupie? The president of your fan club? I'm uploading your performance on Facebook and Instagram, just so you know."

"Duly noted. Now come on. Let's make out on the top of the Empire State Building," he says with a wicked grin.

"I second that motion!" I hop on his back for the rest of the short walk. Avery—well, Todd—sprung for express tickets, so we got to skip the line for the main deck. She told me what it was like, and I've seen "Sleepless in Seattle," but none of that could really prepare me for the sight of New York City from the eighty-sixth floor.

"Welcome to the bird's eye view of the city," Avery says, sweeping her arm up like Vanna White.

"My God, this is the most incredible thing I've ever seen."

James walks up behind me and spins me around. "This is the second most incredible thing I've ever seen." I open my mouth to tell him how sweet he is when he interrupts me. "The most incredible thing was seeing this fifty-three-year-old lady polish off a forty-ounce steak back in Topeka."

"Thanks for spoiling the moment, Romeo." I smack him on the shoulder and roll my eyes, but laugh anyway. He pulls me into a hug and traces the shell of my ear with his lips. I love it when he does that. Avery smiles and makes a fake gagging noise, then walks to the other side of the observation deck.

"Nah, the most incredible thing was seeing this blonde chick practically throw herself at me on my first day of school. I felt bad for her, so I decided to play along."

"Oh, is that how the story goes?" I giggle.

"Yup. I haven't had the heart to tell her I'm not interested, so I'm forced to fake it every day. It's awful." He feigns a sigh. His phone chirps from his pocket, and he angles himself so I can't see the screen. A smile creeps over his face while he responds.

"What's going on?" I try to peek at the message, but he jerks the phone closer to him.

"Nothing! Just telling Fletcher about my gig tonight." He stows his phone in his back pocket and pulls me into his arms.

Fine. Two can play at that game.

"We need our Empire State selfie, Mr. Tennyson." I pull my phone out and snap the picture, then take our heart hands photo to add to my growing collection.

"I'm not happy about the Avery and Fletcher situation, but I'm glad that I get to be here with you," I say, wrapping my arms around his back. He's not quite as muscular as I imagined in my dream the day he first kissed me, but I still have zero complaints. I pretty much hit the jackpot as far as hot boyfriends go. "Do you have any predictions about whether they'll make up?"

His eyes narrow slightly as he scans the view below. "No, nothing so far. It's frustrating to not be able to see memories when I want to, especially when it comes to helping my friends."

I slide my hands to his lower back. "Maybe you don't see anything because they'll patch things up on their own."

"Maybe." He rests his head on mine. I use that moment to snatch his phone out of his pocket then run like hell around the corner of the observation deck while I try to pull up his text messages. He catches up to me in about six strides. "Fork it over, Blondie!" His arms swat at my hands. I twist and duck out of his reach, and my fingers finally land on the green messages icon. The last message was from me when I texted our photo from the Statue of Liberty.

"You erased it!" I stand up and jab his chest in mock indignation.

"Erased what?" he asks with his most innocent voice while tucking his phone in his pocket again.

"Your last text!"

"I have no idea what you're talking about."

"You're up to something, and I'm gonna figure out what it is." I cross my arms. The wind whips my hair around, which makes holding a staring contest next to impossible.

"Doubtful." He gathers my tresses in his hand and gently pulls, angling my face toward his. "But don't worry. You won't

256

have to wait long." His eyes sparkle with excitement as he places chaste kisses on the sides of my mouth.

"Well, it better be good is all I'm saying."

"Oh, it's gonna be better than good. You'll see."

It's official. Avery has lost her damn mind. "There is no way in God's green earth I'm wearing this tonight, Murphy." I can't believe she has me trapped in a fitting room again. This means she's due for some torture, too. Maybe I'll hack up a pair of her precious red-soled heels.

"You can't go to Labyrinth wearing anything you packed," she says from outside the fitting room. "You'll look like a cornhusker from Kansas."

"That's Nebraska!" James shouts.

"Kansas, Nebraska. It's all the same. Anyway, if you hate that top, then try these two on." She throws more fabric over the top of the door. One is covered in multi-colored sequins and the other is ninety-five percent mesh. I pick up my phone and tap out an SOS text to James. At the rate I'm going, I'll be wearing my birthday suit to Labyrinth. Which I'm sure would go over really well with the male population. And some of the females. It *is* New York City, after all. I toss the shirts—do they even qualify as shirts?—back over the door without bothering to try them on.

"Not a chance. Go get something else."

"We're in the city, Ray! Live a little!"

"I'm living just fine, thank you. But I won't be living in either of those."

"Fine," she huffs. "But you're not going out looking like Mother Teresa. We've gotta find a balance here."

"Agreed. I'll get dressed and we'll try again, okay?"

"Don't bother getting dressed," James says from down the hall.

"What do you mean?"

"Here." His voice is right outside the door, and suddenly more clothes appear at the top. I take the hangers and study what he delivered. I don't know what surprises me more—the fact that he went and got me new clothes, or the fact that I actually *like* them. The skinny jeans are some sort of purpley-red color, and they hug me in all the right places. He also brought a shimmery silver tank top that's really soft on the inside and a thin black leather jacket that stops right at my hips. I study my reflection in the mirror, amazed at how well he pulled it off.

"Well?" Avery asks. I don't bother with a response and open the fitting room door instead. "Holy shit, James. Merlot jeans? What do you know about merlot jeans?"

"I know Ray's ass looks great in them." He winks at me, and I bite my lip as heat spreads over my cheeks.

"Seriously. How did you even pull this off?" she asks, gesturing to my outfit.

"Easy. I took the jeans to a sales girl and said I needed something to go with them that wasn't revealing. She took care of the rest." He was right—the top isn't revealing in the least bit. It's form-fitting, which I don't mind, but the neckline doesn't dip too low. I still feel sexy without being exposed.

"I love it! Thank you." I give him a quick kiss, then duck back into the fitting room to change.

"I can't believe I was bested by my Beef's boyfriend. God, I'm getting rusty."

"Don't worry, Ave. You're just off your game a little this weekend, that's all," I say as I put my clothes back on. When I open the door, I link arms with her and walk toward the cashier. "We've still gotta come up with something for James, and you know I'm totally useless."

"That's a fact," she says with a laugh. She hands her credit card to the cashier. Any guilt I had about Todd paying for everything quickly vanishes when I see the total.

"Holy shit! Four hundred and eighty three dollars? I only got three things!"

"Sorry, she's not from around here," Avery tells the cashier, as if she's letting her in on a secret. She scribbles on the receipt, takes the bag, and grins at me and James. "Okay, where to next?"

James and I stare at each other for several beats, then follow Avery out of the store. He starts singing the chorus to *Friends in Low Places* by Garth, only he changes the word "low" to "high." We take turns making up the lyrics on the way to the next shop.

And I won't frown
at those cashiers' faces
When it's time to pay
'Cause Todd will pay
And now we're buying at
all these places
Let's head downtown
to buy crystal vases

And maybe a Benz
or some Hermes shoelaces

"Hermes shoelaces? Really?" Avery asks with a smile.

"Don't be jealous of our lyrical abilities," I say, poking her in the shoulder. She rolls her eyes again and holds open the door to the next store.

Several hours later, we're back at her dad's condo, and I'm doing my best to not fall asleep. I think we walked about eight miles today. Normally, that would be a breeze for me, but combined with all the shopping and sightseeing, I'm toast.

"Here." Avery pops the top on a can of Monster and passes it to me.

"Thanks," I say, clinking my can against hers. "Dude, this pizza is amazing." We grabbed some pies from Freddie & Pepper's on the way home and now I'm ruined. Nothing else will ever compare.

"I've decided I want my dad to ship some down for my graduation party," Avery says.

"Did you ever hear anything from the colleges you applied to?" James asks around a mouthful of food.

"No, there hasn't been anything from FIT and I won't know anything about Parsons until sometime in April."

"And your dad hasn't said anything about a car for you?" I ask. Avery's birthday is on Tuesday.

"Nope. I swear to God after the week I've had, he better not have forgotten about his promise. Sharing a car with Mom is getting really old."

"Well, I wouldn't worry. I'm sure it'll all work out," James says, smiling. He shoves the last bite of pizza in his mouth, then puts his plate in the sink. "I'm gonna take a quick shower so you ladies can have the bathroom to yourselves to get ready. Unless you'd rather get ready now, Ray?" He looks at me with a mischievous smirk and taps his fingertips together.

"Nice try, bud. You go ahead."

He kisses me on the top of the head on his way to the bedroom. I love it when he does that. Avery lets out a sigh and quickly tries to cover it with a cough.

"I heard that."

"Sorry. I'm trying to not be a Debbie Downer." She wrinkles her nose and rubs the space between her eyebrows.

"Why don't you quit being so damn stubborn and just call him?" I ask with a pointed look. "James said Fletcher's pretty tore up."

"He *should* be. I specifically told him lying was a deal-breaker. I know we weren't dating that long, but I thought it could actually turn into something real. Serious. To find out now that he's part of a package deal changes everything."

"Yeah, but you have to admit—Sammy is a pretty awesome package."

"She is. But I don't know that I want to be a stepmom. At least not right now."

"Obviously a kid isn't just something that happens overnight. Do you even know his side of the story?"

"No." Her head dips down in a rare moment of embarrassment. "I left him at the hospital after I knew she'd be okay, and I haven't spoken to him since then."

My head drops to my arm on the table. "Avery, you're killing me," I say into the crook of my elbow. I take a cleansing breath, then lift my head again. "You've got a guy back at home that wants nothing more than to be with you. A good guy. One who clearly doesn't run away from responsibility. And you're willing to throw that all away?"

"Why aren't you trying to at least see things from my point of view?"

"I do. But you're making a bigger deal out of it than it needs to be. Four years ago, Fletcher had a baby. One he's been with *every day* since then. From what I know about him and what you've said since y'all started dating, he's a really great guy. He's not a manwhore. He doesn't do drugs. He even asks for extra shifts to earn more money." She starts to say something, but I hold my finger up to hush her. And then I open my mouth and Gran comes out.

"Hold on, I'm not done. You need to quit looking at what's happening right now and see the bigger picture. Fletcher is the best thing that's ever happened to you. He treats you well. Hell, he's the first guy who hasn't tried to get in your pants since I've known you. You owe it to him to hear his side of the story and give him a chance."

"That's easy for you to say. It's not like James has blindsided you with a big secret."

If only she knew. Psychic abilities has to rank somewhere close to secret daughter, right? "Avery, we all have secrets. But you have to choose whether or not you're going to let that ruin everything. I almost walked away from James because I didn't think we could make a long-distance relationship work at our age. And then a very wise person called me on my stupidity. Which is what I'm doing to you right now. I can't tell you what to do, but don't let your stubbornness keep you from someone who really cares about you." I stand up from the table and give her shoulder a squeeze on the way to the sink. Between the Monster that she gave me and the adrenaline from our conversation, I'm jittery. I feel like I need to keep moving. "Do you mind if I go down to the fitness center in the lobby real quick? I'm all keyed up and I figured I could put a few miles on the treadmill before it's time to get ready."

"That's fine," she says, gathering her plate and empty can. "But you don't need to go to the fitness center. You can use Daddy's home gym. It's down that hallway." She points in the direction of the master suite. Of *course* her dad has a home gym.

"Thanks," I say, walking out of the kitchen. This is as close as we've ever gotten to having an argument with each other, and the air between us feels awkward now. I open my mouth to apologize, but she beats me to it.

"I'm sorry, Beef. I know you're trying to help, and I thank you for that. I'll call him when we get home." She leans and gives me a hug.

"I love you, Avery. I want you to be happy. And even though you've been putting on a good show, I know you're not right now."

"You're right. But I plan on dancing my ass off tonight, so that should help," she says, wiggling her eyebrows. Her attempt at changing the subject doesn't go unnoticed, but I let it slide. "Now go get your sweat on so we can get ready."

"How are we gonna get in to Labyrinth? Do we need fake IDs?" I ask from the backseat of the town car. Todd insisted that

Jensen take us, and I didn't complain. We didn't have any problems on the subway today, but being on it at night creeps me out.

"It's teen night tonight. If you're over sixteen, you can get in," Avery says. She's wearing a sparkly bandage dress that she had hanging in her closet. It crisscrosses in the front and stops mid-thigh. Surprisingly, all of the important places are completely covered. She's paired it with three-inch heels that match the dress. Except, according to her, the dress is champagne-colored and the heels are nude. Whatever. Thankfully, we managed to find flat, strappy sandals to go with my skinny jeans earlier today. I told her I'd rather spend the evening at the club instead of the emergency room with a broken ankle. Besides. I'm tall enough already.

"I don't think anyone's gonna mistake you for being under sixteen tonight," I say.

"Y'all be careful when I'm up on stage, okay? I have no idea what city boys are like, but I've seen a lot of movies."

"Relax, Father James. We'll be fine," Avery says, giving James a reassuring pat on the arm. Jensen stops in front of a nondescript building and opens the door. We get out and I do a complete three-sixty in the street. No lights. No music. No people.

"Um. Avery? Where's the club?"

"It's back here," she says, walking toward an alley. *Great!* I knew I should have packed pepper spray. We make our way between two industrial buildings, the sound of music growing louder as we go. Avery reaches the corner and turns right. Up ahead, a bouncer with muscles that scream "I'm on steroids!" stands outside a blue door with a logo of a maze. Who puts the entrance at the back of the building? Now I understand how the club got its name. We follow Avery inside, and it takes several seconds for my ears to adjust to the volume. The bass from the house music pounds through the floor and up my legs, causing the butterflies in my stomach to flap a little harder. Did I mention I've never been to a club before? From the looks of it, there's about two or three hundred people here. I keep hold of Avery's arm so we don't get separated.

"Where are you supposed to meet Roth and Lenny?" I shout in James' ear.

"The door next to the stage. He texted me in the car and said to have y'all hang out on the upper level on the right side. I should have a clear view of you from the stage."

His words send a shiver down my body. One, because my boyfriend's gonna be up on that stage soon and holy shit, that's *so* hot. And two, because now he has me worried.

"Why do you need to be able to see us? Is there something you're not telling me?" I ask, gripping the side of his black shirt with my free hand.

"No, I just wanna be able to find you when I'm done with my part of the set. And like I said—a man with green eyes has a surprise for you. I wanna see your reaction." He bites his lip and gives me a hopeful smile. Oh my God, he's nervous and so damn adorable. If I don't walk away, I might eat his face right here.

"I'll see you soon, rock star. I'll be the one on the balcony checking out the singer on stage." I wink at him and plant a kiss on his mouth.

"Yeah, Roth is pretty hot," he says with a laugh. "See ya later, Mrs. Tennyson. Take good care of my girl, Avery."

"Yeah, yeah," she smiles. "Break a leg or whatever."

"Thanks!" He squeezes my hand once, then heads toward the door. Avery and I push past a wall of writhing bodies to climb the stairs. The upper level is a little less crowded, but we still have to elbow and nudge our way to the railing. I step in something sticky on the way and pray it's a spilled drink and not dried bodily fluids.

"How many times have you been here?" I ask.

"I used to come here about once a month before we moved." Avery says it like it's no big deal.

"God, we grew up so differently," I laugh. "I've never been to a club and you practically lived here."

"You've never been to a club? I'd say I'm surprised, but I'm really not. That's okay. We'll make up for it tonight." Avery shakes her ass, causing light to bounce off the sequins on her dress.

"You look like a disco ball!" I laugh. She puts her hand on her hips, cocks an eyebrow and gives me a side-eye. "A very sexy disco ball. One that is not actually shaped like a ball, I might add," digging the hole even deeper. *Backpedal, Ray.* "How about 'you look like a smokin' hot island princess?"

"What?"

"Between the color of your dress and the color of your skin, you look all sparkly and tropical." It's true. Her ethnicity means she can pull off so many colors. I'd envy her for it, but I rock the pale blond look. And James apparently prefers that over sparkly tropical anyway. Avery looks at her dress, then back at me.

"Nice recovery, Wheaton. Now, while the house lights are still up, let's see if there's any man candy up here." She turns her head casually, scanning the balcony.

"I thought your man candy was back in North Carolina."

"North Carolina isn't here, and I'd like to forget reality and just dance. With a guy. A gorgeous one, preferably," she adds.

"What if Fletcher showed up here tonight?"

"WHAT?" Her eyes dart around the room like a stage-five clinger who just caught the scent of fresh meat.

"Chill, Avery. I said 'what if.'"

Her hand flies to her heart. "Jesus, Ray. Don't do that to me."

"Don't look so disappointed." If she wasn't sure how she felt about him earlier today, I hope she does now. Her reaction makes it so obvious.

"I'm not." Her hands smooth her dress and she pulls her phone out to check the time. "Arizona Grace should go on in about ten minutes."

There she goes changing the subject again. "I should have asked what songs James was singing. With all the excitement, I completely forgot."

"I wonder what his surprise is. Maybe he'll come out singing Whitney Houston."

"That would be hysterical! James belting out those high notes? I've gotta see that. I'm so requesting that for the next open mic night." I take my phone out and send him a text doing just that. We spend the next several minutes making a mental list of the most embarrassing songs he could possibly sing. *Hit Me Baby One More Time* by Britney Spears, complete with choreography, comes in first. *I wonder if I could get him in full costume, too?*

Cheers from the crowd snap us back to the present and I look down to see the guys walking out. Oh God, he's got a guitar. I repeat *James has a guitar*. The butterflies that were happily fluttering in my stomach when we first got here have all passed out. They didn't stand a chance against the sight of James on stage. I grab onto Avery's arm for dear life.

"He's singing *and* playing! Holy shit!" I fumble in my purse for my phone as Roth takes the mic.

"What's up, everyone? Thanks for showing up tonight so we didn't play to an empty room." The crowd cheers in response. "We're Arizona Grace. I'm Roth, that's Lenny, Bear's in the back on drums and Simon's over there on bass." His New York accent sounds even more pronounced in the mic. "And this guy," he says, pointing at James, "is a hobo we picked up at the 34th Street Station. True story. But the kid's got talent, so he's slumming with us for a while tonight. Give it up for James, everyone!" The girl on the other side of me lets out a loud whistle and hoots. James holds his hand up and waves, then looks up to where Avery and I are standing and winks at me.

"Did you see that, Lexi?" the girl shouts at her friend, jumping up and down. Her boobs nearly spill out of her barely there top. "He winked right at me!"

Please.

James starts the opening chords to a song I don't recognize, but enjoy all the same. Before I know it, he's singing to me about sex being on fire and that phrase does all sorts of things to my ladybits. My body moves to the beat, powered by the raspy voice coming from my boyfriend.

My boyfriend.

Take *that*, Lexi's friend.

The crowd behind us comes to life, dancing and swaying us into the railing. The personal bubble I had before the set started is gone, but everyone seems to be having a good time. I look to my right and see Avery dancing against a guy. His hand is on her waist and she's leaning back into him. He's wearing a ball cap and sunglasses—who wears sunglasses in a nightclub, anyway?—so I can't tell what he looks like. Judging by the way his shirt clings to his body and the way he smells, he can't be a total troll. More importantly, Avery's smiling.

"Looks like you found a partner for the night," I lean over and say into her ear so she can hear me over the music.

"He came up behind me, and I went with it. I'm not turning around though. I don't wanna know what he looks like or what his name is. Right now, his name is Mr. Fun, and that's all that matters to me." She laughs and resumes dancing.

Whatever works.

The song ends and Bear counts the guys right into the next one. I don't know any of the lyrics, but the rest of the crowd sings along. When James sings about using somebody, his voice goes up higher and I wish I could record the sound.

Record! Shit!

I take my phone from my purse again and try my best to keep my hands steady while I take a video for Instagram. I want to hashtag the entire freaking world. #myboyfriend #rockstar #hesmine #backoff #mrstennyson

The crowd launches into applause when they finish the second song.

"Thank you, I hope youse guys enjoyed that little slice of Kings of Leon," Roth says in his thick accent. "Let's take a walk with Mr. Brightside, shall we?" He nods to James, who steps away from the mic and starts the intro. Roth's taking the vocals on this one, and Lexi's friend about loses her mind next to me.

269

"Oh em gee, Destiny! This song is totally for you! Maybe that James guy wants you to call him!" Lexi shouts. They squeal and jump up and down, their boobs in a match to see whose can bounce the highest. I'm almost tempted to let Avery's boobs loose on them just to shut them up, but she's still happily dancing with Mr. Fun.

"Thanks, Labyrinth!" Roth says, once the guys finish the song. "Youse guys have been kind to my hobo friend. He asked us for a favor and being the kind New Yorkers we are, we told him to go fuck himself," he says, grinning wildly. "Nah, just kidding. He asked if he could play a song, and we're gonna slow it down and do that right now."

"Thanks, everyone," James says. "The most beautiful girl in the world is right up there in the balcony and this song's for her. Rachel, I'm still waiting on question twenty. Just ask."

My hands fly to my mouth, and I look at Avery with instant tears in my eyes. She has no idea what the significance of this song is, but she gives my arm a supportive squeeze anyway. Bear, Simon, and James start the intro to the song, and my heart jumps down to my toes and grabs hold of my stomach on the way back up.

I spend the next five minutes absolutely captivated by James' voice. I never thought about him doing a Lake Street Dive cover, especially since Rachael's voice is so iconic. He's dropped the song to a lower octave, and the rock quality he brings to it works for him. *It so, so works*. Three minutes and eleven seconds into it, he closes his eyes and lets his voice go. The crowd whoops and hollers in response and goose bumps sprout all over my body. His voice is fucking magical. The band quiets down when he gets to the third verse, and he sings it directly to me, never taking his eyes off me. If it's possible to fall in love with someone a thousand times in forty seconds, I've just done it. Tears spill down my cheeks, proof that all the emotions inside me can't be contained. When the song ends, he takes the guitar off and hands it to a crew member, then waves to the crowd.

"Thanks guys, we're gonna take a quick break and we'll be back with stuff from our latest album," Roth says.

I turn to Avery and take a cleansing breath. "That was the single greatest experience of my life. I'm just kicking myself for not getting it on video."

"You mean like this?" she asks, holding up her phone. All five minutes of glory are cued up on her screen.

"Avery Jane Murphy, I love you. I promise I'll name my firstborn after you." I lean in for a hug. "Hey, where'd Mr. Fun go?"

"I dunno. He left when the music slowed down." She shrugs her shoulder like it's no big deal. "So you still haven't asked James question twenty? That was like two months ago or something."

"I couldn't ever think of anything good enough." It's my turn to shrug my shoulder.

"Hey there, Mrs. Tennyson." I turn and see a sweaty James walking through the crowd toward me.

"Hey yourself." I take his face in mine and kiss him like I'm drowning and he's my only source of water. I hear Lexi and Destiny huff behind me then shuffle over to the stairs, clearly disappointed that their boobs didn't do the trick.

I love it when the trash takes itself out.

"So did you like your surprise?" he asks.

"The man with green eyes did a *very* good job. Thank you."

"It was my pleasure, trust me. I'm just glad the guys learned the song this afternoon."

"So that's what the mystery texting was all about?"

He wrinkles his face. "Yup. Sorry for lying to you earlier. I know I said I wouldn't do that, but it was for a good cause."

"No apology necessary. I've never had a more perfect song sung to me." Because now I know what question twenty will be.

I just have to figure out the right time to ask.

James

"Hurry the fuck up, dude, or it's not gonna work," I whisper. There's nothing like talking on a cell phone in a public bathroom to make you feel sixteen kinds of disgusting. I needed the privacy, though, and this was the only way I could get it without tipping off Avery. Mandy called before we left New York to tell us she was covering for Devin, who woke up with migraine. I told the girls I'd spring for an Uber instead. Right before we boarded, an image of Fletcher picking us up flashed through my head, so I told Ray about it. She agreed, and I texted Fletcher with our arrival info.

"Relax, I'm pulling into the airport now," he says. "You promise she won't freak out?"

No.

"Sure. See you in a few." I stow my phone in my pocket and walk back to the baggage claim carousel, interrupting a heated discussion between Ray and Avery.

"Nope. No way. Zac Efron beats Channing Tatum every time," Rachel says.

"Please. There's no *way* Zac could have pulled off a Magic Mike role like Channing did," Avery fires back.

"I hate to say it, but you're both wrong. Paul Walker's where it's at, God rest his soul," I say, grabbing our luggage cart. "Now come on, our ride should be here."

"My boyfriend has the hots for Paul Walker?" Rachel asks in a loud whisper behind me.

"You know I have a thing for blondes," I say, grinning over my shoulder. We step outside the terminal and Avery scans the arrivals line.

"What's our Uber driving?"

"A black Nissan Maxima." Right on cue, Fletcher's car pulls up. Avery turns around to pull her suitcases off the cart and misses him getting out of the driver's seat.

Three...two...one...

"What the fuck, James?" she asks, trying to mask her surprise with a scowl. We all ignore her and load our luggage into the trunk. I open the back door for Rachel and slide in behind her before Avery beats me to it. Fletcher opens the front passenger door and makes a sweeping gesture to the interior. She rolls her eyes and flops into the seat. "I *told* you I'd call him when we got home," she huffs to Rachel. "I don't know why you insisted on meddling."

"Hey, you meddled when you told James to write that song. Consider this payback. You're welcome in advance," Rachel says sweetly as Fletcher pulls into traffic.

"Just give me twenty minutes, babe. I'll tell you the whole story and you can ask me anything you want. If you never want to speak to me again after that, I promise to respect your decision." His fingertips tap a nervous beat on the steering wheel.

Avery crosses her arm and narrows her eyes. "Fine."

"Okay." He takes a deep breath and puffs his cheeks out as he exhales. "Almost five years ago, I had a girlfriend named Dayna. I asked her out on a dare and surprisingly, she said yes. I was a freshman and she was a sophomore." He looks over his shoulder to merge onto Interstate 40 and sets the cruise control. "We dated off and on for a few months. The night of homecoming, some buddies of mine scored a few cases of cheap beer. We skipped the last half of the dance to go to my friend Tanner's house and I got drunk for the first time. I also had sex for the first time. My mistake was not wrapping it up. I guess I just thought there was no way to get a girl pregnant since I was a virgin." He rubs his forehead for a few moments, then resumes tapping on the steering wheel.

"A few weeks later, Dayna said she was late. I worked at a grocery store, so I shoplifted a pregnancy test because I didn't want anyone to know what I was doing. I brought it to school with me the next day. I thought the damn thing was gonna burn a hole through my backpack," he says with a quiet laugh. "Anyway, it was positive. I found out on a Wednesday morning that I was gonna be a dad. By Friday, she'd already started researching abortion clinics. I panicked and told my mom. I wasn't ready to have a child, but I wasn't ready for her to make that kind of decision for me, either."

Rachel squeezes my hand, but neither of us say anything. I can't imagine dealing with something like that, especially at such a young age. An image of Stacey from Birmingham crosses my mind, making me shudder. Talk about dodging a bullet.

"Mom, Dad, and I went to Dayna's house and had a long discussion with her and her parents. They didn't want Dayna's life to be over before it started, but Mom couldn't bear the idea of having a grandchild taken away from her. We agreed that Dayna would have the baby and sign over her parental rights if we would cover the hospital costs and not ask for child support. I worried that having a teenage dad would make my kid a target for bullying, so my parents told everyone they didn't want to have an empty nest and decided to adopt. My name is on her birth certificate, but she knows my parents as her parents. I live at home with them and they helped me with childcare so I could finish school, and now when I work. And that's basically it." He takes another deep breath and wrings his hands on the steering wheel. That poor thing is taking the brunt of his anxiety. He exits the interstate, meaning we only have about five minutes before we get into town.

Avery chews on her thumbnail for a few moments then clears her throat. "How do you know Sam is yours? Maybe Dayna was with other guys too."

"Aside from the wicked personality that she clearly inherited from me?" he asks. It's the first time I've seen him smile since he picked us up. "I took a paternity test right after she was born. She's mine." He says it proudly. Definitively. Sam might have a teenage dad, but he's a damn good one.

"Do you plan on telling her the truth?"

"One day, when she's older. Mom and I figure we'll do that with the help of a counselor so we don't screw her up any worse than we already have."

"Do you have any other kids?"

"No. Hell no," he says with a laugh. "I've only had sex once. That first time with Dayna. I've never even had another girlfriend until you."

"TMI, dude," I groan, plugging my ears for fear of hearing anything else. I was all for giving Fletcher a chance to talk to Avery, but I don't want to be the fly on the wall in a mobile confessional booth.

"Sorry, man. I kinda forgot y'all were back there," he laughs. "Am I going to your house or Rachel's first?"

"Hers. I drove there and parked The Beast. Y'all can carry on with your official make up after you drop us off."

Avery asks a few more questions along the way, and Fletcher answers them just like he promised. "Is there anything else you want to know?" he asks, turning on to Rachel's street.

Avery tips her head to the side and narrows her eyes. "Do you have any other secrets?"

"No. Not unless you count the thing where I think I'm falling in love with you, but that's probably not a secret."

Jesus, he's really laying it out there, isn't he?

"Still back here, dude."

"I know, asswipe," he laughs again and pulls into Rachel's long driveway. Like a good Uber driver, he helps get our suitcases out of the trunk and sets hers on the front porch while I toss mine in The Beast.

"Thanks for the ride, man." We exchange one of those guy hug-handshakes. What do they call them, anyway? Hugshakes?

"Thanks for giving me twenty minutes with her as my captive audience." He looks back at the car and smiles then turns back to me. He shuffles his feet for a moment before meeting my eye again. "Hey, can I ask you a question?" He pauses as he struggles to find the words he wants to say. "A few weeks ago, you mentioned Sam having a great dad. How did you know it was me?"

I smile. This is actually a pretty easy question for me to answer. "Dude. You always wanna do stuff with her. You sing her the monster song every night, no matter where you are. And you should see your face when you're around her or talk about her. It's pretty obvious." I shrug my shoulder. My answer is solid, so I don't have any fear that he'll figure out the real reason.

"Huh. Well. Thanks again for helping me patch things up with Avery. I think I actually have a chance."

"She moped around like a sad puppy all weekend."

His face lights up. "Really?"

"Yup." We bump fists and he returns to his car. I walk to the front porch to take Rachel's suitcase inside, but her icy glare stops me in my tracks. If looks could kill, I have about three seconds to get right with God. She's holding her phone in her right hand, and her left hand takes up residence on her hip. I think I might be frightened by my girlfriend.

"What the *hell*, James?" she whisper-yells, presumably so her parents don't hear.

I don't think I touched her phone all weekend. I didn't tell anyone about our sleeping arrangements and I don't even have social media, so I have no idea what she's so pissed at. I'm trying to open up my Spidey senses for any help they can give, but that's no use either.

"What?" I take a hesitant step forward, followed by another. Yes. Definitely frightened by my girlfriend.

Her mom pokes her head out the front door, and Rachel plasters a smile on her face and spins around.

"You're back! Did y'all have a fun time?"

"We did! James was actually just getting ready to leave. I'll be inside in just a sec."

"Okay, sweetheart. It's good to see you again, James." I smile and wave as she pulls the suitcase inside and shuts the door. Rachel jumps off the porch and storms over to the far side of my truck. I follow, feeling a bit like I'm walking to my execution.

"Would you mind explaining what *this* is?" She jams her phone so close to my face that I have to take a step back to focus. I study the screen not having any idea what I'm looking at.

"Um. At the risk of sounding like a total smartass, I can't. And not because I'm trying to hide something. It's because I honestly have no idea what I'm looking at."

"This is my Twitter feed." Well that explains it. I don't know anything about that shit.

"And you're upset about something on your Twitter feed?" What the hell kind of good does having perceptive abilities do if I can't use them when I want to?

"Yes, especially when it comes from Vivien Tanner." She says the name like it tastes bad coming out of her mouth.

"What did she say?"

"Let's start with what I said when I posted a video of your performance at Labyrinth." She taps her screen and I see her post: *Check out the hottie with the great singing voice. #boyfriend #rockstar #nyc.* Then there's a link to one of my songs.

"Okay...?" She taps the screen again, and I see Vivien's page.

"Vivien retweeted my tweet a few minutes ago, and she uploaded a video of her own." Rachel clicks on the link and I hear Vivien's voice.

"Do I look okay, sweetheart?"

And then I hear mine.

"You have nothing to worry about, Vivien. You're a beautiful girl."

The video itself doesn't show our faces. It looks more like she recorded it while her hands were in her lap. Of *course* she did. Oh God. I lift my palms in the air and hope she's open to hearing my perfectly rational explanation.

"It's not what you think." Which is pretty much straight out of the *Guilty: Caught Red-Handed* guidebook. "I promise it's not what it looks like." I'm really digging my own grave here. *Shit.*

"Really? Because Vivien says she'd much rather hear your speaking voice than your singing voice. And that's definitely *your voice*," she says, jamming her finger in my chest.

"Yes, that's my voice. But I wasn't there when she said the first part." I explain to her what happened that night at the animal hospital and tell her about the dream I had in New York City. Then I ask her to play the video again.

"There. See that?" I ask, pressing the pause button. I point to the shift in Vivien's position after she says the word "sweetheart."

"Her hands are different, and the lighting is darker," she says, as relief floods her face.

"Right. She must have recorded that after she left and

edited my part to look like that's what I said to her. I swear to God, Ray, she never asked me that question." I take her face in my hands, searching her chocolate eyes for any sign that she believes me.

"Okay," she whispers a few moments later. Her shoulders relax and she sinks into my embrace. "Sorry for my jealousy-induced outburst."

"Are you kidding? You looked pretty hot." I kiss the side of her head and breathe in the smell of her shampoo. "Even though I was a little scared of you."

"You don't need to be scared of me, James," she says into my chest. "But Vivien should be."

Now that's *hot.*

"She better be in school today is all I'm saying. I will *not* let her get away with that shit." Rachel dangles her legs off the tailgate of The Beast while we wait for Avery. Rachel planned to confront Vivien in the cafeteria yesterday, but she never showed up.

"She'll be there." I can't see anything that happens, but I do see Ray walking out with a smile on her face and her head held high.

She cocks and eyebrow and tilts her head. "Anything in particular you want to share with me?"

"No, but I don't think Vivien will be a problem after today."

"Good." A sly smile spreads across her face, which quickly turns to a squeal when she spots Avery. "There she is!" Ray's already talked to Avery three times since I picked her up this morning. I've heard more shrieking and squealing than I can handle, and it's not even eight a.m. Todd didn't forget about his promise, and last evening Mandy rolled into their driveway in a VW Beetle. A pink Beetle. As in, Pepto-Bismol-had-an-affair- with-bubble-gum pink. It has a convertible top and eyelashes. The car has freaking eyelashes. It fits Avery perfectly. She gets out of her car and they launch into another round of ear-piercing excitement, complete with hugs and a happy dance.

Avery gives Ray a tour, which doesn't take long considering it's a Beetle, while I close the tailgate. Which reminds me—I need to put an up an ad on Craigslist. Hopefully, I can get enough to pay for an electric guitar. I'm thinking of getting a Fender Mustang. Or maybe a Telecaster. Or both, depending on how much money I can coax out of the poor sap who buys it.

"Here, I have something for you!" Rachel reaches down for the gift bag at my feet and thrusts it into Avery's hands. "Open it!" She digs through the tissue paper and pulls out fuzzy dice for the rear-view mirror. They're pink too. Big surprise.

"Lick, touch, grab, above waist, neck, boobs... Rachel, what the hell kind of dice are these?" Avery asks, reading each side.

"They're dirty dice. I saw them at the mall last night and thought you'd like them since you and Fletcher made up." She wiggles her eyebrows and grins.

"My best friend got me sexual dice." She glances down at the gift then looks back at Rachel with a look of shock and pride. "Well done, Beef. Well done." They high five and Avery hangs them on the rear-view mirror. "Now, for the best part." She pulls an envelope out of her backpack and holds it out.

"What's this?"

"Oh, you know. Just my FIT acceptance letter," she says nonchalantly before bursting into another round of shrieks and hugs with Rachel. My ears can't handle much more of this.

"Come on, you cackling hens. It's time to go inside," I say, wiggling my fingers inside my ears. It doesn't help much.

Avery presses the remote lock and the car beeps in response. "Eek! Even the horn sounds cute!" She does another happy dance as we walk toward the school.

"Here," I say, as I hand Rachel the small box she asked me to hold before Avery pulled up.

"Thanks! Avery, this is your real present," she says, passing her box. Avery pulls out a gold necklace with a puzzle piece charm. It matches the one Rachel's wearing.

"Oh, I love it! Thank you thank you thank you! I can't wait to see how it looks!" I follow the girls to their locker since I got my first and second period books before I left school yesterday. Avery's fingers fly over the combination dial while Rachel struggles with hers, as usual. I swear it takes almost as long for her to open her locker as it does to run a mile. I lean in to offer my assistance when something falls out of Avery's locker and lands on my foot. She's too busy admiring her necklace and touching up her lips to notice, so I pick it up and hand it to her just as Ray conquers her lock.

"What's this?" Avery asks, capping her lipstick.

"I dunno. It came out of your locker when you opened it." She reads the paper, then looks over her shoulder into the hallway.

"What's it say?" Ray slams her door shut, spins the dial, and flips it off in a moment of defiance. She's so cute when she's worked up. Avery hands over the note, still scanning the hall.

> **Roses are red,**
> **Violets are blue.**
> **You should ditch that zero**
> **And be with this hero.**
> **Love, Your Secret Admirer**

I don't like this. I don't like this *at all*. The hairs on the back of my neck stand at attention, and my lips form a thin line—pretty much the exact opposite of Rachel's reaction.

"Oooohhh, Avery's got a secret admirer!" she sings in an elementary school tone. "I wonder how Fletcher will feel about this."

More importantly, how does this secret admirer know that they're back together? We got home Sunday afternoon and it's only Tuesday morning. I guess it's possible he didn't realize they were split up for a few days, but my gut tells me I was right the first time.

"Secret notes inside my locker on my birthday? Please. Sixth grade called and wants its lame idea back." Avery rolls her eyes, crumples the note, and tosses it in a trashcan as the first bell rings.

A few hours later, I walk into the cafeteria with Ray and Avery. Her eyes zero in on Vivien's table, and that same sly smile from this morning returns to her face.

"Excuse me. Pardon me. I don't mean to interrupt your lunch," Rachel says, walking up to the table where Vivien and her friends are sitting. "Vivien, I see that you enjoyed James' performance over the weekend. I actually took that video *just for you* since I know how much you care about him." She smiles sweetly at her frienemy. "I did want to give you one small piece of advice, though. Brush up on your video editing skills. That way, the next time you try to make it look like some guy is calling you beautiful, people might *actually* believe you."

No one at Vivien's table says a word, but a couple of them look like they're struggling to not laugh. Red splotches creep up Vivien's neck and her mouth hangs open as Rachel continues her tirade.

"Oh, and my condolences for your dead cat, and for your feeble attempts at fishing for complements. Now, if you don't mind, I'm gonna go eat lunch with my *boyfriend*." She wiggles her fingers at their table, then takes my hand and leads the way to ours.

Holy shit, she's hot.

"Were you taking a video?" Avery asks Gretchen as we pull our chairs out. I quickly look back at Vivien's table before I sit down. The splotches on her neck have moved up to her cheeks, and I can still see her nostrils flaring from here. Serves her right.

"Yup. I'm sending it to Lainey. I swear, she misses out on the best stuff because she's homeschooled."

Rachel, Avery, and I bust out laughing while Gretchen hits "send."

My phone chimes with a text, and I quickly check it between customers. The Sweet Pea is pretty packed on Fridays, and tonight's no different.

> **Unknown: I want 2 check out ur breast 2nite. U free?**

Two more immediately follow.

> **Unknown: BEAST. As in ur truck. From the craigslist ad.**

> **Unknown: My autocorrect hates me.**

> **Me: Ha. It's craigslist, so you never know. I'll be free in an hour.**

We agree to meet here when my shift is over. It's easier to find than my house, and I'd rather not give out my address to a potential breast-seeking buyer.

"Did you see all of the secret admirer messages, or just the first one?" Fletcher asks, plating the order for table three.

"All of them, but they were pretty much the same. Typed, folded, and shoved between the vents in her locker. She just rolls her eyes and throws them away."

"I don't know if I should be pissed or if I should high-five the dude because he has good taste in women." He shrugs his shoulders, clearly not as worried about Avery's secret admirer as I am, and turns his attention back to the grill. I haven't been able to shake my bad feeling or catch anyone in the act. The message this morning was especially creepy. It said "*All I wanna do is dance with you again.*" Avery wasn't terribly concerned, considering she goes to a lot of parties and has danced with half of the student body—her words, not mine. The only person she said it *did* rule out was Smelly Warren, because she's never danced with him.

Gee, I wonder why.

A group of twelve comes in, forcing us to pause our Stalker Gate discussion, and the rest of my shift goes by in a blur. When I walk outside, someone is peering into the windows of The Beast.

"I see you found it," I say.

"I did. I'm Amy," she says with a beaming smile. "This is a beautiful truck." She knocks two metallic thumps on the side.

"Beautiful isn't quite the word I'd use, but okay," I laugh.

"I'm actually a photographer. I plan on using this as a prop in my next photo series." She hands me a card that says *Amy J. Perkins Photography.*

"You're willing to spend fifteen hundred bucks on a prop?" I ask, my mouth hanging open.

"I spend twice that on lenses, easily," she quips. "I've got about five acres. I want to plop this bad boy in the middle of a field and let it die a beautiful death."

"What kind of pictures do you take?"

"Couples. Families. Kids. Pretty much anything that moves." She grins again. "I've been looking for the right truck for a few weeks, but it's harder than I thought it'd be. A couple have been too new, one was missing the bed, and a few more had too much rust. My clients need to be able to interact with the truck and not worry about ruining their clothes."

"Then I guess this is your lucky day."

"Looks like it."

I consider what she said about her photo series as an idea forms in my head. "Amy, how do you feel about doing a partial trade?"

"What do you mean? I know I asked to see your breast, but you're kind of young for my taste."

Laughter overcomes me, and I lean against The Beast as I catch my breath. "Not quite what I had in mind. I'm selling my truck because I'm moving, and it won't make the drive. I'd like to do a photo shoot with my girlfriend before I go. She'd probably like to have some nice pictures of us to look at when I'm gone. How about we take the cost of a session off the asking price?" That should still leave me enough for one electric guitar, so it's a win-win for me and Ray.

"You have yourself a deal. And that's really sweet. Most kids your age don't think of other people like that."

"Yeah, well, I'm not most kids my age."

We agree on a final price—eight hundred dollars, which should be still be enough to get my guitar—and she said I can keep the truck until the shoot. I can't wait to get back to the house and FaceTime Rachel with the good news.

Gran's resting on the couch when I walk inside. She's been more tired lately, though no one has actually admitted it. I guess it's sort of like admitting the Titanic had a weak spot. I kiss her cheek and chat with her for a few minutes, telling her about my busy shift and the upcoming photo shoot.

"Oh, Ray wants to get all of your pie recipes, by the way. She's gonna miss them once we leave," I say.

"You said you're getting your pictures taken on Saturday?"

"Yes ma'am."

"What time?"

"Before sunset. Amy said something about golden light."

"Why don't you invite Ray over that morning? We can spend the day in the kitchen making pies. I can give her my recipe box before y'all leave."

"You'd give her your recipe box? Isn't that something you're supposed to pass down to family?" The ancient wooden box was Gran's mom's. I never met her, but Gran said she was a phenomenal cook.

"What the hell do you think I'm doing? In case you don't remember, finding your soulmate in your teenage years wasn't all that uncommon when *I* was a teenager. Maybe it runs in the family."

"But Mom's adopted. We don't actually share blood, Gran."

"Shut up, boy. Nurture over nature."

"Yes ma'am," I say, laughing.

"There's one more thing. We have a moving date. February 29. Two days after your photo shoot."

That's in ten days.

I'm not laughing anymore.

Rachel

"I have *the* perfect pants to go with this shirt. Why do you have to be so damn tall?" Avery asks, flipping through clothes in my walk-in closet.

"Why do you have to be so short?" I counter with a laugh as I sit on my bed and smooth lotion over my legs. Avery was waiting on the porch when I got back from my twelve-mile run. While I took a shower, she headed for my closet to pick out clothes for my photo shoot tomorrow. I didn't even bother arguing with her. The weather's supposed to be a little warmer than normal, so she's already pulled out a gray ikat patterned sundress and a pair of cutoffs with a yellow peasant-style top. It's like having a pint-sized, boy-crazy personal shopper. "Hey, how are the prom dresses coming along?"

"I'm about halfway done with yours. I'll have you try it on next week so I can make sure the bodice fits right."

"Will you have enough time to finish both of them before prom?"

"Are you doubting my abilities, Beef?" She cocks an eyebrow over her shoulder, trying to look stern.

"Not at all, Vera Wang. I'm actually looking forward to it." I toss my lotion back onto my dresser and start finger-combing my wet hair.

"Well *there's* something I never thought I'd hear you say!"

"Prom means James will be back here to visit," I say, shrugging my shoulders. It still hasn't hit me that he'll be gone in three days. We've spent a lot of time together this week and, for the most part, I've managed to keep the tears in check. At least around him. I asked him if he could see anything about Florida or his new school, but he said not yet. He looked almost upset by it, now that I think about it. And he's still pretty skeeved out about Avery's secret admirer. I had to promise him I'd text pictures of anything else that comes in while he's gone.

"Here, this is the last outfit." Avery walks out carrying a pair of pink jeans and a cream-colored top. "I'll pretend that I didn't just rip the price tag off your pants, which tells me you've never worn them." There she goes again with the stern look.

"You've seen me almost every day for the last year. You know I've never worn them. Hell, I even *told* you I would never wear them when you forced me to buy them last summer. I'm a woman of my word," I say smugly.

"You're a pain in my ass is what you are," she grins. "But your ass will look great tomorrow, that's for sure."

"I just hope I look good next to James. I have no idea what he's wearing."

"You really don't give me enough credit, Ray." She rolls her eyes and flops down next to me on my bed.

"What do you mean?"

"I FaceTimed James two days ago to pick out his clothes."

"Seriously? Why do you act like we're both three years old?" I say, giggling. There's no use in saying I can't believe she did that. Because I totally can.

"Like I'm gonna let a photographer with seventy-five thousand Facebook fans photograph my best friend and her boyfriend without my help in the wardrobe department. Besides, I had to tell him what not to pack."

I guess that makes sense.

"So you're baking pies with Gran tomorrow, then doing your photo shoot?" she asks, changing the subject.

"Yup. James said Gran is really starting to look sick. I hope I don't burst into tears when I see her."

"She'll kick your ass if you do." I can't help but laugh at that, mostly because she's right.

"That's right, just grate the butter into that bowl there, and then we'll add it to the flour."

"How am I supposed to do that if it's frozen?" I ask.

"It works *because* it's frozen. Otherwise, you'd just have a globby mess," she says from a chair next to the counter. "This is easier than dicing the butter, trust me." The fact that she's sitting down and not moving all over the kitchen like she used to doesn't go unnoticed, but James texted me this morning and told me not to mention it. I haven't seen her since she came to my house, and he was right—she looks sick. Like, *sick* sick.

"Gran, this is cold," James protests. He reaches for a paper towel, but Gran swats his hand away.

"You want linty crust, boy? If your sissy hands can't handle a little bit of cold for a few minutes, then use this." She reaches for the butter wrapper and folds it several times before handing it to him. "This will help until you get to the end. Then you're just gonna have to get a big straw and suck it up." She smiles and lovingly pats his cheek. Where her body is slowing down, her quick wit and sharp tongue are still in full form.

"Yes ma'am," he laughs. I can't help but giggle too. I love watching James get put in his place by a woman more than three times his age. We follow the rest of her directions and several minutes later, we're rewarded with two great looking balls of dough. "Okay, what's next?" James asks.

"Cover the bowls with plastic wrap and put them in the fridge. Then grab that box off the kitchen table and set it on the counter next to me." James does as he's told and returns with the box, staring blankly at Gran.

"Well, what are you waiting for?" she asks. "Start packing! I've got a few hours of child labor while the dough chills, and I'm getting my money's worth," she laughs. James looks at me and shrugs his shoulders. Just like with Avery the Wardrobe Nazi, there's no use arguing with Gran. He helps her to the couch without making it too obvious that he's actually helping her, then tosses me a fresh roll of packing tape.

Six hours later, most of the kitchen is packed and our pies sit on the counter to cool under the watchful eye of Lazarus, who is guarding them from the floor below. James passes me a damp paper towel and a glass of lemonade, which I down in about three gulps. I gave up on not breaking a sweat somewhere between the pantry and the lower cabinets. Gran has a ton of shit. I asked her why she didn't hire a company to do all of this for her, but she just grumbled something about thieves taking her stuff.

I set my glass in the sink and toss the paper towel in the trash. "I'm definitely not going to our photo shoot looking like this. Do you mind if I shower before dinner? I can just change into my first outfit now."

"No prob. Mom and I share a bathroom, so you can use all of her girly stuff. Towels are under the sink."

"Sounds good."

"Now, if you don't mind me, I'm gonna use Gran and Grandpa's shower and try to not imagine my hot ass girlfriend naked in my bathroom."

He kisses me on the cheek and walks toward his bedroom, leaving me to compose myself enough to get my bag out of the car. Did he say that because he already knows what I have planned tonight? I press my hand to my stomach to calm the butterflies and walk outside praying that he has the psychic version of bad reception. When I come back inside, Gran sits up, her head barely poking over the back of the couch. She reminds me of the Incredible Shrinking Woman.

"Did y'all leave my recipe box out like I asked?"

"Yes ma'am, it's still on the counter."

"Bring it here, would you?"

I set my bag down, retrieve the box, and bring it around to the front of the couch. Gran pats the cushion next to her, so I sit down and prop my feet up on the coffee table. If I'm not careful, I might pass out from exhaustion right here. Gran runs her fingers over the worn edges of the box, tracing the outlines of dings, scratches and a burn mark in the top right corner.

"This recipe box was my mother's. My father made it for her, and it's lived on the kitchen counter ever since I can remember. It's survived the Great Depression, a few wars and more family celebrations than I can count. She gave it to me when I got married, and I've added to it over the years. My Sunny is wonderful at many things, but she never took to cooking or baking like I did. You're the next girl in the family, so I want you to have this."

She passes the box to me and lays her frail hand over mine. I try to swallow, but a lump the size of a golf ball makes it difficult. Dad's parents died when I was a baby, and we only see Mom's parents once or twice a year, usually on Easter and Christmas. Needless to say, family traditions have never been a big deal in my house, so Gran's gesture is just... *wow*. Especially considering I'm not technically family. And that I'm—.

"Before that teenage brain of yours goes to ruining the moment, yes, I know what I'm doing. Remember what we talked about a few weeks ago?" I nod my head in response, trying to keep the tears in my eyes from spilling over. "Good. Now take this and enjoy adding more to it."

"Thank you," I whisper. I take a deep breath and clear my throat, trying to dislodge the lump. "I don't really know what to say."

"I do. Go take a shower. You look like crap." She smiles and pats my hand as I stand up. I can still hear her cackling when I reach the bathroom.

Amy and her megawatt smile greet us outside the red barn next to her house. She looks even more beautiful than her profile picture. Her short jet-black hair is clipped back, perfectly framing her face, and two cameras hang from her neck. She hands a third one to the girl standing next to her, then gives us a hug. I like her already.

"I'm so excited to see y'all! This is my assistant, Reshma," she says, gesturing to a petite girl who looks to be a couple of years older than us. "James, I'll have you follow us down this path in the truck. You can park next to the oak tree. We'll start there, and we'll work our way back here after the sun sets," she says. The fact that he gave up some of his profits so we could have pictures is mind-boggling. I really, *really* hit the boyfriend lottery.

We grab our bags for our outfit changes and hop into the cab. Since it's a short ride in the country, I skip the seat belt and slide over to his side while he backs up. The reality that this is my last ride in The Beast hits me like a lead brick. "Quick, say something funny," I say, trying to distract myself from the tears that threaten to ruin the little bit of makeup I put on.

"What lies on the bottom of the ocean and twitches?"

"I dunno. What?"

"A nervous wreck."

"Har har har," I say with a laugh as I roll my eyes. He winks, then pulls under the canopy of a massive tree and kills the engine.

"You ready, Mrs. Tennyson?" He holds out a hand to help me down from the driver's side of the truck.

"Yup. I'll be the one getting photographed next to the best boyfriend on the planet. Thanks for doing this for me." He takes me in his arms and runs his hands down the sides of my face before bringing his lips to mine. His kiss is gentle and slow, as if we have all the time in the world to explore each other, instead of just twenty-four hours. Which is why I'm going to make the most out of every hour I can tonight. A light breeze blows pieces of my hair around our faces. He smooths them down in one fluid motion, then wraps his arms around my back, pulling me into a hug. I love that my head fits perfectly into the space between his chest and neck, and I especially love the way he smells right here. It's a mixture of shampoo, cologne, and *him*. It's one of the things I'll miss the most when he leaves.

"Do you *see* this, Resh? We hit a goldmine tonight!" I feel my cheeks flush as I turn toward Amy's voice. I didn't forget that they were there, but... well, I sort of forgot they were there. "Don't move!" she shouts. "James, lean back against the truck and put your hand by Rachel's shoulder. Rachel, keep your eyes on me." She fires off a few shots, then checks the back of her camera and takes several more. She shows Reshma the LCD screen and lets the camera fall back around her neck. "Your chemistry is absolutely off the charts. If the rest of the shoot goes as well as this, you might just be the poster children for this photo series."

I'm not exactly sure what that means, but she seems happy. She spends the next hour positioning us in various spots on and around The Beast, telling us to talk and interact like we normally do.

"If I was thinking about it, I'd have asked you to bring Lucy," I say, leaning on James' shoulder. I'm in my cutoff jeans now, and my yellow top picks up the yellow stripes in his plaid shirt. I was surprised that Avery chose it, considering she's not a big fan of that pattern, but it goes well with the laid-back country vibe of the shoot.

"I meant to, but maybe I can make up for it. If I have a signal, that is." He pulls his phone from his back pocket and pulls up YouTube.

"What's this?" I ask, looking at the screen.

"Before your final race, you asked me about recording songs on my own YouTube channel. Well, I made one. I thought it would come in handy if we ended up going to different colleges. I was gonna surprise you with it at graduation. Once I found out we were moving, I decided to surprise you early." I take the phone from his hand and scroll through the songs, recognizing most of the titles. "These are all songs that make me think of you in some way," he continues. "I think I'm up to about thirty, and I'll keep adding to the list from Florida."

"Is that Fletcher?" I ask, pointing to a thumbnail image.

"Yeah, he recorded a few with me. I just thought this would take some of the sting out of me moving. Between our photo shoot, our FaceTime calls, and this channel, it'll be like I'm still here."

"It most definitely *won't* be like you're still here, but that's okay. I absolutely love it." I thank him with a series of kisses as his version of Ray LaMontagne's *Trouble* plays from his phone. He pulls me to my feet when the second chorus starts, and we slow dance for the rest of the song. When *Just Ask* begins, I raise an eyebrow and poke him in the chest.

"Cheater!" I tease. "You said these were all songs *you* sang."

"Mine's on here too, but I didn't think you'd object to the official version."

He's right, and for a moment, I'm convinced the gods of love and courage have called in a favor. Neither of us says a word as we continue swaying together, chest-to-chest, our feet no longer actually moving back and forth. Verse three starts, and my fingers find their way under his shirt to the words inked along his ribs. I close my eyes and remember the first time he told me about this tattoo. About what the lyrics meant to him. About how they made him feel. Adrenaline courses through my body, causing my heart to beat in double-time. I wonder if he can feel it through my thin yellow shirt. Rachael Price launches into the final chorus, and I take one more deep breath before looking James square in the eyes and ask the biggest question of my life.

"Question twenty," I whisper. I can feel him suck in a quick breath. His hands, which were resting loosely on my hips, tighten their grip in anticipation.

"Will you be my first?"

He doesn't say anything for seven seconds.

Seven.

Long.

Seconds.

And then he smiles bigger than I've ever seen him smile. He spins me around in the grass beside The Beast, then lowers his forehead to mine and kisses me senseless.

"So I'll take that as a yes, then?" I giggle, when we come up for air. He gathers me back into his arms and presses his lips to my forehead.

"That's definitely a yes. With two conditions." His Adam's apple bobs as he swallows. "Not on prom night and not in a backseat. That's so cliché, and you're so much better than that."

"No backseats and not prom night," I echo, my face once again nestled in my favorite spot between his chest and neck. "I was thinking more... tonight. In my room," I whisper. His entire body tenses for a moment before he pulls away and takes my face in his hands.

"How? Aren't your parents home?"

"Nope. Dad got called out this morning to do another overnight trip. His partner has food poisoning or something like that. Mom always goes with him and I stay at Avery's."

"And I take it you're not staying at Avery's?" he asks in a hushed voice.

"I may have forgotten to ask if I could sleep over," I say with an innocent smile.

"Are you sure?" His eyes dart back and forth between mine, searching for any sign of doubt.

"I've never been surer. More sure. Whatever," I quietly laugh. James kisses my cheek and winks at me, and all the nervousness I felt a few minutes ago vanishes.

"Come on, let's get the rest of the photo shoot finished first."

Photo shoot? Oh yeah. That's the second time tonight I've forgotten where we are. I put the blame squarely on James. We turn toward Amy and Reshma, only to see them staring at us with their mouths hanging open.

"So what's next?" James asks loudly.

"Um. Uh... barn. The barn," Amy sputters, shaking her head like she's trying to clear the fog. "Sorry, I'm just over here trying to process the last ten minutes. Y'all are... that was... intense."

Tell me about it. And she didn't even hear what we were saying.

I hope.

"Anyway," she continues, "go ahead and change into your last outfits and we'll walk back to the barn. How do y'all feel about sparklers?"

I admit, I wasn't exactly sure how Amy was going to work sparklers into our photos, but the test shots she showed me look really cool. James and I burned up a few sticks practicing how to write backwards. I think we finally have the hang of it.

"All right. For these shots, you're each going to write one word describing the other person. James, you go first. Rachel, come stand by me and face that way." She points in the opposite direction of James. "You won't see the word until you get your prints back." Excitement dances in her eyes, and it's easy to tell that she's having as much fun with this as we are.

"Hey Amy, can I get another sparkler? I'm not gonna be able to write 'pain in my ass' with just one." James flashes a grin at me before taking his spot in front of the white garden lights that Amy strung across barn. I playfully give him the middle finger and turn away, using the time to think of what word I'll write. How am I supposed to summarize him in one word? He's ridiculously good looking, stubborn, sweet, and incredibly talented. He's an old soul with a huge heart who makes me feel like I won the boyfriend lottery. He's... *everything.*

Amy lowers her camera and jerks her chin toward the barn. "Your turn!"

"Better make it good, babe," James says as we pass each other. "If you need any suggestions, I'm happy to help. Let's see. Gorgeous, charming, body of a god. Take your pick." He tosses the lighter to me and winks.

"Maybe I'll just draw a picture of your big, fat head." I stick my tongue out at him and take my place. James attempts to peek but Amy playfully whacks him in the shoulder. Yup, I really like her.

"Okay, Rachel, ready when you are!" Amy hollers.

I take a deep breath and ignite the long stick, creating a shower of sparks in front of me. When I was little, I was afraid of sparklers. I always thought they'd catch my hand on fire. Thankfully, I got over that. I position my flaming wand at shoulder height and look over at Amy, who gives me a thumbs up. With a beaming smile on my face, I start writing words: Funny. Sweet. Hot. Mine. *It*. Like I said—finding one word was impossible.

Sue me.

My sparkler still has some life left to it, so I twirl around in a circle, raising my arm up higher as I go. Traces of light cocoon me for a fraction of a second until they fade in the warm night air. Then I toss my spent stick in a bucket of water off to the side and walk back to James and Amy.

"Where's your camera bag?" James asks Amy. The two share a brief knowing look.

"It's on the trunk of my car," she answers with a smile. He jogs over to it and reaches inside. I hear something crinkling, but he quickly hides what he pulled out.

"Ray, can I borrow you for a second?"

I approach with trepidation, not knowing what to expect.

"Don't worry," he says, holding out a reassuring hand. I take it without hesitation and he pulls me to the same spot we took our sparkler pictures in. He turns to stand toe-to-toe with me and grabs my other hand, interlacing our fingers together. "It's time for a corny speech," he takes a deep breath. "The last two months have been the best in my life. That's all thanks to you. I know I'm getting ready to leave, but I have no doubt that we're gonna be just fine. And no, that's not something I know because I'm psychic. I just *know*." He touches his forehead to mine. Our lips are millimeters apart, but he doesn't close the space. We stay this way for several seconds. Long enough for our breath to blend together and my stomach to grab ahold of my heart in preparation for whatever is coming next. I can see his shoulders rise and fall with a deep breath, and then he gets down on one knee.

One.

Freaking.

Knee.

Holyshitholyshitholyshit! My insides do a series of flips worthy of an Olympic gold medal. Thankfully, my knees cooperate and keep me upright.

"Rachel Lynn Wheaton, I knew from the moment I saw you that my life would never be the same. I've never been a fan of Economics, but it's been really fun planning our pretend future together. One day, will you do me the honor of being my real wife?"

He lets go of my right hand, reaches into his back pocket, and pulls out a ring.

Make that a Ring Pop.

A red one, if we're getting specific.

I look back and forth between his face and my cherry-flavored symbol of love, and then I burst into a fit of laughter. He stands up and wraps me in his arms, laughing right along with me.

"Oh, God. My side. It hurts so bad," I wheeze, overtaken with another fit of giggles. I step back and wipe the tears that are streaming down my face.

"So I'll take that as a yes, then?" he asks.

"That's a yes," I reply with a smile. He slides the Ring Pop on my finger and kisses the side of my head.

"I love you, Mrs. Tennyson," he says as his arms encircle me again.

"I love you, too." I position my head between his neck and shoulder and take a deep breath. This boy... this moment... it's perfect. I do my best to take in all the details so we can share this crazy story with our kids one day.

Our kids.

The thought makes me smile. I wonder how many we'll have. Will they get my blonde hair or his brown hair? Will they have his musical talents or my love of running? The sound of him clearing his throat snaps me back to the present.

"I think we're probably done here. Wanna... uh... head to your house?"

Done here?

Oh yeah. The photo shoot. I forgot again.

Surprisingly, the drive home wasn't awkward. James kept me mildly distracted with kisses to my neck and the spot below my ear, so that may be why.

"Do you need to let your mom know you won't be home for a while?" I ask, setting my purse and keys on my dresser. I hadn't really thought about the logistics of it all, but I don't want her freaking out because he's not home. James pulls up iTunes on my laptop and sits on my bed with his knees bent over the edge.

"I already texted her and told her I was spending the night with you."

"You *what*?" I squeak. While I'm not at all worried about regretting my decision, it's not something I want to broadcast to everyone else, too.

"Relax, babe," he says with a soft chuckle. "Mom's a hippie at heart. Since I turned thirteen, she's told me she didn't care what I did in my relationships as long as I didn't make her a grandma."

"Oh, God. She's gonna know," I cringe, covering my face with my hands.

"Come here." I walk three steps from my dresser to the open space between his legs. He skims his hands over the backs of my thighs before resting them on my hips. "The only thing Mom wanted to know was if I needed a ride home in the morning. I promise you, she doesn't care and she won't tell anyone."

"You don't need a ride. I'll take you home tomorrow. My parents won't be back until the afternoon, anyway." His thumbs find the edge of my shirt and trace circles on the sensitive skin above the hem. My back arches toward him in an automatic response.

"So this means I get to have a sleepover with you?" he asks in an innocent voice that contradicts the gleam in his eyes.

"Something like that," I say, leaning down to claim his lips. Within a span of about ten seconds, our soft, tender kisses turn deeper, faster, stronger, until we are no more than a pair of frenzied mouths desperate to taste and devour. His fingers tighten their grip on my sides, and a soft groan escapes from his throat. We separate long enough for me to lift my shirt over my head. He wastes no time caressing my exposed flesh with his lips, whispering words of adoration between kisses. His hands trail up my spine, pausing when they reach the clasp of the white satin bra that I bought just for this occasion.

"May I?" he asks, looking up through hooded eyes. His voice is deeper, raspier, and the sound travels straight to my core, pooling in my panties. I nod, not trusting myself to actually be able to form words. His fingers make quick work of the clasp and he lowers the straps over my shoulders and down my arms.

"Christ," he hisses on an exhale. "You're perfect. Absolutely. Fucking. Perfect." He pulls me onto his lap, then stands and turns to lay me down on the bed. He spends the next several minutes—maybe hours, I don't know—worshiping the upper half of my body with his mouth and hands. My hips grind into his thigh, desperate for friction to ease the storm building between my legs.

"A little impatient, are we?" he softly laughs. I can only whimper in response. He sits back on his heels and pulls his shirt off, tossing it somewhere on the floor. I can't help but smile knowing I'm the cause of the bulge in his pants, which is now clearly on display. Without saying anything, I reach up and undo his button and zipper. He rises so I can tug his jeans down, then kneels back on the bed wearing only his boxer briefs. His eyes skim my breasts and stomach before settling on the top of my pink pants. He grabs the button and flicks his gaze back up, seeking approval before unfastening it.

"Please and thank you," I say sweetly, as I lift my hips.

"Cherries?" he asks, pointing to the picture on my matching white thong. "Why cherries?"

"I thought it was appropriate, given the situation," I say with an innocent shrug.

"Well played." Laughter rumbles from his chest as he high-fives me.

"Thank you," I reply, smiling brightly. I know sex is supposed to be, well, *sexy*. But it's also supposed to be fun, and his reaction is exactly what I hoped for.

He hooks his fingers on the straps of my thong and removes it with ease, throwing it off the bed to the sea of discarded clothes below. His eyes scan my entire body with a look of reverence and desire. I've never felt more beautiful in my life.

"I wish you could see yourself the way I see you right now. It's…" He shakes his head back and forth trying to come up with words. "You. This night. It's a gift, and it's not one I take for granted." He strips off his boxer briefs and lowers himself over me, rubbing his length over my sex before straddling my left thigh and working his magic mouth over my neck, shoulder and breast. The tongue swirl thing he's doing to my nipple is amazing. I run my fingers through his hair, one, because I love the way it feels, and two, because I need to keep his head right there. He should always do that. All the time. Forever.

His free hand trails down my stomach until he reaches the apex of my thighs. His fingers brush over the small patch of hair, and he releases my breast with a gentle bite.

"May I?" he asks, with another swipe of his fingers.

"You have incredible manners, Mr. Tennyson," I giggle softly.

"Just making sure you're okay with this, every step of the way," he says against my neck. "You can change your mind at any time."

"I'm not changing my mind. I want this. I want *you*." On that word, his fingers slip into my slick folds. My hips buck in response, and a cry escapes my lips. I won't lie. I've double-clicked my mouse on occasion, but it never felt this good. Not even close.

"James," I sigh, pulling at his torso. The need to feel him on me and in me is overwhelming. "Please."

He reaches back to the foot of the bed and pulls his wallet from the back pocket of his jeans. He tears open the foil packet and rolls the condom on without ever looking away from me.

Sweet Jesus, that was hot.

He places his hands on either side of my shoulders and hovers over me, the tip of his length lightly caressing my sex. His eyes dart back and forth between mine. I lift my hips, urging him to continue, and the corners of his mouth turn upward as he slowly slides into me. He lowers his body to mine and props himself on one elbow, giving me time to adjust to his size. The pain, which I'd heard ranged from a slight ache to a sharp sting, never comes.

"You okay?" he asks. He strings kisses from my lips to my jaw, then down my neck and back up.

"Never been better." And really, I haven't. No amount of health class or reading Cosmo magazine could have prepared me for this. Not just for the moment I lost my virginity, but for all the feelings and emotions that go with it.

His hips start a slow rhythm, testing, teasing, giving, and taking. He leans his head back down to my breasts and alternates his attention between each peak. It's quite amazing, honestly. I can't even chew gum and walk at the same time.

"Oh my God, this feels amazing," I moan on a breath.

"Glad to hear I'm making it worth your while," he says, laughing once against my chest.

"Are we supposed to talk during sex?"

"It's our party, we can talk if we want to. Or lick. Or bite." He demonstrates the last two words on my right nipple, causing me to gasp with a surge of pleasure.

"Well in that case, I want you to flip over, Mr. Tennyson."

"Yes ma'am."

He gives me another kiss, then slips out of me and takes my place on the bed. I settle over him and watch his eyes darken with desire as I lower myself onto him. We sigh in unison. He grips my hips with his hands and rocks me into him once, placing the perfect amount of pressure where I need it most.

"OH!" I cry, not able to help myself. He does it again, and again, his smile growing bigger each time I voice my pleasure.

"That is officially the sexiest sound I'll ever hear in my life," he rasps.

I anchor my palms on his chest, thoroughly enjoying the feel of his muscles constricting beneath me. His hands travel up my sides and cup my breasts as I increase my speed. My breath comes in short bursts through my parted lips, and I can't help but smile.

"Fuck, Ray," he groans. "You can't look at me like that. I won't last much longer." He brings his hands around my back and pulls down on the tops of my shoulders. The movement creates a storm of friction where we're joined, and my hips accelerate as if I'm rounding the final turn of the 1600 meter. Tingles of euphoria spark to life. They shoot through my body, grabbing a hold of each other as they go, getting bigger, faster, stronger. In the fury of motion, my eyes find his and I let go.

"JAMES!" I yelp, bursting into pieces above him. He answers with three thrusts and a loud grunt of his own.

We stay that way, connected physically and emotionally, for several minutes while our heartbeats return to a normal rhythm. As the rush of blood quiets down in my ears, I hear music from my laptop. I forgot he'd turned it on when we came into my room. I lay beside him with my head in my favorite spot between his (slightly sweaty) chest and neck as Meghan Trainor and John Legend sing to us. He runs his hand up and down my spine and together we soak up their words of advice like it's the gospel truth.

James

We survived the first month apart. Technically it was thirty-two days, but who's counting? All I have to say is thank God for Spring Break.

"I think this one's my favorite." I point to the picture of Rachel at mile 20 of the marathon she ran last weekend with her dad. She's covered in sweat and giving the camera two middle fingers.

"Thankfully Mom didn't give me too much shit for that one," she laughs. "I wish you could have been here."

"Me too. But I'm here for about a hundred and seventy more hours." I flip through the rest of the photos on her phone and pass it back as the waiter brings our check. I take out enough money to cover our dinner and the tip, then shove the last bite of chicken and waffles in my mouth.

"You said you were stuffed three bites ago. You'd better not hurl during our date."

"And waste this culinary masterpiece?" I ask, gesturing toward my empty plate. "No way." I wink at her and lead the way out of the restaurant. "You're still not gonna tell me where we're going?"

"Nope. And *please* don't tell me you already know. This psychic boyfriend thing is a real pain in the ass sometimes."

"I promise I don't know. But I recommend staying off of I-40 because there's gonna be a bad accident soon."

She stops in the middle of the sidewalk and glances back at me. "You are *so* weird," she chuckles. "Anyway, we're not driving. We're walking."

Several minutes later, we round the corner and I see the performing arts center.

"You're taking me to see a show?"

"Maybe." Her eyes light up and she bites her bottom lip. Just like she did a few hours ago underneath me when she officially welcomed me back. Christ, now I'm starting to get hard again.

"Who are we seeing?" I ask, adjusting myself slightly.

"I'm not telling you yet. In fact, close your eyes. I'll guide you the rest of the way." She loops her left arm in mine.

"You're really milking this, aren't you?" I try to peek, but judging by the whack to my chest, I guess she was watching for that.

"Absolutely. I only get one shot at this and I want to capture the moment when you realize who's performing."

We stumble through the parking lot and up a few flights of stairs before she pushes me through a set of doors.

"Okay, on the count of three, open your eyes and look straight in front of you."

On cue, I do as I'm told and see a concert poster staring back at me. Holy shit!

"You took me to see Lake Street Dive?" My voice shoots up at least an octave, and I have to fight against the happy dance that's begging to come out.

"Happy birthday!" she squeals, taking a picture. "Are you excited?"

"Dude, my inner school girl is high-fiving herself so hard right now." I take Rachel in my arms and press a kiss against the side of her head. "Thank you. You have no idea how much this means to me. But you're still not getting your present until tomorrow."

"That's fine," she laughs. "Let's go get our seats."

What she didn't tell me was that they're front row seats. She's officially the best girlfriend on the planet. Also, the necklace I got her seems so small in comparison.

An hour later, the band walks on stage and the crowd goes nuts. What's funny is the extreme range of ages. The couple on my right look to be in their 60s and the group of guys behind us are all college-aged. The best part about the night is that Rachael Price sounds even better in person, which I didn't know was possible. I find myself mesmerized by her voice.

"Did I tell you thank you for this? Because it's the best birthday present I've ever gotten," I say into Rachel's ear over the noise from the crowd. She grins back at me like it's no big deal.

"Before we go into our next song, I'd like to take a minute and deliver a message," Rachael says. My Rachel puts a death grip on my left arm. What the hell? "In the past month, a few people have blown up our social media accounts." Now Ray is squealing and jumping up and down.

"Dude, what's going on?" I ask.

"It seems one of my biggest fans has a birthday tomorrow. Are Rachel and James here?"

No.

Fucking.

Way.

Ray shouts waves both arms like a lunatic, but I'm too stunned to move.

"What have you done?" I ask in disbelief.

"Front and center. Excellent," Rachael says, pointing at us. "Bridget, Mike, McDuck, and I hope you have a very happy birthday!" With that, the band launches into the *Happy Birthday* song, and the entire crowd joins in.

This might be the best thirty seconds of my life.

"Holy fuck. I can't believe you did that. I can die a happy man now," I say, clutching my heart. I realize she recorded the whole thing on her phone, but I don't care. My head is so far beyond cloud nine that I'll probably need help remembering the moment tomorrow.

"Did it hurt?" Avery asks, as Mandy brings a box of pizza to the table. Fletcher and I just got done with our last open mic night before prom, and we're starving. This large pepperoni and bacon doesn't stand a chance against us.

"Not really. It felt more like a burning bee sting," Ray responds, running her fingers over the infinity sign inked on the inside of her left wrist. Since we're officially eighteen now, we each got a tattoo this afternoon. Rachel made a comment about finishing all of her bucket list items since we checked off the Lake Street Dive concert last night. We need to brainstorm some more.

"What'd you get, dude?" Fletcher asks in between bites of pizza. I lift my T-shirt sleeve and show them the R on the inside of my left bicep.

"Are you nuts?" Avery shrieks. "What happens if y'all break up?"

"Then I guess I better find another girl whose name starts with R," I say, winking at Rachel. "Let's see. Rebecca. Renee. Rosario. Hmmm. That one sounds kind of exotic." I rub my chin in mock thought, before lifting another slice of pizza from the box.

"I don't plan on going anywhere, so I think you're safe," Rachel says. "I just hope some Florida beach bimbo doesn't woo you away." She tries to play off the remark by making a silly face, but I know she's still a little insecure about me being so far away.

"Well, there was a girl from my seventh period class that kept making googly eyes at me last week, but I took care of that."

"Did you tell her you already had a girlfriend?" Avery asks.

"Hell, no. That's like issuing a challenge. I thought of... another way that will hopefully keep me off of every girl's radar."

"Which was...?" Rachel asks.

In my most nonchalant voice, I say, "I told her I was gay and that if she didn't have a big, thick penis, she was really wasting her time."

"You did NOT!" Rachel shouts before dissolving into a

fit of giggles. Avery, Fletcher, and I follow suit. When Mandy walks back to our table, we're all struggling to breathe.

"What in the Sam Hill is goin' on over here?" She eyes us like we're high on something.

"James is giving us lessons on how to win over the male population at his new school," Fletcher eeks out between bouts of laughter.

"Funny you should mention that," I say. "The next morning in P.E., some kid kept giving me *the eye* in the locker room. It was really creepy." I shudder at thought.

"You brought that on yourself, dude. Looks like you caused more problems than you solved," Fletcher says.

"Speaking of how much money we made tonight," Mandy says, in an obvious attempt at changing the subject, "with tonight's totals, we're at one thousand two hundred and thirty bucks. That's more than enough to do a post-prom party here for about twenty-five guests, and then we'll have some left over. How do y'all feel about raffling off a Sweet Pea scholarship?"

"That's actually a pretty cool idea, Mom," Avery says. "That could be the last thing we do before the party ends. I guess we should go over the invite list, huh? Does anyone have any paper?"

"I've got some in my purse." Ray opens the zipper, removes a small spiral-bound notepad and pen and passes it to Avery. "Here," she says, handing me my phone, which is vibrating from an incoming call. I'd put my phone on silent and tucked it inside her purse before our set began, but forgot to get it back afterward. One glance at the screen has my stomach dropping to my toes.

"Shit."

I try to swipe to answer Mom's call, but it quits ringing before I can. With shaky hands, I manage to unlock the screen and see I missed three other calls and four text messages.

Mom: River, call me ASAP.
Mom: Where are you?
Mom: Why are you not answering?
Mom: CALL ME NOW.

I use one hand to grab Rachel's and use the other to dial Mom. She answers on the first ring.

"Mom, what's going on?" I ask, even though I already know.

"Honey, I'm sorry. I'm s-so sorry," she says between sobs. "Gran is g-gone."

Her words punch me in the gut. Gran's health steadily declined once we got to Florida, but I thought she'd be okay until I got back. I offered to stay instead of coming up here for Spring Break. She told me I wasn't allowed to quit living my life because hers was coming to an end. Then she threatened to put me on diaper duty if I didn't go to North Carolina to see my woman. That was the last thing she said to me. I kissed her on the cheek and left for the airport right after that.

"R-river, are y-you there?"

"Yeah," I manage to squeak out. Fletcher and Avery exchange worried glances with Rachel, who squeezes my hand harder. "I'm here, Mom. Do you need me to come home?" Rachel gasps, and her free hand flies to her mouth as she figures out what's going on.

"No. She'll be c-cremated in a c-couple of d-days. W-we'll spread her ashes a-after you come b-back."

"Okay. Thanks for telling me," I say around a massive lump in my throat. I end the call, lay my head on top of my arm on the table and let the sobs overtake me. I can't believe this woman, one of the few constants I had in my life, won't be waiting for me when I fly back to Florida. What's even weirder is that I had no idea that today was her day. No flashes. No memories. Nothing. I'm sort of glad though. Had I known, there's no way I would have come—diaper duty or not. Ray pulls me into her arms, and together we weep for our biggest champion and the huge hole she's leaving in our lives.

Several minutes later, I pull away and grab a stack of napkins from the dispenser on the table, keeping a few for myself and passing the rest to Ray.

"Sorry, guys," I say, blowing my nose. "I didn't mean to get so emotional. I knew she was sick and wasn't going to last much longer, but I guess that still doesn't prepare you for actually hearing the words."

"Don't apologize, James. We all loved Gran," Avery says, wiping her own eyes.

"Dude. She's probably giving St. Peter a run for his money," Fletcher says, laughing softly. "I can hear her now—'My name is Pearl, you buffoon! Let me past my gate!'"

"Or fussing about where her chef's kitchen is so she can start making some more pies," Ray adds with a small smile.

We share more stories about Gran and make the invite list for the post-prom bash, which the girls are calling "Party at the Pea," while Fletcher and I finish the last of the pizza. When we're done, we head to the front door and wait for Mandy to lock up. I grab Ray's hand as we cross the parking lot. She's riding home with Avery since I'm staying at Fletcher's, so we have to say our goodbyes here. Lame.

"What the hell is this?" Avery asks, pulling a folded white piece of paper from her windshield.

There's still time to choose the better man.

"Really? Why doesn't this asshole get the hint?"

"Mouth, Avery," Mandy says with a raised eyebrow.

"Seriously, Mom. I'm so over this seventh grade sh—stuff." She wads up the paper and walks it to the trash can in front of the restaurant. My gut churns as I turn in a complete circle to scan the parking lot. Nothing seems out of place, but that doesn't stop my mind from flashing to the man I saw across the sidewalk in New York City.

"You okay?" Rachel asks, tugging on my arm.

"Yeah, I'm fine." I rub the back of my neck to smooth down the hairs that are standing on end. I really, *really* don't like this.

"God, I've missed you." I drop my carry-on at my feet to catch Rachel as she jumps in my arms, which earns a series of "Awws" from the people standing nearby. Our mouths collide, making up for the three weeks we've been apart. It takes me a few minutes, but I manage to remember that we're in baggage claim and not a bedroom. "Easy killer, I don't wanna jump you in an airport," I say with a laugh against Ray's cheek.

"Let's grab my stuff and see about an early check-in." Prom's at a ritzy hotel in Durham. Mom sprung for a room there as an early graduation present. Since it won't be our first time, I'm completely okay with spending prom night with Ray, especially since this will be the last night I have with her until graduation.

"I need to remember to thank her. Hopefully I can keep the blushing to a minimum," Rachel says.

"You're really cute when you're embarrassed, you know that?" I give her a quick kiss on the nose as my suitcase drops onto the baggage carousel. I pick it up and walk out the door marked "Short Term Parking." I took the earliest flight I could today to maximize the time I have with Rachel. I fly out tomorrow at three in the afternoon.

"How do you like the new vet's office?" she asks as we make our way to her car.

"It's pretty cool. Dr. Folsom is gonna give me a letter of recommendation for school. I called Dr. Brooks last week and she said she'd love to have me back at the animal hospital once I move back up after graduation."

"So it looks like I'll be the one married to the hot veterinarian instead of the hot firefighter," Rays says teasingly.

"Yup." I lift my bags into her trunk and settle into the passenger seat. "Did you remember to bring those notes?"

"They're in the glove box." Rachel punches the hotel address into the GPS and backs out of the parking space.

"So they stopped a week ago?" I flip through the stack of nine messages. All of the messages are harmless, so it's nothing I can take to the police. Still, that uneasy feeling is simmering away in my gut. I'd hoped that by touching the notes, I'd get a flash of something worthwhile, but it didn't work. I'm still just as clueless as I was before.

"And Avery put tape on the vents of her locker?"

"Yeah, she got some 'Do Not Enter' duct tape and wrote 'NOT INTERESTED.' The messages stopped after that."

"Hmmm. Well, enough of that." I return the messages to the glove box and take Rachel's hand. "What's the plan for the rest of the day?"

"Avery's doing hair and makeup at four, then y'all will pick us up at her house. Mom and Dad will be there to take pictures. Prom's in the Holden Ballroom from six to ten. We're doing Party at the Pea from ten to midnight."

I glance at my watch. It's only eleven thirty in the morning.

"So that means we have four and a half hours to kill."

"Yeah, did you have anything particular in mind?" Her eyes never leave the road, but her cheeks flush slightly and she licks her lips.

Busted.

"Actually I did."

I dropped Ray off at Avery's house right at four then went to Fletcher's to get dressed. An hour and a half later, I'm back on her front porch. When Mandy opens the door, I find myself unable to breathe. Rachel's dress is done in varying shades of blue, and her hair's pulled up in a messy bun with a bunch of curls hanging down. She looks like a really sexy mermaid. I've never seen her wear makeup like this either. Her eyes are... wow. And her lips, which a few hours ago were all over me, are now covered in a shimmery gloss. She looks like she's ready for a night at the Oscars, not prom.

"Holy shit."

"Mouth, James," Mandy cautions. "But you're right." Her smile lets me know she's forgiven me for my language. She opens the door wider so Fletcher and I can pass through. His tongue is practically hanging out as he takes in Avery's bright red dress. I have to admit—she's smokin' hot too. The girls look at each other and giggle, then do a slow spin so we can see the rest of their dresses.

"Did you really make these?" I ask.

"Did you doubt my abilities?" Avery counters with one hand on her hip and an eyebrow lifted.

"No, I just didn't know you were this... good. These dresses look like they're off the rack of some fancy store."

"Nice recovery, James."

"Anyway. Y'all both look beautiful. And Fletcher and I have something for you." The first box is small. We each hand them over, and the girls bust out laughing when they open them.

"Ring pops? Why am I not surprised?" Rachel giggles as she slips it on her finger. We made sure to color-coordinate with their dresses, which I was pretty proud of. Fletcher helps Avery put hers on while Rachel's dad clicks away from the side of the living room.

"Okay, now for your real gift," Fletch says. "Since the dresses were handmade, we decided to skip the corsages and do something else that's handmade. Plus, I know you hate flowers, Avery."

"Finally, someone who gets me!" she laughs.

The girls open the second box and share matching gasps. Nestled inside each box is a bracelet made out of guitar strings and a pick. Ray's pick is engraved with J + R and Avery's says F + A.

"This is *perfect!*" Avery exclaims.

"I love it so much. Thank you!" Rachel squeals. Fletcher and I fasten the bracelets and pose for the obligatory prom photos. Ray's dad is going over the list of do's and don'ts when the doorbell rings.

My heart starts galloping in my chest as I glance around at everyone in the living room. I'm the closest to the door, so I open it and see Derrick standing on the front steps wearing the same aviator sunglasses I saw that day in Battery Park. He looks so different from the day he came into the Pea. Maybe it's because he's wearing a tuxedo instead of baggy pants. His hair is shorter, too. Every inch of my body is on alert. When he tries to push past me, I shift to the right to block the door.

"Can I help you?" I ask with as much threat in my voice as I can muster.

"No, but she can," he says, pointing at a shocked Avery.

"What the HELL are you doing here?" Avery shouts. For once, Mandy doesn't give her a language warning.

"Picking my date up for the prom." He smiles and gestures to the white limo on the street in front of the house. "Come on, babe."

"*Babe*? What the actual fuck, Derrick? I have no idea why you're here or why you think I'd be willing to go anywhere with you. We're over. We've been over. You're not even a blip on my radar. If you were on life support, I'd unplug you to charge my phone. What part of that can you not get through your thick skull?"

It's been a while since I've seen Avery fired up. I forgot

how much she scares me. Derrick doesn't look the slightest bit fazed by her words.

"You don't mean that. You just need to remember how good we were together. That's what all my notes were for. To help you remember." He holds up a clear plastic container with a corsage made of red roses.

"You're the one who was leaving me notes? How is that even possible?"

"I started chatting with a kid who goes to your school in an online gaming forum. He said he'd be happy to help me win my girl back. Don't you see the lengths I've gone through to get you back?"

"Who?"

"His name's Warren."

Smelly Warren? God, this is getting creepy.

"Like I've told you a thousand times before. I. Am. Not. Interested. I never will be again. You had your chance and you blew it. I deserve better."

"You certainly didn't act like you weren't interested at Labyrinth," he says in a steely voice.

"What the hell are you even talking about?" Avery's eyes narrow. "How did you know I was at Labyrinth?"

"Because I was dancing with you. Right behind you. With your body pressed against mine as you let loose."

"That was you?" She looks physically repulsed.

"It was. So don't tell me that we aren't still good for each other."

"Go to hell, Derrick. Go straight to hell and don't ever come back." She grabs Fletcher's arm. His fists are clenched so hard that his knuckles are white and the muscle in his jaw is twitching back and forth. Based on that look, Derrick has about thirty seconds to leave.

Now it feels like ice water is pumping through my veins.

"Fine. But this isn't over."

He turns and storms down the driveway into the open door of the limo.

"Are you okay?" Ray asks, rubbing Avery's arm.

"I'm fine, I promise. But I *really* don't know what I ever saw in that asshole," she laughs. "And Fletcher, I promise I can explain what he's talking about. It's really nothing like it sounds."

"Babe, you don't have to explain anything. That guy is delusional and that's all there is to it. Now let's get outta here so I can show off my hot girlfriend."

"My feet hurt so bad," Rachel groans. "The next time Avery tries to talk me into wearing three-inch heels, smack me please."

"Aww, poor baby," I say, twisting her around in the booth to face me. It's the same one we sat in the first day she met me to go over our Economics project. That seems like forever ago. I take her foot into my lap and press my fingertips into the arch. "You know, your feet probably wouldn't hurt so much if you weren't trying to show off on the dance floor in front of Vivien Tanner," I tease. I hope the playfulness of my voice covers up the growing sense of dread I'm feeling. All I wanna do is get Ray back to the hotel, more for her safety than for any of the activities I have planned.

"And miss out on rubbing it in her face that we're still together? No way. The foot pain is well worth the scowl she wore all night. Besides, you didn't seem to mind being pressed up against me for four hours." She flicks an eyebrow at me in a mock challenge to prove her wrong.

"I don't regret one second of it." My knuckles knead the pad of her foot, and she sighs in relief.

"I've officially died and gone to heaven," she moans. "If you need me, I'll be the one in a massage-induced coma at the Sweet Pea." I carefully lay her foot down and pick up the other one to give it the same treatment. "I just really wish you didn't have to leave tomorrow."

"Me t—"

"Can I have your attention please?" Mandy shouts from the other side of the room. "We'll announce the scholarship raffle winner in three minutes. Or however long it takes me to find where I put the basket of tickets." She spins around, checking the tables near her. "Avery, will you go in my office and see if I left it there?"

Avery walks off the makeshift dance floor with Fletcher in tow, headed to the back of the diner. I reach for the ticket in my jacket pocket when pain shoots from the center of my chest outward to my fingers and toes.

"AAAHH!" I shout. He's here. It's happening. It all makes sense. I have to get Rachel out of here.

Now.

She jerks forward and runs her hands over my face, her eyebrows drawn together in a tight line. "Are you okay? What's wrong? You're seriously freaking me out."

"Rachel, RUN!" I can barely get the words out before I'm shoving her out of the booth. We make it about five feet across the empty diner floor when the door jingles and Derrick storms in.

With a gun.

"Where is Avery?" he bellows, his eyes darting wildly around the room.

Screams echo across the diner. The people who were standing by the stage duck behind two rows of empty booths. Mandy and another group of students dive behind the main counter. Most of the girls are crying, and one behind me says, "I don't want to die on prom night!"

Ray and I are caught in the middle of the floor with nothing to protect us. I carefully step in front of her as I try to keep Derrick calm, which is hard to do considering he's got a gun and my insides feel like they're liquefying.

"She's not here, dude. She didn't feel good and she left. We're all getting ready to leave. Why don't you lower the gun and I can try to get her on the phone for you?"

"That's bullshit!" he shouts, waving the gun in the air. "That fucker's car is outside, so I know she's still here. AVERY! It's time you come out and be with the one you're supposed to be with."

Derrick is too far away for me to tackle, but too close for me to be able to run at without being shot. Still, I have to do something. I reach behind me with my left hand and grab ahold of Rachel's left arm. We're about seven steps from the main counter. If I can get her even halfway there, she can dive for the counter when I lunge toward Derrick. I just pray that Fletcher and Avery are calling the police in the back.

Rachel and I take one small step to the left. As if he can hear my thoughts, Derrick aims the gun directly at me.

"Don't even. You and the whore behind you have been filling Avery's head full of lies. Telling her she should be with that douchecanoe instead of me. Telling her she should throw her flowers and notes away. Telling her she's better off without me." His hysteria climbs higher and higher, but it's getting harder to hear him. The pain that burst in my chest when he walked in is now pulsing through every inch of my body. "Let's see how you like living without the girl you love." Blood rushes into my ears when he takes a step to his left and points the barrel at Rachel. I dive to cover her half a second before Derrick fires his gun.

The bullet pierces me right below my chest.

Of course, the fucker's aim would be spot on.

The sounds of everyone screaming almost blocks out the sound of the second gunshot.

Almost.

Derrick falls to the ground and I fall back onto Rachel. She lays me on the black and white checkered floor and rips my shirt open, all good signs that she wasn't hit too. She shrieks and presses her palm over the bullet hole. It should probably hurt, but oddly, it doesn't. I guess that's the adrenaline?

"JAMES! Please stay with me. Stay here." She lifts her head toward Derrick. "He shot himself. He's gone. You're safe. You kept me safe. I can't believe you did that. I'm gonna kick your ass when you get better."

"Ray," I whisper. "I love you."

"I love you too." Tears roll down her cheeks and mix with the blood pooling on my stomach. I didn't expect everything to feel so warm, but it feels kinda good, so I close my eyes.

I see Gran's face.

"What are you doing here?" I ask, genuinely confused. As far as I know my psychic abilities never included seeing dead people.

"I'm here to take you home."

"I am home. Right here, with Rachel." I look down at her, still clutching my body.

"Looks like you're moving again, son." A sad look crosses Gran's face for the briefest of moments. "Don't worry. I promise this will be the last time."

Rachel

He's gonna be okay.

He's gonna be okay.

He's gonna be okay.

Maybe if I repeat it enough, it'll be true. The power of positive thinking, right?

"James, the EMTs are here. You stay with me," I cry as they move me out of the way. Avery lifts me up and hugs me when they start working on him. Fletcher is on James' phone talking to his mom, relaying all the info we have. Which isn't much.

"I'm so sorry, Rachel. This is all my fault. I had no idea he'd do something like this," she sobs into my chest.

"No one did, Avery. This is not your fault. This is Derrick's fault." I squeeze her and watch helplessly as the EMTs intubate James. I only catch half of what they're saying, and understand even less than that.

"Pulse is weak and thready..."

"Alert the trauma team…"

"Forty-five caliber…"

"Call for LifeFlight…"

They bring in a stretcher and load James onto it. Sensing that this is my last chance to see him before we get to the hospital, I rush over when they get him belted in.

"You hear that, James? You're going on a helicopter. That's the last thing on your bucket list. So tomorrow we're gonna think of more things to add." I reach for his hand and squeeze it, trying to transfer all of my strength to him. "I love you. Please don't leave me."

"Excuse me ma'am, we have to go," one EMT says. I step aside and watch as they run out the door to the helicopter waiting in the field across the street.

"He's gonna be okay, Avery," I say, gripping her arm.

"He's gonna be okay," she repeats.

Five Years Later

"Are you ready for your first day?" Avery asks, entering my new office. It's just outside the gymnasium and still smells like fresh paint. Dad worked with the developers that built the new Glenn Farms community. As best as I can tell from the before and after aerials, Tennyson Elementary School is situated right where their house was.

I take a deep breath and look around the room. My UNC diploma hangs proudly above my desk in between two framed newspaper articles.

April 30, 2016: Murder-Suicide at Local Diner Stuns Small Town

August 26, 2018: New Elementary School Named After Teenage Hero

"Yup, I'm ready. It's not exactly the way I planned on becoming a Tennyson, but I feel good."

"He'd be so proud of you," Avery says quietly. "This is your dream, and you did it." She crosses the room and hugs me, which is getting harder to do these days. Her belly is huge. Only, don't ever tell her that. She gets mean.

"Thanks, Beef. How are you feeling?"

"Like I'm thirty-eight weeks pregnant," she laughs. "Sammy is so excited she can hardly stand it. Although yesterday she asked where babies came from and wasn't happy with the generic answers we've been giving her so far, so *that* was an interesting conversation."

I think back to the months after the shooting and the dark place Avery slipped into. She blamed herself for James' death and pushed everyone away, including me and Fletcher. Thank God we're stubborn. She eventually found a good counselor and worked things out with Fletcher. They got married a year and a half ago, around the same time she changed her career path. Now she designs clothes as part of Thrive + Blossom, an organization that supports victims of domestic violence. All of her models are survivors, and many of them started working there too.

"James would be proud of you too. I know I am," I say, rubbing her belly. "And I can't wait to meet this little guy. Have y'all decided on a name yet?"

"Last night, finally. It was Fletcher's idea, and I can't think of a more perfect name. In two weeks, you'll meet your godson, Henry James Strickland."

My eyes instantly fill with tears. "It's beautiful. Thank you for honoring him," I whisper before clearing my throat. The first year at UNC was tough. Especially after I discovered that James had been accepted and would have been there with me. I missed him with such an intensity that some days it was hard to breathe. I felt like I had a boulder on my chest that wouldn't budge. Eventually I started finding my happy. Little things along the way would happen like hearing a song from James' YouTube channel when I was missing him more than normal or some random item would appear completely out of the blue, like a guitar pic on the sidewalk. It was like James was right there with me, reminding me to be happy. I owed him that much. I also started volunteering at an animal shelter and even adopted a mangy looking puppy that stole my heart. She's feisty and sweet. I named her Pearl.

"Now you better go home and prop your feet up before Fletcher gets mad at me for keeping you here so long. And I'll be on the lookout for Sammy later this morning. I promised her she could be my helper during P.E."

"Which means we'll hear all about Aunt Rachel's gym class during dinner," she laughs, wiping her own eyes.

I walk Avery to the door and give her one last hug, then turn back to the row of photos I put up last week in preparation for the first day of school. The first picture is of Mom, Dad, and me at my college graduation. I'm wearing the UNC flag Dad draped around my shoulders. He's smiling even bigger than I am. This year for Father's Day, I got him a "Proud Dad of a Tarheel Grad" T-shirt. I think he wore it for a week straight.

The next picture is of me and Sunny the last time she stopped in town. Grandpa died about a year after James did, and Sunny dealt with the loss as best as she knew how—she bought an RV and she and Lazarus started driving. I get a postcard every few months from a new location, talking about the odd jobs she's done and the people she's met.

Next is a picture of me at my first guitar lesson. Sunny gave me Lucy, James' guitar, a couple of years ago. Learning to play has been so much fun, and now I'll be able to incorporate music into my P.E. classes.

The next picture is from the photo shoot James and I had before he moved. Amy delivered the prints to my house a week after James' funeral. It was the first time I saw the sparkler word he wrote to describe me.

Everything.

That day, I realized our love was a lot like the sparklers we used in our photos—instant, quick burning, and over way too soon. Last year, I was on a fourteen-mile run wondering if I'd ever find someone who made me feel the way James did. I mean, how can a person have a love like that twice in their life?

That's when I heard Gran's voice.

"Quit looking at what's happening right now and see the bigger picture."

Two months later, I met Adam outside the campus library. And by met, I mean I tripped on the stairs and crashed into him, sending us down the last several steps in a tangle of knees and elbows.

I was bruised for weeks.

He joked that I knocked him off his feet, and we've been a couple ever since. It was strange at first, making room for another man in my heart, but Adam was more than understanding as I processed my emotions. With the help of counseling, I've learned that no one will ever make me feel the way James did. He was my first love, and that can't ever be duplicated.

I step in front of the last picture on the wall and smile. Adam is on his knee holding a small blue box, his face beaming with love and excitement. My hands are covering most of my face, but there's a smile underneath, I promise. Our wedding was small. Our parents and ten of our closest friends traveled to St. Croix to watch us get married on the beach. It's been four months, and Avery has almost forgiven me for wearing a tank top and cutoff shorts. Even though we got married in paradise, Adam insisted we go on a honeymoon. He kept our location a surprise, and Avery helped him pack for what I would need. When we got to the airport and I discovered the honeymoon he had planned was to Fiji, I crumbled into a weeping mess of tears. I told Adam about James' prediction five years ago that the man of my dreams would take me to Fiji.

James was right—the man of my dreams *did* take me there. I'd like to believe he had a hand in placing Adam in my life. I rub the infinity tattoo on the inside of my left wrist, thinking about how the meaning has changed over the years. I got it to symbolize my unending love for James, but now I know that it represents the love my heart carries for two wonderful men— each part just as great as the other.

Where one ends, the other begins.

Without either side, I'd be incomplete.

Acknowledgements

To anyone who's made it to the back of the book, thank you for taking a chance on a newbie. (And I hope we're still friends.) There are a million books out there, and I'm humbled that you chose to spend some time with James and Rachel. Thank you for being the biggest part of making my dream come true.

Mom, thanks for always reminding me that you loved this book because of the writing, and not because you're my mom. I'm still working on believing you. (But you're still the best mom I've ever had.)

To my husband, your support has never wavered. That means the world to me. I'm sorry for all the times I yelled that I didn't want you to read over my shoulder. I still love you. And you can be my friend. To my kids, whether you know it or not, you inspired me every day to keep going. Some days writing was hard, but I kept picturing your faces when I could say the words "I'm done." I love you!

Sam George and Mandy Grifka, the best road trip buddies EVAH, I don't think I'll ever be able to express the gratitude I have for each of you. Who knew all of our DYKing would turn into a lifelong friendship? I love the shit outta both of y'all. Thank you for encouraging me and believing in this book. I can't wait to get Chased with you! 1 2 3 | 4 3 2

To the authors I've met and befriended along the way (and by befriended, I mean you let me fangirl all over you and still answered my messages), thank you for being awesome. Stacy Kestwick, Kim Holden, Erin Noelle, CM Foss, BN Toler,

Kathryn Andrews, and Ashley Christin, I appreciate your words of advice and encouragement more than I'll ever be able to say. Fist bumps all around.

(And speaking of Kim Holden, the book Gran mentioned in Chapter 15 is real. It's called *Bright Side* and you should add it to the top of your TBR list right now, along with Gus. He's my number one book boyfriend, but I'm willing to share.)

To the Happy Hour gang, y'all ROCK! I'm so glad I get to share this corner of the Interwebs with so many awesome people.

To my early readers—Karen Allen, Tara Genova, Miriam Green, Julie Hardy, Lisa Marie, Gina Mary, Ali Montoya, Kearsie Murphy, and Alicia Neil, thank you for your feedback and encouragement. That alone is worth its weight in gold. (And Ali, thank you for my hug!)

Tatiana Hardy, thanks for helping me keep it real at the end. Muah!

Jennifer Van Wyk at JaVa Editing, thanks for polishing this turd! You're a delight to work with, and I'll Be the One is a better book because of your edits. And I'm really sorry for making you cry. Mostly sorry. Okay, not sorry at all. Hahahaha!

Kay Springsteen, thank you for your eagle eyes! You're so great at what you do.

Sofie Hartley at Luminos Graphics, thank you for the beautiful cover and graphics (and for dealing with my nitpicky ass). I love them all so much.

Elaine York with Allusion Graphics, LLC, thank you for the finishing touches that took this book to the next level.

To the phenomenal bloggers and friends who shared this book, God bless you. I owe each of you a Ring Pop and a Diet Coke. Thank you thank you *thank you.*

This book was a labor of love. I knew how the story ended before I ever started writing it, but it didn't make the final chapters any easier. I love James with all of my heart and I was so sad to have to say goodbye to him. If you have a Derrick in your life, or know someone who does, please tell someone. It could make all the difference.

About the Author

I'm a proud Army veteran, Army wife, and my greatest loves include my family, lip gloss, Diet Coke, and the beach. I believe 90s music is the cure for most bad moods and chocolate after 9 p.m. doesn't count. I'm a self-professed bibliophile. If reading burned calories, I'd weigh -20 pounds. Hang out with me at facebook.com/realhazeljames.

I'll Be The *One* Playlist

Ed Sheeran "Thinking Out Loud"
X Ambassadors "Unsteady"
Smashing Pumpkins "Ava Adore"
Kings of Leon "Sex on Fire"
Kings of Leon "Use Somebody"
Chris Stapleton "Tennessee Whiskey"
Ray LaMontagne "Trouble"
Lake Street Dive "Just Ask"
Charlie Puth "One Call Away"
Alexander Jean "Roses and Violets"
Meghan Trainor Feat. John Legend
"Like I'm Gonna Lose You"
Half Moon Run "Need It"
You Me at Six "Cold Night"
You Me at Six "Carpe Diem"
You Me at Six "Wild Ones"
Imagine Dragons "Bleeding Out"
Death Cab for Cutie "What Sarah Said"

Made in the USA
Middletown, DE
02 June 2016